"*Forget Me Knots...from the Front Porch*...will take you back to your childhood. Back to the days when life was slower and simpler. On one page you will smile, on another you will cry, on still another you will be laughing out loud. If you close your eyes from story to story, you can almost hear the neighbors walk by and come and 'set a spell' while they drink a glass of ice cold lemonade.

"I am very proud to be a small part of this anthology. It will tug at the strings of your heart."

—Janet Elaine Smith, Author of *House Call to the Past*

"Memories are made from the moment we take our first breath; we create them for our parents. Our memories, in turn, are created as our parents guide us through our lives, kissing our hurts and explaining our fears.

"As I read *Forget Me Knots...from the Front Porch*, I rode an emotional roller coaster, taking me through the dusty caverns of my mind where memories long forgotten rose up to fill me with wonder once again.

"This heartwarming collection of memories from around the world will leave an indelible print in your mind. As you relive your own memories, more will surface, and you will begin finding those pieces of yourself you thought lost forever.

"*Forget Me Knots* is a must read for everyone who believes in family and especially for those who don't."

—Georgie DeSilva, Author of *Next Stop* and *If I Would Love Again*

"Author Helen Kay Polaski has done a wonderful service in compiling the stories in her book, *Forget Me Knots*. It's more than a collection of stories. It's a sprinkling of memories that will spark your own and warm your heart. *Knots* gave me a sense of 'how it must have felt' living through the Kennedy assassination and war, with stories like 'That November' and 'War Through the Eyes of a Child.' The stories are gripping and emotional, entertaining and uplifting.

"Like a box of chocolates, *Forget Me Knots* is a delightful combination of 'flavors' and each story should be savored for its uniqueness. 'Broom-Swinging Grandma' made me laugh and cry, as did so many of the others.

"This is a book to be read and reread, whenever your spirits need a lift and your ov... e nudging. Simply a delightful and in...

...f *I Never Held You*, a book about ... and recovery, and *Jackie's Heart*

Forget Me Knots... from the Front Porch

An anthology of heartfelt stories from around the world

Compiled by Helen Kay Polaski

Obadiah Press

607 N. Cleveland Street
Merrill, Wisconsin

1826 Crossover Road, PMB 108
Fayetteville, Arkansas

Forget Me Knots...from the Front Porch

Published by Obadiah Press

Compiled by Helen Kay Polaski
Preliminary story selection by Helen Kay Polaski
Edited by Tina L. Miller

Cover art by Melissa Szymanski

Page layout by Tina L. Miller

ISBN: 0-9713266-8-1

Printed and published in the United States of America

Thank you, Lord, for being with
me every step of the way.

Forget Me Knots...
from the Front Porch
is dedicated to my parents,
Harry Philip
and
Stella June Szymanski.
Because of them,
my front porch memories are sugar
coated and steeped in magic.
I couldn't have asked
for better parents.

Table of Contents:

Acknowledgments

I would like to thank my husband, Tom, for allowing me to be me. It if wasn't for him, this book might still be one more dream too far away to reach. To my children, April, Alissa, and Nathan—I send a genuine thanks. Even when I brushed them aside to edit one more bio or read one more story, they understood how important this project was to me. They're the best.

I'd also like to thank my sister, Veronica Joan Dickerson, for her unwavering belief in my abilities; my sister, Melissa Jane Szymanski, who did a wonderful job on the cover art; and my niece, Jillian Sue Liedtke, and her dog, Sassy, who grace the cover with their smiling faces.

In addition, I would like to thank all of the *Forget Me Knots...from the Front Porch* authors. Without their wonderful stories and continued patience and understanding, there would have been no book. A heartfelt thanks also goes out to the authors whose stories had to be cut because of space constraints. I wish we could have included them all.

Finally, I would also like to extend my appreciation to Tina L. Miller, my editor and publisher, who was available just about every time I emailed or called to interrupt whatever she was doing, and my good friend, Vanessa K. Mullins, who listened to my whining. Tina took the time to answer all of my questions, no matter how many times she had to repeat herself, and Vanessa listened to me repeat what Tina had said, over and over again until I thought I understood what it was I was supposed to be doing.

Thank you from the bottom of my heart.

— Helen Kay Polaski

1

Moments Frozen In Time

Some memories are printed indelibly on our minds, never to be forgotten.

That November

By L.L. Rucker
Campbell County, Tennessee, United States

I have returned many times to my childhood home. There are so many memories here—some good, some bad, but all precious to me. My favorite place at the old home is the huge front porch that runs from side to side across the front of the house. It was here that I read my first book, lying stretched out in the swing, here that I received my first kiss, and here that I tried to make sense of a tragedy that affected all of us. It holds so many memories of so many different and significant times in my life, and that November day was no different. I can remember like it was yesterday…

I was in English class that afternoon when Mr. Johnson, his voice hushed and strained, came over the P.A. system.

"This afternoon President John Kennedy was shot and killed in Dallas, Texas." He spoke just a single sentence, but the words sent a shiver of fear down my back.

I heard my teacher gasp and saw her cover her face with her hands as she tried to hold back the sobs.

Around me the whole class sat in stunned silence, disbelief and fear etched into their faces. No one spoke.

Finally we heard the crackle of the P.A. system again and Mr. Johnson quietly spoke.

"The buses will be arriving shortly to take you home. Please leave your classrooms only when you hear the bell.

There will be no school tomorrow. May God have mercy on us all." And then a barely audible click as the P.A. was turned off.

We sat still and silent in our seats looking to our teacher for guidance. She took a deep and shuddery breath, wiped her eyes with the back of her hand, then got slowly to her feet.

"Please gather your books and..." Her voice broke and she began to cry softly.

We looked at each other or at our folded hands, not knowing what to say or think or feel or do.

Finally, the bell sounded and we quietly gathered up our books and belongings and streamed out into the hallway. The other teachers were in various stages of stunned disbelief. Some were crying, some stood stoically silent, their faces a mask of sorrow and something more. There was anger, too.

The eeriest thing was the total lack of talk. No one said a word. Even the most boisterous of students were silently making their way down the hall and out to their buses.

On the ride home, there was none of the usual horse-play. Everyone stayed in their seats and whispered quietly among themselves.

We were scared. Period. The President of the United States had been assassinated. Where did that leave us? We had no leader. We may have only been children, but we did on occasion listen to the news.

We knew that we, the United States, were involved in what was termed a "Cold War" with Russia. Just what that was wasn't exactly clear to any of us, but we knew it wasn't good. We knew that our parents feared this Cold War and many of them had built bomb shelters to house us in should the worst happen. But being children we had no clear idea of what the worst was. When you were 12 years old, politics was a foreign word and you had no need to worry about things like bombs and Khrushchev. Whoever he was.

A great many of us only knew who John Kennedy was because he was the President. We had no notion of his role in the workings of our government or what his assassination would mean to the country and the world, but we were about to find out.

When I got home that afternoon, my mother was in tears. She had the TV on and was watching the coverage of the events. I didn't ask her what was wrong. I knew. I listened to her and my granny talking, and they were afraid.

Slipping out of the house to the front porch, I climbed up into the swing and pulled a throw over me. The cold wind was blowing through the leafless trees, moaning mournfully as clouds scudded across a steel gray sky.

Then I became afraid. We were without a leader for a brief time, and anything could happen to us.

What would happen to us if we didn't have a President? Would Russia drop bombs on us? Would we all be killed? I didn't know. I huddled under the throw on the front porch swing and cried. After a time, I went back inside and called my best friend. She and I talked for a few minutes, but neither of us had any answers. As I got ready to hang up, she said, "Linda I'm scared. What are we going to do?"

"I don't know, Mary. I don't know. This is bad. Real bad." I said. She began to cry as she hung up, and so did I.

And that was to be only the beginning of the million or so tears I shed over the next five days.

The television carried little else but the news of John Kennedy's death. We watched as Lyndon Johnson was sworn in as the new President on board Air Force One. We saw the place where John Kennedy was shot, and they showed the newsreel over and over again of him slumping in the seat of the limousine with Jackie screaming and trying to crawl from the moving car.

They showed the shocked and grieving faces of the people along the parade route when the news reached them that the President had been shot. And I cried.

Not out of fear any longer, but out of grief—grief for the President, for his family, for the nation.

For five days the world watched as the leader of the greatest nation on earth was laid to rest.

I was amazed by Jackie's calmness. I couldn't understand why she wasn't crying. I thought she should have been sobbing hysterically. I didn't understand the meaning of decorum and dignity. I was a bit angry that she showed so little emotion, when I, a 12-year-old kid was sobbing brokenheartedly.

I watched and cried as thousands of people paraded past the President's coffin on display in the Rotunda. Leaders from all over the world came to pay their respects to our fallen President, some openly crying, and I cried.

By the time the day of the funeral arrived, I was cried out, or so I thought. Daddy was home from work, and we all gathered in front of the television to watch the first Presidential funeral to ever be televised. We gathered to watch history in the making.

And then the procession began, and the drums started playing, and forever after whenever I hear a drum cadence, I will remember that cold and dreary November day.

A horse drawn caisson carried the President's coffin, draped with the American Flag. The horse was saddled, and in the stirrups of the saddle were boots turned backwards, signifying the death of the Commander in Chief.

The drums beat out the cadence as the coffin was drawn down Pennsylvania Avenue. The streets were lined with mourners.

As the coffin drew abreast of the President's family, little John Kennedy, Jr., "John-John," solemnly saluted his father. It is a picture I will carry in my memory for the rest of my life, a simplistic gesture that spoke volumes and endeared that child, a son of Camelot, to the people of this country till his own death.

At Arlington Cemetery, they interred the president. His brother, Bobby, lit the eternal flame that burned brightly in the gloom of the cold November day. The band played taps, and the President was laid to rest forever. And a memory was born.

I will never hear the sound of taps again that the picture of that little boy saluting his father one last time won't pop into my head and I will remember the million tears I shed.

That was my first introduction to loss and death and grief. Sadly it was not my last, but over the years, I could always find some small measure of comfort sitting in that swing on our front porch.

Wildflowers

By Nancy Baker
College Station, Texas, United States

I sat on the trailer steps, elbows on my knees, chin in my hands, the picture of dejection.

Idly, I picked up the ball to my jacks set and bounced it a few times, but didn't bother to retrieve it when it rolled under the trailer. Unbidden, tears slipped from my eyes and threatened to become a full-fledged rushing river as I pondered the things I hated.

I hated California.

I hated living in a trailer.

I hated my new school. The teachers were mean and the kids were snobs. The more I thought, the more my dejection turned to anger.

Without thinking, I scooped up my jacks and threw them against the side of the trailer. The harsh tinny sound of metal against metal caused me to cover my ears and then my eyes as the sobs came in earnest.

The screen door squeaked, and I felt the weight of someone settling on the steps beside me. I expected my mother to offer me words of comfort, as she had so often during the last few months, to pull me into her arms and tell me it was okay to cry, that she understood. But there was only silence.

The quiet stilled my sobs, and I peeked from behind my fingers, trying to comprehend what was happening. My dad sat gazing off into the distance, his elbows on his knees, hands clasped in front of him.

Was I in trouble?

Fearfully, I glanced at the side of the trailer to see if any of the jacks had marred it. Not that I could tell. Maybe he was going to chew me out for being a crybaby. Even if I was girl, he didn't like me to be a sissy.

The silence grew longer, punctuated by an occasional uncontrolled sniff from me. What next?

Finally, I could stand it no more. "I'm sorry," I whispered in a tiny voice, glancing at Dad and then quickly away, afraid of what I would see in his eyes.

Still the silence continued. I began to wiggle my foot and clear my throat. My eight-year-old mind was confused, no longer focusing on my "hates," but on my dad. What was coming? At last, after an interminable period of stillness, Dad spoke.

"Nancy, when I'm as sad and mad as you seem to be this morning, I usually try to take my mind off of it. Think about pleasant things, do pleasant things. Replace the sadness and anger with happiness. How does that sound to you?"

"Fine," I replied hesitantly, carefully studying my bare toes. I raised my eyes questioningly to his. "But how?"

"Well, tell me something you'd like to do."

"Go back to our house in Texas," I responded immediately.

Dad's infectious laugh exploded from his chest. "No, something that's possible."

"I don't know." I was still unsure of where this was going and what he wanted me to say.

"Think about a time when you had fun. What were you doing?"

I deliberated for quite a while. Fun times drifted through my memory. My mood began to lighten just thinking about those good times. I wanted to pick the very best one.

I looked at Dad waiting patiently, his blue eyes reflecting the color of the sky on that lovely spring day, and remembered the time he had taken me to see Texas bluebonnets. There had been field after field of the blue-purple flowers, blending with the distant sky.

"I want to go see wildflowers," I burst out.

With a smile as wide as the Mississippi, he slapped his knee and exclaimed in a booming voice, "Excellent choice!"

So we set out, Dad and I, to see if California wildflowers could equal Texas bluebonnets. The windows were down in the car, and my hair was blowing every which-way. I felt free and light. The weight of my "hates" disappeared, and in its place was a delicious feeling of anticipation. As we climbed higher in the mountains, the air was cooler, but the steadily rising sun promised warmth.

"There!" I yelled. "There on the side of the road. See them—those yellow ones." I may as well have found gold.

"Let's take some back for your mom to see," Dad suggested.

I scrambled out of the car even before it rolled to a stop and began gathering my golden gems. Dad was right beside me, pointing out the most beautiful flowers.

"We have to leave some for others to see and enjoy," Dad cautioned.

"Let's see if we can find a different kind."

It wasn't long before I was pointing out the tiny pink ones nestled in the rock crevices. "We'll never get to them," I moaned. "They're too high up."

"Sure we will." Dad pulled a thin length of rope from the trunk. "Come on, I'll tie us together. Then, if one of us slips, the other can stop the fall."

I stood very still as Dad tied the rope, watching his capable hands deftly secure the knots. My heart began to race with both fright and excitement at the adventure before us. Had it been anyone other than Dad, I might have refused the challenge, but I trusted him, and I wanted him to be proud of me. Besides, we were bound together, my dad and I.

Up the incline, Dad in the lead, picking out the easiest and safest route to the tiny pink flowers. Jump across the crevice, land on the shelf, watch for loose rock. We repeated the process until we reached our goal.

"Won't Mom love these?" I exclaimed, happily filling the basket we had brought. Dad sat on the hard surface, head thrown back, drinking in the sun.

"Remember to leave some," he reminded me.

"I know."

I harbored no fears of the descent, having accomplished the ascent without incident. Once again, Dad led the way. As he attempted to leap across the first gap, the handle of the basket caught on an outcropping, causing him to lose his balance. He landed on one knee, his other leg dangling into the opening.

"Daddy!" I screamed, fear clawing its way into my stomach. "Daddy!"

The cry came a second time. Then I turned and ran as fast as I could away from Dad until I felt the tug of the rope between us. My legs kept churning, even though I could go no farther. I was not going to let my dad fall. We were to save each other.

"It's okay, Honey. I'm okay. Stop running." I turned to see Dad sitting on the edge of the crevice, flower basket intact, breathless, but smiling. "You saved my life!" he proclaimed, eyes glistening at the attempt of a 70-pound girl to pull her 195-pound father to safety.

"I love you!" I cried throwing myself into his arms.

"I love you too, Sweetie," he said ruffling my hair.

I would have gone home immediately after this

terrifying mishap, but Dad wouldn't hear of it. "There are more wildflowers to be found and picked," he declared.

We spent the rest of the day searching for flowers. Some he knew the name of, like the ice plants that grow so profusely on the California coast. Others were just the tall purple ones or the white puffy ones. Much to my surprise, we found that lupine (known in the Lone Star State as bluebonnets) grows in California, too.

We even found a yellow one. Imagine that—a yellow bluebonnet.

By the time we started home, the back seat was loaded with wildflowers, the intoxicating aroma enveloping us. My mother oohed and aahed appropriately, and then we set about filling every vase, pitcher, and glass we owned with flowers. Our tiny trailer was festooned with our bounty.

Lying in my bunk bed that night, thoughts fairly danced through my head as I relived the adventure we had, my dad and I. It was then that I vowed to always find something beautiful to chase away the "hates."

The Village Boy

By David Ritchie
San Juan Islands

I remember that I was trying to be quiet. But the night was dark and sound carried far. Rifling through garbage cans outside the little clubhouse where the Boy Scouts met was not exactly something I wanted others to see. The sweet rotting smell of banana peel was strong in the air. I could see inside the cans due to the pale light coming through one high window and was excited to find an old red Boy Scout neckerchief some boy had probably discarded for a new one. I rose fast, stepped back, and tripped over a garbage can lid on the ground. My fall into the tin cans announced my presence to everyone within a quarter mile. In a few seconds, the entire troop was standing around me. I was stunned with embarrassment.

I pulled myself up quickly and tried to walk away with dignity, but the laughter and "Village Boy" taunts hurt so much that when I reached the darkness, I ran wildly. Then the tears came. I knew boys didn't cry, but I could not stop.

I lived in Alabama Village. I knew it was for poor people, but it would be years before I realized it was what people from the north referred to as *The Projects*—a place for the really poor—primarily single mothers.

When I got to the duplex where my mother and I lived, I sat in the back yard against the house, breathing hard from the humiliation and the hard run in the summer heat. I wanted the tears to disappear without trace. In the darkness, lightning bugs lit the bushy yard like stars lit the night sky. The air smelled of freshly mowed crabgrass, and the perfume of honeysuckle was strong.

Later, I rose and went around the house. Mother was sitting on the front porch in the old rocker that had belonged to her daddy, and when she heard me, she set her iced tea on the table beside her. I heard the tinkle of ice. I barely heard her say, "Love you, Dahlin'," as I walked past her.

My bed was a mattress on the floor. Beside the bed was a wooden box within which I kept my important things. I opened it and fingered the Boy Scout flashlight with broken lens and then an old mess kit one of the Scouts had discarded. I folded the red neckerchief and placed it in the box. We couldn't afford for me to join the Scouts, but I loved the uniforms, patches, and gear. During summer months, I watched them gather at the little Boy Scout building and pack their camping gear, then march high-stepping into the woods like an army of little boys. Many times I felt the heat of almost formed tears at my aloneness when the last scout disappeared.

It took only moments before I was asleep.

I woke up when the sun blazed through a tear in the roll-down window shade. I smelled coffee, so I knew Mother was up. I slipped on my canvas pants and t-shirt and went to the kitchen.

"Hi, Momma."

"Mornin', Dahlin'. Went to sleep a little early for summa vacation time, huh?"

"Yes, ma'am. Guess I was just tired."

"Well, you smell a little ripe, too! Why don't I start more au lait while you take a shower."

I went to shower, but I usually enjoyed watching Momma make coffee. She made it the way old-time southerners made it. Bring a saucepan of water to boil, then lower the heat and pour a cupful of French Market Coffee and Chicory blend into the water. When the water looked like coffee, she dropped large pieces of eggshells into the water. As the shell pieces sank to the bottom, it settled the grounds; then you dipped your cup into the coffee. She always added milk when it was a chicory blend. Momma was sipping hers when I returned.

"Sit down, Dahlin'. I'll get you a cup."

She frequently let me drink a cup of this southern liquid. I loved it with a little sugar added.

"Thanks, Momma."

When she sat back down with my cup of au lait, she put her hand on my forearm.

"Ben, you want to tell me 'bout last night?"

I was startled by the question. Momma always seemed to know when something was wrong.

When I looked up at her, the sun streaming through the kitchen window shadowed half her face and yellowed the other half. It was spooky. She had one yellow-brown eye, one gray, bright yellow-auburn hair on one side, gray on the other. When the yellow eye blinked, it brought me back to the moment.

"Ben, were you over to the Boy Scout hut last night?"

"Yes, ma'am."

"What happened?"

"I was just hangin' around—they were singin' songs, and I, uh, looked around for stuff."

"Oh, I see! You were looking through the garbage again, huh?"

"Yes, ma'am. And I found a—"

The disappointment in her face stopped me. Then she softened and leaned in farther.

"Ben, why do you keep hangin' around that place? If I could afford to buy the uniform and all the gear those boys have to buy, I would, Son. But I can't. You know that."

My eyes glistened, but I would not cry.

"I'm sorry, Momma. Last night I tripped on a lid and fell. All the boys came out and laughed at me. I ran home and sat outside for a while."

I saw something in Momma's face. Just for an instant. She looked away just for the briefest moment. When she looked back at me, she was softer.

"Well, Honey Boy, y'all go on and play outside today. Be careful in the bayou—watch out for them cottonmouths. They don't take to barefoot boys steppin' on them, you know! I'll make you a grilled-cheese sandwich for lunch."

My friend, Bobby, and I walked to the other end of Pritchard where the little store had big stalks of sugar cane for sale in a barrel outside the front door. We each contributed five cents we earned from redeeming pop bottles and purchased a six-foot cane. We broke it at the knuckles and had seven pieces. Bobby took four, and I took three.

We sat on the curb in front of the store and began shaving the ends of the cane with our penknives. We were after that incredible, sweet core. We chewed and sucked on the cane 'til we had our fill. As we stood, one of the boys we knew from school walked up.

"Hey, Ben."

"Hey, Stubby."

"Hey, Bobby."

"Hey, Stubby."

"Would ya cut me a round a cane?"

We knew Stubby had the money to buy his own. But Bobby gave him a round, or plug, from his. He pulled his penknife out of his pocket and started to cut it into four smaller pieces.

"Saw you at the hut last night."

"Yeah. I was just listening to y'all sing. It sounded like fun. When I stepped on a can to look in the window, I fell." I lied and tried to make it sound funny.

"We're going into the woods to build a campfire and roast weenies Saturday. Why don't y'all come go with us?"

"You know I got no uniform or stuff to do that with. I go'n join next summer though." I lied again.

"You old enough?"

"I'm 'leven!" I said defensively. Sweat drops moved down my face slowly, like little wet bugs. It was hot and, as always, humid.

"You nine, maybe ten!" Stubby said.

"Well, I'll be joinin' next year anyway!" I said a bit too defensively.

Stubby folded his knife. That it had a Boy Scout logo on it didn't for a moment escape me. He put it in his pocket and thanked us for the cane and left.

"Lets go look for snakes or turd-roller bugs." Bobby said. The fun had been taken out of my day.

"Lets head back. Momma'll wonder where I been. Hey, you want to come over tonight?"

"Nah. My dad says I caint stay over anywhere for a week. He punishin' me."

We walked back home together. Bobby was a Village Boy, too.

"Hey, Momma."

"Hey, Hon. You hungry?"

"A little. I had some cane today, with Bobby."

I laid the last segment on the kitchen counter.

"Here's a piece for you."

Momma made cowboy stew for us that evening. It was made from the commodity foods we were allowed to pick up at a warehouse in the Village. It was potatoes, onions, and turnips fried up in a pan, with melted Velveeta Cheese over it.

"You want some bread with that, Benny?"

"No thanks, Momma."

Pause.

"Momma, the Scouts goin' into the woods near Pritchard Saturday. Stubby told me 'bout it. I have an old mess kit, and you know I'm okay in the woods—I'd like to follow along and cook somethin'…"

"Well, I don't think that's a good idea Hon. I…."

"But it's only for the day—only for lunch! I wouldn't be—"

"I don't think—"

"Please, Momma, please!"

She looked at me for a couple of minutes. I could tell she was thinking hard about it.

"Okay. Just this one time. And if you aren't back b'fore dark, and I mean this house, your ass is mine! Do we understand each other, Mr. Davy Crockett?"

"Yes, ma'am, yesum. Thanks, Momma." I knew better than to push it right now. I'd wait 'til later to talk more about it with her. After dinner, Momma washed and rinsed, and I dried. We were standing at the kitchen sink. I was drying the last dish.

"Momma, do we have any weenies?"

Mother immediately got the hysterical giggles. I didn't have a clue why, but when she snorted, I got them, too. For the next few minutes we bounced around the kitchen laughing like crazy people, barely able to stand. I still didn't understand what got her started.

"Well, Mr. Ben, I think you mean for the trip Saturday, right?" wiping tears from her eyes.

I nodded. If I spoke, I might snort again.

"I have a much better idea. I'll pack you a big pork chop in wax paper and pack a little Crisco for you to cook it in. How's that sound?" She smiled big.

"That sounds great, Momma. Thanks!"

Mother thought it sounded great because we had no weenies, no money to buy them, and four pork chops in the freezer.

The following days went by slowly. All I could think about was the camping trip. But finally it was Friday night. I opened my little box and pulled out all my Scout stuff. I folded the red neckerchief into a triangle, and smoothed it with my hand. Momma had washed my jeans and a light cotton shirt and left them by my mattress. She also put her Big Ben alarm clock by my bed. It was set for six o'clock.

The clock was ringing, and when I woke I couldn't even remember my head hitting the pillow the night before. I turned it off, jumped off the mattress, and showered quickly. It was already hot. The light coming through the tear in the window cover was pale orange. Very pale.

Mother had everything packed in a little canvas bag in the refrigerator. I was just about to leave when I handed the neckerchief to her.

"Momma, would you tie this around my neck for me?"

There was that look on her face again. Her eyes were telling me she loved me. And I knew she wished she could afford to buy the Boy Scout clothes. She tied the ends in a knot since I did not have the little wooden clip the Scouts all had.

"You have fun today, Mr. Davy Crockett. Be careful when you make your fire—dig a decent pit and all, okay?"

"I will."

She bent down, and I kissed her on the cheek. She took my face in her hands and kissed me on the lips. "I love you, Ben. When you come home, I expect you to tell me all about your hike."

I smiled at her and left through the kitchen door.

I stood off about 50 yards from the Boy Scout hut. Soon about a dozen boys and two adults came out. They were all in those beautiful red and tan uniforms and had little backpacks on. They got in a line and marched smartly into the field that was on the edge of the flat pine woods. When the last boy reached the trees, I stood and started off behind them.

It was only about two hours later that the group stopped to build a fire pit and sing songs. I was still keeping a distance of about 50 yards between us. I found a clear spot to dig my pit and set my bag down. I had my old hunting knife on my hip.

I dug a pit about 1' x 2', about eight inches deep. I put in a few dried pine needles, struck a match, and when it caught, put some pinecones on to hold the fire while I slowly put on some limbs that were scattered around. It burned nicely.

For most of the morning, I watched the scouts doing various things, but I couldn't tell exactly what. I pulled out my penknife and carved interesting little pieces of wood. The pork chop was on my mind. When they finally started building their fire up for the weenies, I did the same.

I put about a cupful of Crisco in the little pan and set it over the fire to melt. It didn't take long until it was bubbling over the sides it was so hot. I reached in and grabbed the handle. I didn't realize the handle would be as hot as the pan.

When I grasped the handle, it was like sticking your finger into a light socket. The shock! I drew back my hand quickly, but the handle seemed to be stuck to my hand, and the jerking motion spilled the boiling lard onto my right thigh. I opened my mouth to scream, but it didn't seem like any sound was coming out. The shock was immediate. I jumped and ran, trying to scream—back to town or home to mother. The pain was searing, my vision became surreal, and then darkness.

I woke up in the little clinic near the Village. Mother was sitting near me, as were the two Scout leaders I saw on the trip. When I spoke, it was like I had cotton in my mouth.

"Momma."

She rose from her chair and sat on the bed next to me. She put her hand on my face, bent down, and kissed me.

"Hi, Mr. Man. Had a hard day, huh?"

"What happened?"

"Well, it seems the Scouts heard you screaming and went to help, but you were running so fast they couldn't find you until you passed out. Mr. John here—pointing at one of the two men—carried you back to the clinic. They are all worried about you."

I looked at Mr. John.

"Hey, Ben."

"Hey, Mr. John. Thanks."

He smiled and nodded his head. He walked over and put his hand on my arm. I didn't know how to react.

The pain was getting worse, so they gave me some kind of shot, and I went to sleep again. I woke again early the next morning. The sun was barely up, and the room was that beautiful summer color of yellow and orange. Mother was asleep in the big chair. I looked down at the bottom of my bed. There scattered all over the white cotton cover were various Boy Scout badges, knives, a working flashlight, a pack, a genuine Scout shirt, and other Boy Scout items.

I felt the sting of tears.

War Through the Eyes of a Child

By Violet Apted
Queensland, Australia

Introduction: My granddaughter, Samantha, was invited to give a talk at school for Remembrance Day and asked me if I had a memory of the war she could use. Pleased, I began telling her some of my experiences. She was enthralled and wanted to hear more.

It was as if I had turned on a verbal tap. The words gushed out almost tumbling over each other as I relived some of the most frightening moments of my life—during my own schooldays.

Samantha's talk was a great success, and her friends all wanted to ask me many questions when I met her after school later that day.

I promised Sammi and her brother, Steve, I would write my war story down one day. That is how "War Through the Eyes of a Child" came to be in your hands today.

There have been so many war stories written, perhaps you wonder why I bothered to write another, but of all the stories I have read, I have never felt that a child's point of view was really considered. Maybe the old adage "a child should be seen but not heard" is something adults really believe, but this story is about the war through the eyes of a child.

It is about the scars I have carried for a lifetime. Mental scars that go so deep they still cause a physical reac-

tion, like the sound of a machine gun in a film. You know it's only a film, yet your whole body goes cold with fear.

I dedicate this story to my three children, Maureen, Stephen, and Beverley. I will always thank God they were given a childhood free from all that goes with being a child somewhere in the middle of a war.

There was no fear, but then why should there be? War was only a word to an eight-year-old child. The fact that we were at war with Germany appeared to have upset all the adults on the street. Everyone was outside their homes, all talking about the terrible announcement that had just come over the radio. Mothers were crying, dads were trying to calm their wives. I remember my big sister telling me that now we would have to eat black bread and there would be no more sugar for any of us.

She had, of course, heard our grandparents speaking of the previous war.

I only laughed and told her it wouldn't worry me and to prove it, I would go without sugar from that day on, so when it did happen I would not have to suffer. If war only meant we had to go without sugar and eat black bread, it wasn't all that terrible.

People were making so much fuss all around us that we ran off to finish our game, blissfully unaware of the tragedy that was about to engulf our lives—unaware that the announcement of war was to steal our childhood away from us. No wonder our parents let us play…after all were they not children of war themselves?

My father was already in the army when war was declared, so we were used to him being away. His last leave home from France is the one I remember so clearly, because of the beautiful gold cross and chain he bought me. He had come laden with gifts for all of us six children. I thought my cross and chain was the most beautiful thing I had seen in my life. I could not understand why my mother put it away until I was old enough to take better care of it, and I had cried bitterly.

That cross was to become so very precious to me.

I answered the door the day the telegram was delivered. I heard my mother crying and knew it had been bad news, but all my questions were brushed aside. We accepted an adult's words in those days, so it was not until I was helping my mother with the shopping that I first heard the words, "missing in action, believed dead," when a friend of mother's stopped her to say how sorry she was to hear about Alec. In her grief, Mum forgot I was there and said Dad had been at Dunkirk (which I had heard the adults talking about).

Those words gave me a cold chill inside. I knew fear for the first time and cried because I knew something bad had happened to my father, yet not understanding what it was. As she became aware of me beside her, Mother gripped my hand and comforted me. She also made me promise I would not tell my younger sisters and brother. I listened and tried to understand that "missing, believed dead" was the way the army had to do it until they had real proof of death.

She explained tearfully that proof could come at anytime.

I kept my promise to my mother, never telling the younger members of the family, suddenly feeling much older. Crying in my bed about three months later because there had been no word from the army, Mum came into my bedroom and, without a word, handed me the gold cross my father had bought for me.

That was the first time I knew what it was to really pray. As I lay alone in my bed that night, I just knew my father had to be alive.

Twelve months after that awful telegram, we got the news that Dad was alive and in a prisoner of war camp in Germany. He had been on the beach, one of a gun crew, when they were hit by shells. All his mates had been killed, Dad's identity disc lost, and he'd suffered amnesia for a long time. He was to remain a prisoner for the rest of the war, but he was alive, and to his little girl back home, that was all that mattered. To me, my faith in my cross had saved my Dad. I believed I had reached him through it, bringing him back to me. My mother sent him my photograph to help him get his memory back, because I did not want him to forget me. He carried that photograph with him throughout the war and brought it home with him. It still has the prison camp mark on the back (Stalag XXB).

War soon became an everyday part of our lives. We soon lost our fear in hearing the air raid and Observer Corp spotter's warnings that told us the enemy planes were overhead. It became a game to brave it out. We only went down into the shelters if we were made to go and used to stand on the front porch to watch the planes above us being shot at and shouting encouragement to our pilots to kill the enemy.

Carrying a gas mask to school became as natural as carrying our satchel. Gas mask drill became as common as fire drill.

There was an old railway carriage at the fire station that was converted for use as a gas mask testing station. We all had to wait outside for our turn, file inside, put on our gas masks, and stand there while tear gas was released to test the mask for leaks. We were scared even though we had been told it was harmless. Before they would open the door, we had to remove our masks. There was a sharp stinging sensation, and our eyes watered badly, but we were told it was a harmless form of gas. Though that wasn't pleasant, we thought it was fun when we were pulled through a long dark tunnel, lying flat on a low trolley, as a practice means of escape and rescue. It was thought that by training us, we would know what to do and not hamper any rescues we might have to be involved in.

School attendance became governed by air raids. We could not leave for school if there was a raid on, and if the siren went as we were on our way, we were told to run as fast as we could to get to the school shelters as quickly as possible. If there were any spotter's warning or planes overhead, we had to run to the nearest house for cover. I never once did so, wanting to see the enemy that had caught my father shot down in flames as often as I could. There was no fear or realization of the danger in doing so.

The sirens went off one afternoon, and the primary school teacher hurried us all into the shelters. Forms were placed down each side of the shelter, and we all sat facing each other. Soon we heard the spotter's warning, and the planes were overhead.

We could hear the guns and the shells exploding. The teacher got us all singing, so we would not be frightened. There was a big explosion close by, and the teacher ordered us under the forms. We lost no time in obeying her order. Everyone was scared, and some children were crying as we all squeezed under the forms. Our teacher was a very large lady, and it looked so funny when she tried to get under with us that we started to laugh. Because of our reaction, she exaggerated her movements, squirming and wriggling to make us laugh some more. For a while, we forgot the frightening things going on outside at the sight of our big fat teacher stuck fast in a most unladylike and "un-teacher-like" situation. Because of that wonderful teacher, Miss Willis, that was one scar less we would carry.

It was thanks to that same teacher and the headmistress, Miss Adams, that all the children in that school were saved when the school took a direct hit in a raid a few months later. By then, I had gone on to high school, but my younger sister and brother were among those saved.

One day my friends and I decided to go to our gang's secret den that we had built in a gnarled old tree in a field by the river. The field was a child's paradise with lots of abandoned materials from an unfinished bridge scattered everywhere—piles of sand and ballast and some V-shaped girders. We girls changed into our swimsuits in our tree, then plunged into the river with the boys, some of whom were not so modest. After our swim, we decided to play in the sand among the girders instead of sunbathing on the top of the unfinished bridge. That decision was to save our lives.

We ignored the air raid warning, and when the spotter's warning went immediately after, we could already see the enemy planes overhead. We ran for cover, but even as we did so, a German plane dived toward us. We threw ourselves down on the ground as the German pilot opened fire with his machine guns. Bullets ripped into the ground around us as we fell. Somehow no one was hurt, but all six of us were very frightened. My young brother started to cry.

The two older boys, Maurice and Charlie, took charge telling us to quickly turn over the V-shaped girder and get underneath. They didn't need to tell us twice! They flung themselves in after us just as the German plane attacked again. Bullets struck our makeshift shelter. We were petrified with fear and huddled together. I was trembling as I held my young brother tightly in my arms. Maurice reached over and held my hand, reassuring me we would be all right. After the third hail of bullets had hit our shelter, we heard the sound of another plane. It had a different sound than the German plane, and although we could still hear machine gun fire, no more bullets struck our shelter.

Suddenly Maurice and Charlie began to shout at the same time, telling us it was a Spitfire.

"He'll get him! Come on!" Maurice shouted.

We scrambled out of our shelter to see vapor trails crisscrossing the sky. The Spitfire was on the German's tail. We shouted and screamed encouragement, but fell strangely silent when smoke and flames belched out from the German plane. I felt an immense sense of relief when the pilot's parachute opened, and he drifted slowly down.

We ran to where he landed, which was not very far from us. The German was unconscious and covered in blood. Soldiers with fixed bayonets appeared. One took my brother from my arms and put a comforting arm around my shoulders. He asked me if I was all right. I could not answer. I was looking at the face of the German pilot. The soldiers were lifting him onto the back of the jeep when he regained consciousness and our eyes met. He had tried to kill me, my little brother, and my friends, yet strangely I felt no hatred. He could not have been many years older than we were.

For as long as I live, I will remember that day, the day I lost my childhood.

Another day that lives on in my memory is the day of the terrible bombing of our town. We were all kept at school until someone could collect us or teachers could check if, in fact, we had homes to go to. No one came for me, and I was sent home with the instructions to find a relative or friend until I heard from my mother. If not, I was to go to the police station.

When I reached the corner of my road, I understood why. Half the street was demolished. There were so many people—still looking dazed and crying, ambulances and NAAFI, police and soldiers. People still searched through the rubble that had once been beautiful homes. It was routine to keep searching until everyone was accounted for.

I could not find my mother! I searched the sea of faces and knew the worst fear I could ever know.

Where could she be? Was she one of the bodies they had found? Worse still…yet to be found?

Was that why no one had come for me? Perhaps there was no one to do so?

Panic welled up, and the tears began. *Please God let me find my mother.* I became one of a crowd of dazed crying people. I knew that one brother and sister were in the school that had been hit. My two older sisters worked in the factory that had been hit. Were they all…? That was it! That was why no one had come for me. There was no one to come.

My baby sister attended the infant's school—she should be all right, but they would not have let her come home alone. Just as I was thinking of my little sister, I saw her! She was sitting in the child's seat, on the back of a woman's cycle. It was her teacher.

I called out and ran over the road to her. I must have been quite hysterical by then, because I can remember greeting them as if it was a normal day and laughing.

The teacher had located my mother and was waiting for her to get a cup of tea from the NAAFI van nearby. I walked over to the van and saw Mum standing in the queue about to be served. She looked so tired and was covered in dust and dirt. I remember thinking how terrible it was that the woman could not give Mum a cup of tea without sugar, because the big urn of tea was sweetened. I understand now that it is the usual thing to do as it helps in cases of shock, and there were plenty of those that day.

Mum hugged me to her as we stood talking to the teacher who had brought my sister home. She knew our street had been badly hit and had checked up on the casualties before bringing her home to find Mum. I learned then that Granny and Granddad were both alive but in hospital, and Mum had been digging through the debris—that was once beautiful houses—to find her family and the many others who were trapped underneath, including friends and neighbors who had been killed. No wonder she looked so tired and sad. How she must have suffered that day on top of all that was going on there.

She knew where the bombs had fallen, and the not knowing if she had lost most of her children, as well, must have been horrific. When she saw the teacher with my sister and I, she thought her worst fears were true—that maybe we were the only two to survive. I remembered my own fears earlier that day and started to cry.

Later that day, we were taken to a Rest Center that had been allocated as temporary accommodation for all the people who had been left homeless by the bombing. My brother and sister, Bert and Jean, joined us later. They were luckier than some of our friends who had no home or family to return to. My two older sisters, Rose and Joan, arrived shortly after. We had been allocated a room, supplied with beds and blankets. It looked like a dormitory by the time we were through.

After a meal, which left me still hungry, we children were tucked into strange beds, but little sleep was to be had. We each told our story of the day, each of us recalling our own horror and wondering what tomorrow would bring. Our biggest fear now was that they would send us away from our Mum.

Tomorrow would never come for some of our friends. They, too, were children of war. They would not carry their scars into the future as we would, but maybe the scars their parents now carried would be so very much harder to bear.

The Cousin Danny Story

By Maureen Allen
Newcastle, England

Aunt Eileen and Uncle Earl were snobby people. They lived in a lovely home in an exclusive community, had the correct friends, belonged to the right clubs, and their children grew up to be exactly like them. Everything about my aunt and uncle was perfect, from their manicured lawns to their spic 'n span clean home.

But my most lasting memory about them has little to do with them. I fondly remember their porch. It went three quarters of the way around the house, it was screened in, and it had the most comfortable furniture in the world.

Entry to the porch was from the front door, the back door, or a side door that opened out from the living room. The front door was a bit odd because it was at the back of the house. The house faced the pond, away from the street. No one ever used the front door when we visited my aunt and uncle—we always entered through the back door. The only time the front door was used was when someone wanted to get into the back yard.

I spent many lovely summer days on that porch when I was a child. Being the retiring type, I stretched out on the floral patterned, deeply padded chaise lounge to read a book while my sisters and cousins splashed around in the pond, played badminton, or had a game of hide 'n seek in the aromatic and plentiful fuchsia rhododendrons.

Aunt Eileen and Uncle Earl lived in Hingham, Massachusetts, in a house that was designed to be a summer home. For months after they bought the house, they spent every weekend painting it, weatherizing it, and making it into a palace. When it was ready to live in, they brought in the antiques they had acquired from my uncle's family.

My grandfather was a plumber. He added two bathrooms to the second floor and erected a shower near the pond so everyone could clean off the mud and grass from their feet and not track it into the house. (God forbid, if Aunt Eileen had mud and grass on her carpeting!) Gramps was also an accomplished carpenter, and he helped Uncle Earl add and enclose the porch.

The porch acted as a corral for the youngest cousins. My grandparents had 27 grandchildren, and keeping them all in one place, particularly at mealtime, was a challenge. Only at Aunt Eileen and Uncle Earl's house could all the cousins be accounted for readily. With everyone on the porch, it was easy to figure out who wanted hamburgers and who wanted hot dogs by looking for a show of hands.

When the meal was over, the kids were scooted off the porch and shuttled onto the back and side lawns for game playing under the watchful eyes of the grown-ups. The side lawn had a badminton net set up, and we could play croquet if we wished. The back lawn contained a volleyball net, a basketball hoop, and several swings and slides.

If this sounds idyllic, it's no accident. It was constructed to be a heavenly place to take advantage of a cool breeze from the nearby pond on a hot summer's day, a place where children could play in safety away from the street traffic, and a place from where the owners and their visitors could enjoy the view of the pond at sunset.

Let me give you a little background detail about my family. They were of the old school where children were to be seen and not heard. For them, it was an adult's world, and the children of the family were to know their place. For the most part, we were a good lot who didn't get into serious trouble. What trouble we did get into was filtered through the eyes of the old school. We were just kids being kids. Sometimes, though, being a kid was not an acceptable profession.

One of my fondest memories includes a bit of trouble. The entire family was at Aunt Eileen and Uncle Earl's house for my grandparent's 60th wedding anniversary. Three of my female cousins, Rita, Christine, and Mary, my two sisters, Chris and Janet, and I were sitting in the red breakfast nook in the kitchen drinking Coke and chatting. My cousin Rita's Coke fizzed up when she opened it, and it sprayed all over me. By the way she said, "Sorry, Maureen," I knew she wasn't sorry at all. I retaliated by spraying her with my Coke. Then it became a free-for-all with all of the cousins plunging their thumbs into their bottles, shaking them, and spraying the others with Coke. There were shouts of "Stop!" "Hey, not all over my new blouse!" and "Look, Christine doesn't have any Coke on her!"

When the Coke was gone and we were catching our breath, our grandmother walked into the kitchen. Each of us drew a sharp intake of breath, because we knew then that we were all dead meat. Nana was the matriarch of the family, and her word was law. We could get away with some infractions with the aunts and uncles, but we never got away with anything when Nana was around. It was her job to make sure we all stayed on the straight and narrow, acted like civilized human beings, and remembered our manners at all times. She loved us, and we knew it, but she was not the warm and fuzzy type at all.

She stared at us with her "Will you ever become civilized?" look, went to the sink and fished out several sponges, handed them to each of us, and said, "I want you to clean up this kitchen before your Aunt Eileen sees this awful mess you've made." We did what we were told, and then we ran upstairs to laugh about it. It just wouldn't do to let Nana hear us laughing, so we buried our faces in the bed pillows and howled. I think we laughed as hard as we did because of our relief at being allowed to live, rather than the hilarity of the Coke fight. Regardless, the story remains one of my cherished memories.

Aunt Eileen and Uncle Earl were fastidious. Germs knew better than to invade their home. If any germ did happen to wander into Aunt Eileen's gaze, it was eradicated quickly. And, Uncle Earl was just as bad. He was a butcher who showered three times a day: first thing in the morning, when he got home from work, and then again before going to bed. Being that clean, I wonder how they ever got four children out of the deal. But, I digress.

Shortly after the porch was completed, my Aunt Alice and Uncle Walter, along with my grandparents, came to visit. Aunt Alice and Uncle Walter brought their children, who at that time numbered four. It was when they were relaxing after having had a barbecue that the unmentionable Cousin Danny Story took place. No one in the family talked about what happened that day because of: 1) the subject matter and, 2) well, you just don't talk about those things in our family. It was only recently that I heard the story, and it happened 12 years before I was born!

Danny was a precocious child whose middle name was trouble. Everyone who knows him is amazed that he has lived to his present age because of all the punishment he accrued for being truant from school. Nana and Gramps and all of the aunts and uncles were sure that Danny would become a member of some radical political organization, spend time in prison, or end his days selling aluminum siding in Tijuana.

But no, he surprised everyone by finishing school, going to college, and getting a Ph.D. in Education. He now teaches teachers how to teach. Ha! There was a method to his madness all along.

Let's go back to when Danny was about 18 months old and playing on Aunt Eileen and Uncle Earl's porch. Danny hadn't yet learned that it was not acceptable to interrupt his elders, and after being reprimanded by one of the grown-ups, Danny contented himself and plotted his revenge by playing with his favorite toy–his diaper. His filled diaper was a source of endless entertainment for him and an embarrassing trial for his parents.

Sitting quietly, like a good little boy—and left to his own devices—Danny proceeded to smear the contents of his ripened diaper all over Aunt Eileen and Uncle Earl's porch screen. It was a work of art. A large work of art. A large, smelly work of art.

Had his parents, his aunt and uncle, and either of his grandparents been paying any attention to him, it would never have happened. But with the old school values regarding children being what they were, it was bound to happen. I'm glad I wasn't there to smell it, but I do wish I had been there to see the looks on everyone's faces!

He Sat Alone

By Steven Manchester
Somerset, Massachusetts, United States

It was an early spring afternoon, the sort where only die-hard Red Sox fans would endure the bone-chilling winds of the open park. So there I sat with my brother Randy, ignoring the cold, but suffering the ancient curse of the Bambino. By the end of the seventh inning, the heroes of Fenway Park were on the bottom end of another bad spanking. Most fans stood up to stretch out, scattering peanut shells everywhere. Randy and I took it one step further. We caught one last glimpse of the Green Monster and left.

Not two steps from the smells of stale beer and hot dogs, I noticed that my brother and I weren't the only people who had taken enough. The filthy streets were flooded with thousands of dissatisfied customers, and many were not prepared to conceal their disgust. Randy, a glutton for punishment, headed for the ticket office. I teased him about his misguided loyalty, and then took a seat to wait. It was then that a harsh reality hit the only home run of the day.

It was an ordinary Saturday in Boston. The streets exploded with hoots and hollers. A closer look, however, revealed that no one was engaged in conversation. Men and women alike kept their eyes either on the ground before them or focused straight ahead. Then I saw him. An elderly man was sitting alone on a front stoop. Curious, I wandered over for a better look. A shiver traveled the length of my spine.

Unfortunately, the temperature was not the cause of the horrible sensation.

Amidst a flowing river of Nikes and Timberland boots, the nameless man wore shoes that had worn through long ago. Dressed in threadbare rags, he held a silver coffee can in one trembling hand and his sign in the other. It read: "Hungry Korean War Vet." As if already dead, the man's eyes were sunken deep in his head, while a gray tinge painted his somber face. I was reminded of the sacrifices I made for my country in Operation Desert Storm. For a moment, I thought that my stomach might actually kick up the two hot dogs I'd just devoured.

People circumvented the man as if he were a leper. Instead, they hustled toward the sausage vendors' heckles and the loudmouths that pushed souvenirs. Not one person stopped to help. Obviously, it was easier to assume the man a con artist than to find the truth in his tormented eyes. I somewhat understood. There were still many truths people did not want to know. In this case, that truth only defined a cold and uncaring society.

Other passer-bys went above and beyond apathy. They were mean enough to leave behind an insult or a laugh to stab the poor man's heart. The Vet was too old and weary to strike back at the masses. Each time a harsh word was offered him, his eyes closed briefly and then opened again, as if he'd completely absorbed the cruelty.

Fifteen endless minutes elapsed, and although the coffee can remained empty, I witnessed a fellow human being suffer more embarrassment and humiliation than deserving of an entire lifetime. Whatever dignity remained was greedily and brutally stripped away by those who, somewhere along the line, were hardened and left blind.

Suddenly, another unfortunate soul captured my attention. It was another elderly gentleman—this one, confined to a wheel chair. The man slowly approached a curbstone and then worked his chair back and forth in a courageous attempt to clear the lip. It was no use. Determination and effort were quickly replaced by frustration and mumbled curses. Through it all, hundreds of patriotic baseball fans herded around him and proceeded onto their different ways. I stood paralyzed with shock.

As the numbness wore off, I took two steps to assist, but was one step too late. The homeless man placed his sign and empty cup on the stoop and went to help another who needed more. My eyes filled. There was still some good left in the world. Strangely enough, it always seemed to come from those who were in desperate need of what they themselves gave so selflessly. For his trouble, the Korean Vet received a donation. The two shared a genuine smile that apparently only those in need could understand. The pauper returned to his stoop and the judgmental gaze of a million cruel eyes. The man in the wheel chair pumped his arms to another of life's obstacles. I stood amazed.

I placed a crisp twenty-dollar bill in the beggar's can and received a nod for my generosity. I felt a tap on the shoulder and turned to see Randy's eyebrows rise in disapproval.

During the lengthy ride home, I explained the tragic scene and the topic led to some unusually deep discussion. We were in complete agreement on most points—not supporting a person's drug habits and the genuine possibility of being scammed, but Randy shared the strong opinions of most. I, on the other hand, was less suspicious. There didn't seem a need for it.

We traveled a good distance in silence, as my thoughts remained with the homeless vet. I decided that as long as my own intentions of helping were pure, then I didn't see any risk of injury to anyone. For the price of a scratch ticket, I'd rather give the man the benefit of the doubt. The odds seemed better. Besides, it was one of society's problems that more people should be taking personally. With thousands being swallowed up by unemployment and homelessness each day, it could have easily been anyone sitting on that same lonely stoop. Then, placing myself in that man's worn shoes, I only hoped that someone would be kind enough to take a chance on me rather than the state's lottery.

Reaching the Airport Road exit at Fall River, my traveling companion broke the silence with a very innocent question. Though he expected no answer, Randy asked, "Steve, don't you ever wonder why God has given so much to so few and so little to so many?" Surprised that my brother's thoughts mirrored my own, I smiled. The answer seemed so easy, so obvious.

To Randy's surprise, I responded, "I think that God has given enough. The problem is that people have forgotten how to share His generous gifts."

The rest of the journey was driven in silence, the Boston Red Sox continued to lose, and somewhere on a very cold front stoop a needy man sat alone.

Popeye in the Outhouse

By Darlene Zagata
Uniontown, Pennsylvania, United States

I spent my childhood growing up on a farm. It was a wonderful place, and I loved being able to roam the wide, open spaces. Summer was always my favorite time of the year, and I enjoyed being outdoors. We always had fresh milk and eggs, and there was a small pond at the edge of the field where I loved to go and sit when I wanted to be alone. Sometimes I sat there for hours, lying back in the green grass, the sun warming my face and the wind caressing my hair as I dangled my bare feet in the cool refreshing water.

I was a friend to all of the animals on the farm, as well as the household pets. The dog ran with me through the field and accompanied me to the pond, and I enjoyed helping my uncle with the daily chores, which didn't seem like work to me at all. To me, it was the perfect place.

Most farms had plenty of cats to keep the rat population down, and we were no exception. We had several cats, but I developed a special bond with one particular kitten. His name was Popeye. He was black and white with one blue eye and one green.

Popeye was always getting into some sort of mischief. He tended to wander off for a few days at a time, but we had become accustomed to his wandering and didn't worry when we hadn't seen him for a few days. We knew he would find his way home when he was through exploring.

Popeye had been gone for three days on his latest excursion and we were expecting him to return at any time.

Now everything about living on the farm was wonderful, except for one drawback. The old farmhouse was not yet equipped with indoor plumbing, so the only "facilities" that were available was an outhouse. One hot, summer afternoon in particular, my aunt had gone to the outhouse. We were all sitting on the front porch enjoying the summer afternoon when we heard my aunt's sudden scream. We immediately ran in the direction of the outhouse to see what all the commotion was about. We found the door open and my aunt standing half-clad screaming and shaking her rump.

She shouted hysterically through tears that she had been bitten on the bottom by a snake. She was shaking and flailing her arms about in such a way that it was hard to see if there was anything on her bottom or not!

It was difficult to see, being that the only light was the bit of sunlight entering through the open door and the bit that had filtered through the tiny cracks in the roof. My uncle stepped inside the outhouse to try and calm his frazzled wife and to see if he could find any trace of the snake that she said had bit her. Once he had calmed her enough to look around, he reached behind her and pulled up, not a snake, but Popeye, who apparently had fallen in during his latest exploration! Popeye had reached out to grasp at his only means of escape—and that just happened to be my aunt's derriere!

My uncle, my mother, and I burst out laughing, but my aunt did not find the situation amusing in the least bit. She had just been half-scared out of her wits and did not see anything funny about it. She proceeded to reprimand the three of us for our outburst and insensitivity. We tried to regain our composure, but it was still hard to stifle the giggles.

My aunt was furious, to say the least, and more than a little embarrassed. She ended up spending the rest of the afternoon in the hot, blistering sun with a bucket of soapy water, scrub brush in hand, and a wet and reeking Popeye getting the bath of his life. Most cats have an aversion to being bathed and Popeye wasn't at all pleased, nor was my aunt, who had other things she would have much rather been doing.

Popeye didn't get into too much trouble after that, and he and my aunt seemed to make up and be closer companions from that time on. I think they both shared the memory of that frightening and embarrassing moment.

Shortly afterward, my uncle had indoor plumbing put into the old farmhouse. I guess he decided it was time to make a few changes. Even though he never came straight out and said so, I would guess that my aunt had been instrumental in moving those plans along.

We used to spend our summer evenings on the front porch looking out over the resting field and listening to my aunt while she recalled the day's events at work or listening to my mother tell her very vivid and sometimes chilling ghost stories, but now there was a new story to tell. Whenever friends or family dropped by, they heard the latest happening, and those who weren't familiar with Popeye would be given a formal introduction as he occupied the honored seat in the middle of my aunt's lap and she told the story in the midst of laughter. The event that had so embarrassed my aunt now became a favorite topic of discussion. She loved relating the story to others and would hardly let any of the rest of the family say a word. The story soon died out, like most tales do, but the memory lives on.

They are all gone now, but when I think of any of them, I remember moments like this when we shared our lives, love, and laughter. I can smell the fresh cut grass, feel the cool, refreshing water on my toes, and see them sitting there on that big front porch telling stories and laughing while

Popeye and I chased lightning bugs. And I can still see the old outhouse sitting there, even after the indoor plumbing had been put in.

Burning Memories of Dad's Easy Chair

By Avis Townsend
Western New York, United States

The first time my parents left me alone, there was a fire in the living room.

It was 1957, and I was 10 years old. One of my father's co-workers had died, and I begged my parents to let me stay home. They'd been dragging me to funeral homes since I was a baby, and enough was enough. It was time to put my foot down.

I was an only child born to middle-aged parents. Overprotective and very old fashioned, they fretted all day whether to hire a babysitter for an hour or let me stay alone. It wasn't the worry of an intruder that bothered them, it was the worry of old wiring catching fire and burning the house down or me falling down the stairs and not having anyone to help me. There was never a thought about careless smoking causing disaster.

Nothing in the place spelled danger to me.

I loved that big old country farmhouse with its pitted plaster walls, high ceilings, and a huge bay window in the living room. And the long front porch was haven to my collection of plastic farm animals, barns, and gates.

They agreed to let me stay alone, but not without an hour of lectures and instructions and promises from me to obey all the rules. "Don't let anyone in. Don't open any doors. Don't go outside. Stay in and watch television. Don't call anyone on the phone…"

By the time they were finished with all their admonishments, I was considering the funeral home alternative. Staring at some unknown dead person couldn't be as bad as this verbal drill instruction. But I stayed, and they went, and all was good for about 10 minutes. That's when I noticed the fire.

My father smoked heavily, one cigarette after another. His old pedestal ashtray had stood like a silent soldier next to his easy chair for as long as I could remember. Sitting on his lap, breathing in coils of blue second-hand smoke was an everyday occurrence, and no one thought to blame his smoking for my constant bouts of asthma or bronchial infections.

Because of the heavy smoke odor in the living room, I didn't notice his chair burning as soon as I might have, and by the time I did, smoke was pouring from inside the seat cushion and tiny flames danced across the seat.

I stared open-mouthed at the smoldering chair, panic-stricken. What could I do?

I remembered all of their instructions. I couldn't call, I couldn't go outside, I couldn't tell anyone what was going on. I might have to stay in the house and burn up with the chair. How could I fix this problem without breaking the rules?

I ran to the kitchen and filled a tall glass with water, then ran back and poured it on the cushion. Steam rose, and the smell was horrendous. That wouldn't do. Taking deep, scared breaths of rancid air, I forced myself to think. The porch! That's it—the porch.

Breaking one of the "don't" rules, I opened the front door as wide as it would go. Then I began to push, pull, kick, and tug at the chair, working it toward the doorway, coughing and gagging from the putrid smell of the burning stuffing. The chair wouldn't go through. Fortunately, the water had put out the flames, but it caused more smoke and steam to rise out of its stuffing.

The chair stood stubbornly in front of the door, wider than the doorframe itself. That didn't make any sense to me at all. The chair came into the house once, I reasoned, so it had to go back out. I stared at its Queen Anne legs, wondering how I could cut them off. Then I got a brilliant idea. I flipped it on its side and slid two legs out first, and then the rest of it followed. It was now out of the house and on the front porch. I shoved it toward the steps, and with one adrenalin-filled heave sent it flying down the stairs to the ground below. There it lay in a smoking heap, dead. Dead as the man my parents were seeing in that funeral home.

I stayed on the porch and watched the chair, waiting for it to explode. I feared the house would go up in flames, as well, even though the source of the trouble was out on the ground. I also feared what my parents would say when they got home. I had disobeyed. I had opened the door. Now my father's favorite thing was lying in the front yard, a victim of accidental arson.

After what seemed like forever, our old Ford pulled in the driveway. I could see my parents staring. My mother's mouth was going a mile a minute. My father was squinting, peering into the darkness at his beloved chair. I remained a sentinel on the porch.

Rather than driving around to the back of the house like he always did, my father stopped the car, and both parents leaped out, rushing toward me with so many questions pouring out of them I didn't know which one to answer first.

After I explained, my mother's first response was, "I knew we should never have left you alone," to which my father countered, "If we hadn't, the house could have burned down."

The scenario of what might have happened played like a movie across her face, and she grabbed me and pulled me to her. Now I was being squeezed to death.

They hugged me individually—then came a huge group hug. We all stood on the porch staring down at the chair.

"You and your damn cigarettes," my mother said to my dad. "You could have killed her and burned the house down."

He defended himself. "Well, I didn't, and she was smart enough to know what to do."

They left the chair on the lawn for the evening, and by the time I awoke the next morning, it was gone. I never asked what they did with it. I didn't care. Out of sight, out of mind was my motto.

After breakfast we all went shopping. My father got a new easy chair. My mother got some new porch furniture. I got a new toy horse and more fencing to add to my collection. I played with them a lot, creating farmlands under the new porch furniture my imagination called mountains.

My father loved his new chair. It looked pretty good next to his old upright ashtray. I think the shopping spree was to celebrate the house not burning down. My gift was my reward for saving it.

With new porch furniture, we spent more time entertaining there than in the back yard, the way we used to. The porch became our new entertainment center, and a lot of warm remembrances were created there.

It was a while before I stayed alone again, and that was my choice. Why tempt fate? And I never stepped out on that porch again without mentally replaying the scene of the steaming chair tumbling down the steps. I guess you could say it was burned into my memory forever.

2

Child's Play

The innocent days of childhood, lost in playtime and carefree fun, will remain with us long after that childhood has passed away. Reliving those memories in our minds brings out the child in us all.

The Cave

By Anne Watkins
Vinemont, Alabama, United States

When I was a child, we didn't have video games, color televisions, or computers. In our rural part of north Alabama, there weren't even many children close enough to visit, so my favorite playmates, besides my brother, were books borrowed from the Book Mobile that passed through our community every two weeks or so, and the various critters on our farm. My days were filled with climbing trees, fishing for frogs and crawfish in the icy waters of a nearby spring, and scuffing my toes against the grayed wooden boards beneath our front porch swing as I lazily swayed back and forth. But by far, my favorite pastime was to climb around in a cave deep in the woods on my family's property.

It wasn't really a cave, but rather a huge bluff with gigantic overhanging rock formations. Not many days went by that I didn't make my way across the pasture and down through the woods to visit my special place.

A lot of times I took along a picnic lunch, my dog, and a book, and enjoyed the stillness of the spot. In the quiet company of the trees, I read to my heart's content or basked on a boulder in the sun daydreaming. Then one afternoon, to my amazement, archaeologists asked for and received permission from my daddy to dig the area.

It was fascinating to watch the scientists conduct the dig. It was even more fun when they allowed me to dig, too. I was given a small trowel and shown how to sift the tiny shovelfuls of dirt through the screens the team had brought with them. These devices looked like window screens fastened to short-legged wooden frames to keep them high enough off the ground to allow the dirt to filter through. Whatever was too large to pass through the holes in the screen was carefully examined for artifacts.

I was thrilled to discover a perfect flint spearhead, a bear tooth that had once been part of a necklace, and two pieces of broken pottery that fitted neatly together. I even learned how to distinguish between pottery shards and pieces of regular rock.

Hundreds of artifacts were found, and it was determined that several families had once inhabited the shelter. I stared at the rock walls and ceiling, trying to imagine what it must have been like to live under a bluff. Was all the black soot on the ceiling left over from ancient campfires? Had Indian children played on the same big rocks over which I now scampered? My active imagination created all sorts of scenarios.

Finally, the excavation was done, and the team left us. While it had been exciting to have archaeologists working the bluff, I was glad to see them go. I missed having the place all to myself. In honor of the occasion, I summoned my younger brother, Graham, and my cousin, Glenda, a city girl, to a meeting on the front porch. They were delighted when I asked them to join me at the cave for a marshmallow roast.

One chilly afternoon we hiked down the wooded, leaf-covered path to the cave. To get to the mouth of the bluff, you either climbed the "long way around," which was for sissies and old people, or you grabbed onto a tree that grew right next to a sheer rock wall and then scaled down. We always opted to hang onto the tree and half-slide, half-climb down. The daredevil possibility of breaking our necks added to the sense of adventure.

It was so cold that our fingers were stiff and our breath hung in hazy clouds before our faces, but getting warm again was no problem. I kept a small glass jar filled with wooden matches stashed beneath one of the rocks of the bluff. As we neared, I dug it out. The matches inside were nice and dry, and one immediately popped to life when I struck it against a stone. We made a small campfire from the supply of sticks and branches piled in the back of the cave and huddled around it to thaw our frozen fingers.

Glenda was fascinated with the cave. She listened intently as we told her about the Indians who had once made the bluff their home. We discussed the possibility that they had cooked their meals on the very same rock where we now had our campfire and wondered where among the huge stones they made their beds. Then I hauled out the packet of marshmallows I had brought along.

We each peeled a stick and poked the fluffy white candies onto the ends. Graham and Glenda liked their marshmallows barely singed and melted, but I preferred mine burnt almost to a crisp with a gooey middle. Licking our sticky fingers after eating most of the bag, we all agreed that nothing came close to the taste of a marshmallow roasted to perfection over a campfire in the woods.

It had grown steadily colder, and the sun had almost disappeared. Suddenly Glenda gasped, "Listen!"

Tiny spattering noises sounded from the trees surrounding the cave. As we peered into the darkening woods, we were delighted to see snowflakes filtering down through the few brown leaves still stubbornly clinging to the branches. Hard, grainy snow crystals bounced against the bare limbs of the trees and struck the dead leaves carpeting the ground.

Breathless, we watched as the snow crystals fattened into big flakes and drifted through the woods. Fingers of wind swirled and danced and blew the flakes into the cave to kiss our cold-reddened cheeks. For a brief moment, I sensed the presence of others. Children like us, perhaps, who had once huddled near a campfire and stared into the darkness as snow fell gently outside.

We lingered until it was almost too dark to see, then extinguished our fire and put away our matches and marshmallow sticks. Reluctantly, we headed home, our feet pounding as soon as we cleared the trees, trying to make it back to the safety of Daddy's well-lit front porch before we were overtaken by night.

Though that marshmallow roast took place nearly 30 years ago, the memory has never faded. These days I sit on my own front porch swing, just a few hundred yards from the old house where I grew up, and cuddle my little grandson in my arms. Some day I'll tell him all about the cave waiting down in the woods. Maybe he'll hang onto that tree and scale down the mossy rock wall I once knew so well. And when he's done, I hope his feet will thunder a path up through the pasture and straight to his Grammie's waiting front porch.

Five Dollars Up

By Helen Kay Polaski
Milan, Michigan, United States

We moved as a unit—each running so close to the next it was a miracle no one was trampled. And then, just as quickly, we separated as each child scouted out his or her own spot on the lawn and stopped, waiting.

There was nothing unusual about the ragtag assortment of loosely fitting plaid shorts, cotton pedal pushers, and flowered sundresses that dotted the lawn. This was our evening ritual. A sense of rightness shimmered in the air around us. We lived minute to minute, hour to hour. Yet as surely as we knew the sun would come up in the morning, we knew this or some other lawn game was what should occupy the last moments of each day just before the screen door on the front porch slammed one final time.

We kept our eyes on Veronica as she tossed several practice throws into the air. We watched, estimating the exact time her foot would connect with the ball. As the sun's last rays shot pink and orange Kool-Aid colors into the western sky, the ball sailed off the end of her right foot, and we gave chase. The shimmering evening sky, now dotted with lightning bug flares and the sound of peepers singing in the rain-soaked ditch, tucked in around our shoulders like a favorite sweater.

With the wild abandon of youth, we determinedly raced after the ball, our bare feet sliding on dew covered grass. Faces grew red and shiny, and wayward strands of blonde hair found their way out of long braids and short pigtails as the game progressed.

"Mine!" I shouted at the top of my lungs. "This one's mine!" I spread my arms wide to receive the ball. Three feet above me, my older brother, Harry, Junior, plucked the ball from out of the air. I jumped anyway, collided with him, and fell to the ground empty-handed. I rolled over and glared up at him.

"Another dollar," he yelled. "That makes five for me. I'm Up!" Without question, Veronica gave up her claim at the front of the group and raced to take Junior's place in the yard.

I frowned. Junior was always Up! And now we had to start counting all over again. He spun the ball in his hands as he confidently strutted before the group.

Curling my hands into fists, I took a deep breath. *Next time it's mine!* As if he heard my silent shout, Junior turned and looked at me, a wide grin on his face. Then with precision, as if he'd practiced long and hard for just this moment, he pulled his leg back and kicked with all of his might. I dropped to the ground in agony. There was no way *that* dollar was gonna be mine.

Like a bird taking flight, the ball rose. Just when I thought it might disappear altogether, it plummeted to earth. It bounced hard, hit the depression in the ground used as second base when we played kick-ball, and veered to one side. The older kids all darted after it, bumping and nudging one another out of the way. By the time anyone was near enough to catch it, it had settled down to a slow roll. Teresa scooped it up seconds before it landed in the muddy ditch. She only got 25 cents.

Junior clapped his hands together in glee. The longer it took for anyone to count up five dollars, the longer he was Up. After checking the wind and setting up more strategy for making sure no one caught a fly ball, he kicked again. This time the ball bounced once, twice before Susie grabbed it, calling out "50 cents!" and throwing the ball back.

The next one is mine! I stomped my feet and batted away several mosquitoes. "Kick the ball," I wailed impatiently. But when he pulled back his leg a third time, the sound of tires crunching gravel filled the air, momentarily silencing the peepers and bringing the game to an immediate halt.

For a split second, no one moved. Before another breath was drawn, the yard emptied.

"Daddy, Daddy!" We screamed in unison, running to greet the dusty red pickup as it coasted down the driveway. Almost before the wheels stopped moving, Daddy opened the door and unfolded from the driver's seat. Giggling, the youngest of the group all stepped on his shoes and wrapped our arms around his legs, being carried along as he walked. Daddy chuckled. He held his lunch bucket high in his right hand and used his left to ruffle the nearest heads and pat little backs in greeting.

I looked up at him and grinned from ear to ear. He smiled back. "Here Chief," he said holding out the bucket. "Take this to the house." He waited long enough for me to step off his foot, take the bucket from his big hand, and let someone else take my place on his foot before the group was moving again toward the lawn. I watched as he raised both hands to chest level in silent request for the ball. Reluctantly, Junior tossed it into his waiting hands, and amid squeals of delight the game resumed.

In seconds my feet had covered the territory from the truck to the front porch. Jerking open the screen door, I yelled excitedly, "Daddy's home!" Racing into the kitchen, I dropped the bucket on the table with a clatter, but before I could race back out, a tantalizing aroma stopped me dead in my tracks. Strawberry jam! I watched in fascination as Mom stirred the bubbling concoction. Smiling, she dropped a spoonful on a plate and let me dip my fingers in the hot jelly. Raising my fingers to my lips, I sucked voraciously.

"Who made that noise?" she asked innocently, her eyes wide. I giggled and buried my face in her lap, the excess jam on my fingers transferring to the front of her apron. She swatted me playfully on the behind and nudged me toward the door. "Go play. This is for later."

Instantly, as if someone had pushed an On/Off button, my attention zoomed back to the game outside, and I raced to reclaim my spot on the lawn.

A short while later, the screen door screeched and Mom stepped onto the porch with the babies in tow. Karen sat on her lap chanting, "Da-Da, Da-Da," and Mary sat at her knee.

"Momma, did you see?" I asked an ear-to-ear grin on my face. "I caught one!"

Mom looked up, nodded, and twisted to the side in time to grab Mary before she fell off the porch.

"Here's one for Bam-Bam," Daddy called, and I raced forward to try and get it before my little sister, Pam, did. I was too late. The ball floated into her chubby arms, bumping her on the nose and knocking her backward.

Dad held his breath while Pam rolled over like an armadillo bug. Mom stood up from her chair and wandered to the edge of the porch watching, but Pam wasn't hurt. She hadn't even let go of the ball! Seconds later she was skipping toward the front singing, "I'm Up, I'm Up!"

I tugged at her shoulder, nearly knocking her down again. "You're not Up. That was only a dollar." *Besides, it's my turn next!* Pam shrugged my hand away and raced toward the shelter of Daddy's arms. I frowned and turned away angrily as Daddy let her have one turn at kicking before he remembered the real game.

"This one's for Judy." The ball sailed up. "Catch it," he called as the wind pulled it sharply to the left. Judy caught it on the first bounce, 75 cents for her. The next one was for Veronica, and then Rosie.

Then it was time to start all over again.

For the next half hour, everyone gave chase, and for some reason it no longer mattered if anyone caught dollars or quarters or 50-cent pieces. In the blink of an eye, the importance shifted from who caught what, to who was in our midst. It wasn't often Daddy had time to play.

Falling over ourselves in fits of laughter and shrieks of delight, our senses hummed, capturing the scene in our memory banks for later recall. Careful not to squander a single moment of the velvety night, we attentively waited on the ball.

"Me! Me next," echoed from one child to the next.

All too soon, the game was over. As if the ball was no longer important, Daddy dropped it to the side and scooped Pam into his embrace. As I watched the purple and turquoise colors turn end over end, slower and slower, the ball called to me as it always did. "Helen, Hel—en , Hel…en." A secret smile crept across my face. I would be Up next time!

I reached for the ball and heard my siblings' shouts of "Mom made strawberry jam!" Ignoring the ball, I scampered toward the house. Even purple and turquoise balls could not beat strawberry jam on thick white bread. Sweaty, jabbering, and overexcited, we burst onto the porch, fighting to be first in line as we entered the house one step behind Mom.

A dozen jars of freshly made jam stood at attention on the kitchen counter. One stood open. My mouth watered as Mom began spreading jam over slices of warm bread.

"Me! Me next!" The words echoed again from child to child as Mom refereed the distribution.

After a while, she pushed her steamed up glasses higher on the bridge of her nose. “Who didn’t get one yet?”

Carousel

By Veronica Hosking
Avondale, Arizona, United States

Remember what it felt like when you went to the amusement park and heard the carousel music playing?

Palms itched to feel the reins in their grasp, and your heart began beating faster in anticipation of the adventure. Was there ever a little girl or boy who could resist its whimsical melody? Everyone wanted a chance to ride his or her horse off into a world of their own creation. Little girls pretended to be princesses, and little boys pretended to be brave knights.

Until I took my daughter on her first carousel ride, I had forgotten what hold this simple ride could have on a person.

It did take a bit of coaxing to get her on the first time, and even then she wouldn't go up on a horse. But once the carousel started turning and its music began playing, the magic took over, and a wide-eyed three-year-old girl looked around in fascination.

"Mommy, why are the horses going up and down?" She asked with eyes glued on the horses in front of us.

I laughed and pulled her closer to me. "It's supposed to feel like you're riding a real horse."

She stared in awe at the horses. "Oh," she sighed in love. "Can I try one?"

"Of course you can," I replied with a smile.

When the ride stopped, we turned around and got back in line for another go. The second time was even better than the first. This time she sat up on a horse with reins in hand and laughed through the whole ride.

Now, she pretends to be on a carousel wherever we go.

One day while we were playing in the neighborhood park, she came running up to me with a huge smile on her face. "Mommy! Mommy! I want to ride the carousel," she pleaded, pulling me onto the grass.

"Rachael, there isn't a carousel here to ride," I explained as I tried to figure out where she was leading me.

Rachael pointed in the direction we were going and said, "It's over there, Mommy." She stopped in front of a tree and said, "See. It's a blue horse. Can I ride it?"

Most of the trees in our park have a base trunk and then fork off into two separate trunks, making a V pattern that is easy for a child to straddle. After Rachael pointed out the horse to me, I realized this was what she wanted to do. I stood there in total bewilderment as to how her little mind saw this tree as a horse.

Rachael tugged on my shirt again. "Put me on, Mommy. Put me on!" I picked her up and she straddled the tree trunk and held on to the part that was in front of her. "You have to start the ride, Mommy."

"Okay, Sweetie. It's started." I replied.

"No it isn't. The controls are over there." She pointed to a storm sewer cover.

I shook my head and then walked over and stood on the cover of the storm sewer. "Here?" I asked with raised eyebrows.

"Yes!" She kicked her horse. "Turn it on."

I grinned and pretended to push a button in the thin air in front of me. "There it's on," I said, shaking my head in disbelief.

"Yay!" She squealed in amusement. Then she began patting her horse's mane. "I have the prettiest blue horse on the carousel, Mommy."

I was still standing on the storm sewer cover, envious of my daughter's vivid imagination, because all I saw was a little three-year-old straddling a tree trunk, and I wondered what others might think if they came walking through the park at that moment. I gave Rachael another smile and simply replied, "Yes you do, Sweetheart."

After a little while, Rachael looked at me and said, "Okay, the ride's done."

"Okay," I said and proceeded to help her out of the tree.

"No, Mommy!" She screamed. "You have to turn it off!"

Silly Mommy; she forgot we were on a carousel! I stepped back on the storm sewer cover and pressed another pretend button.

Rachael smiled wide and patted her horse again. "You were a good horse. Thank you for the ride."

I leaned over and helped Rachael out of the tree, and she ran over to another tree and said, "I want to ride the gray horse now."

For the rest of the afternoon, Rachael ran from tree to tree and announced which color horse she wanted to ride. She was crestfallen if she came to a tree that forked off too high for me to get her in the saddle.

When I carried my exhausted little girl home, I knew the magic of a carousel ride would inspire her for a long time to come, because as we crossed our front porch into our house, Rachael lifted her head off of my shoulder and offered me a weary smile.

"That was the best carousel ride I never had, Mommy." Then she laid her head back down on my shoulder and closed her eyes.

I smiled and brushed my hand over her hair. Rachael had no idea how prophetic her words were. I never did see the horses she rode so enthusiastically all afternoon. Someone should figure out how to bottle the heart-racing imagination of a child. It is something spectacular to witness first hand.

Do you remember how magical your first ride on a carousel was? Think about it some summer evening while you watch your children play and you keep yourself secluded on the front porch.

One afternoon, when our first carousel ride was just a distant memory, my daughter and I were watching Arthur on TV. Arthur and his family went to the amusement park, and Arthur's little sister, DW, wanted Arthur to ride the carousel with her. But Arthur told her, "No way! The carousel is a ride for babies. I'm going on the hurly-twirly." Poor DW's heart was broken, and Rachael looked at me, "I'll go on the carousel with her, Mommy."

Once again I shook my head and laughed. The world would definitely be a brighter place if we could only capture the magic found in a carousel ride and share it with everyone.

A Place Called Home

By Vanessa K. Mullins
Michigan, United States

When I think back to my childhood home, I remember many things. I vividly remember the house and the yard with its flowers and trees, but I especially remember our front porch. It was the perfect place to be young.

You had to walk up nine steps to get to the porch landing, which was surrounded by a black metal railing that traveled all the way down to the bottom of the steps. The porch itself was brick and had a white concrete layer over the top. It stood about six feet off the ground above our drive-way.

My house was in the middle of all the houses with kids in our neighborhood. This meant our house was the one everyone was allowed to come to, even if they weren't al-lowed to go to anyone else's yard. Our yard was open, and moms could see where their kids were, so naturally, our porch was the base for playing hide 'n seek or cowboys and Indians. We used it as the jail when we played cops and robbers, and since it was so tall, we dared each other to jump off of it in order to prove our bravery. We were very lucky no one ever got hurt.

Sometimes we took several blankets and stretched them out from one side of the porch to the other and made a fort. We also used to jump up and try to hang onto the top railing. The one who could hang on the longest was the winner. Usually it was my neighbor, Scott, who was also the oldest.

At the time, it seemed like a really big place, but now as I reflect on growing up in that house, I wonder if the porch really was as big as it is in my memory.

The porch was also a great place for spying. If someone else sat on the porch, like my little brother and his friends, my group of friends and I snuck around the back of the house and climbed over the locked fence and behind the bushes to spy on them. We could also sneak around the other side and inch closely along the house to stand beside the porch to spy on them. Spying was one of our favorite games.

My front porch was also the best place to rest. It was the time-out place when we were tired of running, or the place to go to take a break from the heat.

Three very important events stand out in my mind when I think about my childhood years.

One has to do with the 4th of July and my cousin, Cindy. It was 1976, the Bicentennial year, and Cindy and I were sitting on the porch. Excited about our independence, we went out into the street and created chalk graffiti all over the white pavement. It all pertained to the holiday and was harmless, but I'll never forget the liberation I felt at having done that. After we finished, we went back and sat on the porch and talked about the kinds of things teenage girls talk about.

Another time, when I was a teenager, my mom left me and a couple of friends home alone overnight. Of course, we stayed up nearly all night. It was just about morning, and we were playing music really loudly and singing "*Someone's knocking at the door, somebody's ringing the bell,*" when all of a sudden we heard the screen door open and a loud noise sounded against the inside door. Whoever it was had to come up the walk and onto our porch to get to the door! We immediately ran to the door to make sure it was locked. Then I banged loudly on the inside of the door for whoever it was to go away. Screamed, in fact! Finally, after what seemed like forever, we opened the door to find that the paper boy had left the newspaper between the doors. Talk about fear and relief all within the span of a few minutes!

Another big memory I have of our front porch is both sad and sweet. Since my house was at the entrance to the cul-de-sac (which we called a court), I could see everyone coming and going. I remember one night when the ambulance drove down my street, lights and sirens blaring. I sat petrified on the front porch as it moved down the court to The Cookie Lady's house.

That was the one house in the neighborhood where all the little kids went, rang the bell, and waited until The Cookie Lady answered the door and gave them a cookie. On that night, we all stood on our porches and watched as the men got out of the ambulance, quickly went into the house, and then came back out. As if it were yesterday, I remember hearing one of the men announce over the ambulance loud speaker that Mr. Starkey—The Cookie Lady's husband—had died. After his death, the Cookie Lady rarely had cookies to pass out to the kids in the neighborhood anymore. Mrs. Starkey's house looked just like mine, porch and all.

It was also sad when my friend Angie, who lived right next door, moved away. I stood on the front porch and watched them pack up and move. I stood there and cried, and I knew it would all be different then. And it was. She was the first of my best friends to move away, but not the last. My family lived in that house for many years. When we finally moved away, I was 18 and had just graduated from high school.

I kept these and many other memories of my first house with me all through my life. To this day, I have the wrought iron house number sign that adorned the screen door, in my possession.

Years later, when it was time for my family to buy a new home, it was very important to me to buy one with a big front porch. At the time, I didn't know why this was so important to me, but now after writing this, I do. A front porch is something I want my kids to remember when they are adults.

I want them to remember the games they played in the yard, the talks they had with their friends, and the secrets they whispered on the phone while sitting on their front porch. A front porch is more than wood or concrete, more than brick or stone. When you step onto your front porch, you are stepping out into freedom while still having the security of the family home, just beyond its cornered boundaries. The front porch is the first place you set your feet on when that feeling of being home after a long trip hits you and the last place your tears tumble to as you leave into adulthood.

Stop Wishing Your Life Away

By Margaret Marr
Bryson City, North Carolina, United States

Now that I'm an adult, it's hard to think back over the years to when I was a child and didn't have any problems other than deciding what to do on a lazy summer afternoon. I used to wish those days would fly by so I could become an adult and do my own thing without Mom and Dad as my boss. I didn't know how good I had it back then, even as poor as we were.

One evening, after a long day playing in the yard, I trudged into the house and flopped down on the couch, dusty and tired. "I wish Friday would hurry up and get here, so we can go to Ghost Town," I said, kicking my legs back and forth, my heels thumping against the bottom of the seat.

Mom looked up from the cloth squares she was piecing together to make a quilt. "Stop wishing your life away, Margaret."

I scowled. "I still can't wait until Friday. It's boring around here," I complained and slid down on the couch, half of me on and the other half off.

Mom shook her head, sighed, then returned her attention to her sewing.

Boy, what I didn't know then that I wish I didn't know now certainly would apply.

I'd often wished for a specific day to hurry up and get here—like my birthday, the first day of school, or a planned trip to Ghost Town in the Sky, an amusement park in Maggie

Valley, North Carolina. Whenever Mom would tell me to stop wishing my life away, I never knew what she meant exactly. I just thought it was something dumb that grownups said.

But now I know better.

With age comes wisdom. In my haste to reach my next birthday in a week, a month, or a year, I failed to treasure the days in between.

Now I wish I had more days to skip rocks across a tranquil lake, skip rope on a dusty driveway, and go fishing in the dark and listen to the frogs croak and the catfish jump and splash in the water. I would love to go back and hear the snap and pop of a campfire, roast marshmallows until they melted off the stick, and eat so many blackened hotdogs off a broken birch limb that my stomach feels like it's about to explode. Or see who could sit next to the fire the longest until our legs turned red and we had to jump up and away to let the night air cool our hot skin.

One of my favorite memories is going swimming with my cousins in the Little Tennessee River at two a.m. because the camp's ground was too hard to sleep on. I awoke stiff and sore, having only slept for maybe an hour. I heard laughter coming from the direction of the river, so I crawled out of my blankets—we didn't own sleeping bags—and went off to investigate.

A sandy trail wound down to the river, and I followed its path. Small saplings and bushes snagged me as I walked, but I brushed them aside until I reached the water's edge.

"Hey, what are y'all doing?" I called to my siblings and cousins where they splashed around in the cold water.

"Swimming," Tony, one of my cousins, called back to me. "Come on in, it's not half bad."

The crickets chirped and lightning bugs flashed on and off around us. A bullfrog croaked nearby. I grinned, waved away the gnats and mosquitoes, and jumped in. After the initial shock of frigid coldness, my body grew numb, and I relaxed as the river rushed over me and on downstream. Nothing feels quite as invigorating as a cold mountain river late at night and the laughter of children having the time of their lives. Of course, the camping trip was one of those things I had wished would hurry up and get here!

After my little swim, I returned to my blankets and gazed at the stars and thought about how small I was compared to the universe, but at the same time I felt protected by a higher power, by God's love. I wondered what was beyond the stars and pretended I could fly up to soar with the birds and look down on creation. I made wishes on the brightest star and fell asleep with the gentle fingers of a cool night breeze caressing my skin, imagining they were little angels sent to watch over me as I slept.

Now that I'm older and return to my childhood memories, at least I have many to choose from…

Ah, spring! Green apples, yellow daisies, and fields of tall grass. Gentle rains and dew drops on morning glories. April showers and squishy mud holes to run through. Blowing on dandelions…I always imagined they were little men parachuting from the sky. Tumbling down a newly mown slope, standing up all itchy from the grass, climbing back to the top to do it all over again, giggling all the way.

Then summer rolls around, and it's too hot to do anything but be lazy most days. As a child, you could do this without guilt. Oh, but I dearly loved to wade barefoot in a cold creek or swim in the cool, green lake, racing my brother and sisters to the other side. We respected the water but didn't fear drowning. Diving off rock cliffs, doing the cannonball, and seeing who could hold their breath the longest under water.

Thunderstorms with lots of lightning were always my favorite, especially late in the evening. I'd sit on the front porch and watch the sky light up and listen to the crack of thunder.

"God's rearranging His furniture," Grandpa Dills would say.

My eyes grew wide. "Really?"

"Yep, He doesn't like to look at the same setup all the time either." My white-haired grandpa, dressed in coveralls, grinned at me, his teeth big and white in the gloom of the day.

I giggled and stared out at the storm with a child's unstoppable curiosity.

Sometimes the wind blew the rain in, dusting my skin with a light film of water, and goose bumps popped up on my flesh. I'd rush inside, grab a blanket, and rush back outside wrapped in it to watch the rest of Mother Nature's fury. The sound of rain drumming on a tin roof is one of the most peaceful sounds in the world!

Fall always smelled nostalgic and made me feel sad. Summer was dying. Soon winter would take over. But here, too, I loved the red, orange, and yellow trees, smoke from a chimney, leaves swirling down and dancing in the wind, and the harvest of potatoes, corn, green beans, and apples. Fall is the perfect time to catch lightning bugs, count raindrops, and listen to the sound of crickets late at night. I loved crunching dead leaves under my feet on a hike across a mountain trail. Fields of hay...ummm, smell that sweet scent...and cloudless skies where you could see for miles and miles. There's nothing quite like falling asleep in the season's last warmth of sunshine on the edge of a creek bank with the gurgle of water over rocks to lull you.

But let's not forget winter! The sound of silence after a new-fallen snow and sliding down the driveway on an inner tube, piece of plastic, or an old cardboard box if that's all you could find. Crowding around the stove to warm cold hands, cold noses, and cold feet only to pull gloves back on and "hit the slopes" again. Building snowmen, catching snowflakes on tongues, and making snow angels, and best of all, I loved to see my cousins trudging up our driveway, ready to slide in the snow with us, build snow forts, and play war with snowballs as ammunition.

When the day in the snow was done, it was especially cozy to put on soft, dry clothes—sweatshirts, wool socks, and sweatpants—and curl up next to the fire with a good book or to watch TV—usually Hee-Haw or Walt Disney—with a hot mug of cocoa. Later we snuggled down under handmade quilts and slept the night through, safe and free from worries.

My youth seems so far away, but all I have to do is think back, or better yet, live it again with my children.

Mother was right. It's not a good thing to wish your life away.

The Dollhouse

By Martha Dillon
Brownstown Township, Michigan, United States

My daughter and I were sitting on the front porch, talking about the yard sale we had just been to and about all the things people were getting rid of that still were in very nice condition, when she suddenly turned to me.

"Did you see that computer? Don't you wish you had one of those when you were young?" She asked, honestly believing that life without a computer was incomprehensible.

"No, I had enough things when I was young," I said, and her jaw dropped.

"I thought you said you didn't have *any* toys when you were a kid!" She corrected me, knowing my memory wasn't all that great even when I was young. "You said you didn't!"

"I did say that," I replied, leaning against the upright railing of the porch. "I said it, and it's true. But I had enough, too. Don't you remember me telling you? Sit close, and I'll tell you again.

"I can't say we grew up in a one-room shack with only an outhouse. I can't say we never had enough to eat. I can't say I never had new clothes, shoes, books, etc. I can't say any of that, because it isn't true. But we didn't have a lot of new stuff, and the house wasn't really big enough for all of us until my dad added a wall here and a room there. And we may have had an indoor bathroom, but there were six of us—mostly females—and only one bathroom. And anyone with half a brain knows that the optimum ratio of women to bathrooms is 1:1, right?

"We didn't have many toys, but that was in the days when playing outside was considered the normal thing to do. Gangs were good groups of kids who got together and mowed lawns, raked leaves, and shoveled snow. Gangs played baseball, touch football, hide 'n seek, and tag. We had fun. No computer. No Gameboy or PlayStation. Heck, half the families didn't even have televisions, and what was on them was mostly black and white! But we managed to survive.

"We were normal and got bored occasionally, and we also often wished we had some of the stuff that the rich kids got. Being female, I always wanted dolls and a dollhouse, but we didn't really have the money, and there were three of us girls, and that would mean three of something, either dolls or houses. So buying a dollhouse was out of the question. Enter dad's skill and mom's creativity.

"My dad had some fantastic building skills, and in his spare time, he'd built cabinets, tables, dressers, and even a deck. This time, he was building a dollhouse that had to be sturdy—we were young—and it had to fit the imaginations of three *very* different girls. We couldn't agree on how many rooms, or what rooms, or where to put them, so he created a convertible house. It was topless, changeable, flexible, and movable.

"The walls were made of pegboard, that weird wood-like stuff with holes. We had lots of 12" squares of pegboard. There were probably three dozen of them. That may be just a slight exaggeration, but I don't think so. We had lots of L-shaped and straight brackets to join the walls and lots of screws and lots of nuts. That was our dollhouse. The screws and nuts could be connected without screwdrivers, if necessary, and were inexpensive to replace. We could move those walls anywhere. We could have long rooms and short rooms, square rooms, rectangular rooms. We could combine a couple walls at irregular lengths and make halls. Dad eventually cut some pieces of pegboard to shorter sizes for halls and small rooms. We could pack up our dollhouse pieces and take them anywhere. We could build two! Three! We had dollhouses, and we loved them! And furniture—

"Mom used to carve neat little figurines out of balsa, although she doesn't do it much anymore. So she started to carve furniture for us, small pieces of furniture that we could use in the dollhouse. By the time she was done, we didn't even care that we didn't have dolls!

"She carved beds. She carved pillows. Small scraps of fabric were available to double as blankets, towels, and cloths. She carved couches and chairs and tables. She carved a tiny dresser with drawers that pulled out. We filled those drawers with a selection of folded pieces of fabric to resemble clothing, and a few years later filled it with Barbie Doll clothing when we were learning to sew. Some of the furniture was painted; some was varnished. Some was even proportional, but I don't think it was planned, and I don't remember any of us ever caring one way or another. It fit in the house and that was the important thing.

"She carved a refrigerator and a stove. She made the doors to both with hinges—tiny hinges so they could be opened. She used pieces of those plastic strawberry baskets as shelves in the fridge and racks in the stove.

"She carved food."

"Food?" She asked, her eyes wide as saucers.

"Yep, milk cartons and cereal boxes and cheese. And dishes! Well, pans, anyway. She carved a frying pan—painted black, of course, like cast iron—and then she carved a fried egg—painted just exactly like sunny-side-up—that fit right in that frying pan. She carved all kinds of little box-shaped things that looked like whatever kind of food you could imagine and painted them to resemble—vaguely—various popular brands.

"And she carved a toilet. That was the neatest toilet I've ever seen, and there isn't a dollhouse today that can compare. She carved it so carefully that it looked exactly like the toilet in our bathroom, and I have only now begun to wonder just how much time she spent in that bathroom checking out her artwork.

"The toilet seat and lid both could be lifted. The tank had a removable cover. The handle was glued on, although I'm sure she tried to make it move! In the tank, she placed a piece of clear plastic to look like water. In the bowl she placed another piece of plastic, again to look like water. That was the coolest toilet! I wonder why she never made a plunger…

"Kids from the neighborhood all came around to see our dollhouse and play with the furniture. No one else then or now ever had a dollhouse like that. No plastic furniture has ever come close to the ingenious furniture we had. But then, no one has ever had a set of parents quite like mine."

Getting up from the porch, my daughter gave me a hug.

"Grandma sure is cool, isn't she?"

"Yes, she is definitely cool." Weird, but cool, I thought to myself.

My dad's gone now, and the dollhouse and furniture were lost in a fire many years ago, but Mom is still going strong. Not too long ago, she decided to carve a toadstool. She's still got that wonderful imagination, so you'll believe me when I tell you that the finished product was an intricately carved frog with four, straight and very sturdy legs. Toad...stool…go, Mom!

(And they wonder about me!)

3

Grandpa and Grandma

They raised our parents, and they often helped raise us, as well. They passed down their values and beliefs, and a legacy of wisdom we will carry forward for generations. Grandparents are priceless!

My Summer Job

By David Ritchie
San Juan Islands

At exactly 10:00 a.m. my grandfather honked his horn. I was sitting in the glider on the back porch, and the easy movement of the swing had lulled me into a morning stupor. The sound startled me—I jumped up, grabbed my "New Orleans" straw hat, and raced out to the alley where he was waiting in his old van. The sweet honeysuckle along my back fence briefly conflicted with the putrid smell of the sun-heated trashcans in the alley. The big black van reminded me of a hearse, but I climbed in beside Granddad every Saturday morning. It was my summer job.

Granddad was a vegetable salesman, and he, too, wore an old, white Jazz straw hat that was *de rigueur* in New Orleans. He always smelled of Red Man chewing tobacco. Granddad would lift the sides of the van and then prop them open when he was parked on a street for business.

I always wanted to be like Granddad. He always had money in his pocket and had a lot of friends. I've never seen him in a suit and tie, and he drank beer and had a new girlfriend every week. What I wouldn't give to be like him.

My mother and father had always told me that he was a dangerous man. They said he drank too much and ran around with bad men, and they told me I should pay more attention to getting an education and not have to sell vegetables from a van in the summer and work in the commercial fishing fleet in the bad weather months.

But drinking, working on boats, and girls. That's exactly what I wanted to do.

Galveston, Texas, was hot in the summer, but being an island, the humid Gulf winds cooled us some. Most of the women wore sundresses and the men mostly t-shirts.

Our days always followed an exact route from which Granddad seldom varied. We went first to the street behind the old, garish Bishop's House. The house was huge, painted a pale shade of pink, and it was a Galveston landmark since all the tourists had to pass it when entering the city.

Granddad would stop, go to the street-side of the van, and prop the side open. By the time this was done, a line of customers halfway down the street had formed. As usual, all were men. They wore baggy pants and the string-shoulder type of undershirt. Most were dark skinned and wore thongs on their tanned feet. Today was pretty much the same.

"Hey, Slim! Bring that boy along to help you count your money, did ya?"

"Slim" was my granddad's street name. Granddad was 6'4" and weighed about 250 lbs. His real name was Claude, but no one—and I mean no one—called him that.

Granddad pulled a huge knife out of his back pocket and waved it at the guy. "Betsy here is the one who counts my money, boys! You only get one chance with her!"

I thought that was so cool.

The whole group howled. My granddad was as ornery and tough as they come, and they liked him.

"Royce, what you want today? Light or dark?" Granddad asked.

A wiry old guy, his face a dried up riverbed, stepped up and croaked. "Two of the light ones, Slim. Same price?"

"Yep. Boy pull that top drawer out and hand me two jars."

I moved the yellow squash aside and pulled open the top of two hidden drawers and extracted two small Mason jars with a clear liquid in them.

Granddad snapped open a paper bag, put the two jars in the bottom, and put a few vegetables on top.

"Two-fifty, Royce."

The line diminished rapidly with me pulling the jars and Granddad taking the money. Then we closed the side of the van and drove to our second spot. It was near West Beach and a block off the waterfront. The houses there were all white and built up off the ground due to the floods from hurricanes. Most of the windows had shutters, but these were kept open during the summers, and the little palm trees were bent slightly landward, away from the Gulf of Mexico just a few hundred feet away. It felt cooler, and the salt smell was strong. There were big clouds with anvil bottoms in contrast to the pale blue of the sky. There was another long line waiting for us.

"Hey, Slim."

"Hey, Thump," Granddad said to a huge man.

"Vegetables lookin' good today, man!" The man said with an attempt at humor.

"You're still the ugliest guy on the island though!" said one of the other men in the line.

They all laughed, but the little guys all stepped back. One never knew how ole Thump would react. Today he laughed, too.

Later, when there were still two or three men in the line, I saw them move away slowly—like they were just passing by.

"Get in the van, Boy."

At no time did I question Granddad, ask him "why," sass him, or fail to respond immediately. You just didn't second guess Granddad. I was in the van in about two seconds, and I saw a black and white Galveston police car come to a quiet stop beside Granddad.

"Afternoon, Ronnie," Granddad said calmly.

"Hot, ain't it, Slim?" asked the cop fanning himself with his hat.

Granddad nodded, then turned and spit tobacco juice.

"How's the criminal life, loser?" said the younger cop at the wheel of the car.

The other one gave him a quick, sharp look, then turned to Granddad. "You got any a' that dark stuff left?" The other cop asked in a much friendlier tone.

"You bet. How much you guys need?"

"It's towards the end of the shift. Anything you can spare would be great, Slim." Granddad opened the lower of the two drawers and pulled out four of the Mason jars. He snapped open a bag.

"Don't bother with the bag, Old Son—that stuff won't live to see the sunset!" The older cop laughed at the joke.

Granddad handed them through the window, and the cops opened the jars without delay, and started sipping. The danger here was thick, and even I could sense it. I saw Granddad's right hand caress the knife in his back pocket several times during the encounter.

"How much we owe you?"

"One thin dime."

"That way they cain't say it was a gratuity, ya' see," the older one said to the younger.

"Well, Slim, got the boy again this summer, huh?"

"Yeah, he does the pulling for me. Grandson. It's his summer job." Granddad said, sharing a chuckle with the policeman he seemed to know. "Gotta go, Ronnie. We'll see you later."

"You bet. Make sure that boy learns to cook that stuff right. Wouldn't do to have a bunch of rot gut on the street, you know."

Granddad smiled as they pulled away. The older cop waved. Granddad put the side down and got in behind the wheel.

"Granddad, that scared me."

"Don't worry, Boy, those guys want it as much as the regulars. They just don't like to pay for it. And I don't mind—they pretty much stay away from me when I'm out selling my 'vegetables,' you understand?"

I nodded, but my heart was pounding.

He put his big hand into his pocket, and as was his custom, flipped me a silver dollar. It was always the highlight of my day with Granddad. The heft of the silver dollar made me feel like I had a jewel or something special in my pocket. Sometimes I walked around with my hand in my pocket gripping the silver dollar. No few comments were made about how that looked.

"Boy, Royce invited us to stop by on the way home this afternoon. I wouldn't mind listening to a little Cajun music and drinking a little shine. How about you? The music, I mean. Not the shine."

I had never been invited to do this before. I was ecstatic. "Granddad, I'd really like to! I like Royce."

"Okay, but your mom and dad would be really pissed if they find out. Can you keep your mouth shut?"

"Yessir."

"I ain't worried so much about your dad, but, God Almighty have mercy on us both if your momma finds out! You know what I mean?"

"Yes—Sir," I said with understanding.

We parked the van about a block from Royce's house. When we got to the house, we went around back to an old barn. Granddad opened the big front door, and we entered.

"Holy cow!" I whispered.

Granddad smiled.

Inside were a sawdust floor and several picnic tables scattered around with red and white checked vinyl tablecloths on them. At some sat men playing Dominoes or just listening to the music from a large, beautiful old jukebox. Along one wall were several iceboxes.

"One of those iceboxes is full of my corn liquor, Boy," Granddad said, pointing with a sausage size finger.

I was unable to speak.

From a table in the corner, Royce motioned for us to come over.

"Hey, Royce."

"Hey, Slim. Sit down with us. Who's your pal there?"

Granddad looked at me.

"Hi, Royce. Don't you remember me? I'm his grandson. I work with him every summer now. I saw you—"

"I'm jus' kidden, son. I know who you are. Sit down with us a bit. Slim let you sip the stuff?"

I was confused, but just for a moment. "No sir."

Royce acted very surprised. "What! Slim, how's this boy ever gonna grow up right!"

"His momma would kick my—" He didn't finish.

As they talked, I noticed the men around me looked dangerous. They had what Momma called "jailhouse" tatoos. Two stopped arm wrestling and stared at me. I wasn't sure what they were thinking, but something instinctive made the hair on the back of my neck stand up. I was afraid.

"Oh, hell. The boy's here with friends. Let's make a man out of him, huh? It's only three o'clock; nobody'll even know it happened. What do you say?"

All the other guys looked at us and encouraged Granddad.

"All right, let him try the clear stuff! Where's it at Royce?"

The next thing I knew, a jar of the clear liquid was set in front of me. I was nervous and happy all at once. As I brought the jar to my lips, I could smell nothing. But when the liquid hit my tongue, it was boiling hot—or so I thought. There was no way l could let this stuff go down my throat. Some of it dribbled out—some of it spewed out. The entire room broke out in screaming laughter. I was mortified.

"Boy, don't drink it like water!" Granddad said. "Watch me."

I watched him as he brought the jar to his mouth. First, he looked at the jar from several angles.

"Lookin' for floatin' pieces, so's I can get 'em out."

Then he brought the jar to his lips and gently licked the screw part of the glass.

"Gets the drippin's off, so's it don't drip down on your shirt."

The he made a big deal out of smelling the liquid.

"Ahhhh. Then you smell the bouquet."

Well, this brought the house down. Even I got the joke now. And Granddad, smiling, sipped a small amount of the stuff.

"Thanks, Granddad," I started tasting the hot liquid. That's the last thing I recall clearly.

Then sounds in the room became a whisper, like at Mass in a chapel with high ceilings. I could hear the noise, but it didn't quite reach my ears. The faces of all those around me morphed into replicas of a Dali painting—melting faces with big round eyes. All sense of touch was lost. When I wrapped my fingers around the jar to have another sip, I had to use both hands to make sure I didn't drip the precious liquid.

The most unusual thing, however, was my inability to speak English. My lips and cheeks were completely numb.

"Grahhhhh, mmy lppsss..." They all looked at me like I had just stepped off a space ship. And then they laughed so hard I think one of them fell off the bench. "Nna, wwhasss."

Granddad leaned over and wiped the drool off my chin and shirt. "Told you it was good stuff, boy."

I was beyond speech. I saw Granddad's face change several times as I looked at him—and it seemed that my head was moving side to side, under its own control.

"Royce, time to go. I better take the boy to the levee for some air before I take him home. Thanks for the invite. See you next Saturday, if not before."

Royce waved and nodded.

Granddad took me by the arm. I could see it, but I couldn't feel it, and I still had no speech.

"Boy, what's your head nodding back and forth like that for?"

I couldn't answer.

In the next instant, I was in the front seat of the van with my face in my lap.

"Good God, Boy, sit up before you break your back, will you?"

I knew he was talking to me, but I didn't get the meaning of the words. Granddad was driving along the road to the East Levee with one big hand on the wheel and the other across my chest to hold me upright. I could see my arms jumping around like rag dolls. We parked near the water at the levee. Granddad came around and helped me out of the seat.

"Damn, Son, your momma's going to kill you. Right after she kills me."

He took me to the sandy beach and took off my shoes. He put my feet in the water hoping it would help sober me up.

I threw up. I threw up with such force that it surprised Granddad. He splashed saltwater on my face, took my shirt off, rinsed it in the gulf, and laid it on a levee rock to dry. It was so hot it would dry in minutes. Then he walked me around the beach, and this seemed to help some. I was starting to get my speech back.

"Granddad?"

Pause.

"Granddad?

"How you doing, Stud?"

"What. Happened."

"Had a sip or two, Boy. You'll be fine in a few minutes."

"Mom."

"Yeah, she'll be really pissed if we don't get you up and around."

"Mom."

"Okay. I have a plan. When we get to your house, I'll carry you in, and we'll tell your momma that you are sleeping. I'll put you in your bed and get the heck outta there. What do you think?"

All I could do was nod.

When we got in the van, the smell of booze, vomit, sweat, and chewing tobacco made me feel like I was going to throw up again. Granddad parked the big van in the alley at the gate to our yard. As he carried me to the house, I again smelled the putrid trashcans in contrast to the sweet honeysuckle.

My senses were dulled, but after he put me in my bed, I could hear voices.

"Boy worked hard today, and, brother, was it hot. Just wore him out. Listen, I'd love to stay and talk, but got things I gotta do. Tell him to call me tomorrow."

That was the quickest exit Granddad had ever made.

I vaguely remember someone checking on me in the night, but I don't think I moved at all until the next morning when Mother leaned into the room. "C'mon, breakfast will be ready in two minutes."

God, that sounded terrible. My head hurt, and my stomach was cramping, but I couldn't let Mother get wind of last night's events. I washed my face, went downstairs, and sat at the table with her. After a while I asked, "Momma, tell me again what you think I should be when I grow up."

Just Lavender Polish

By Glenys O'Connell
Ireland

I finally found you again—inside a tin of lavender furniture polish.

It took three countries and thousands of kilometers, but I found you. Right there in the household goods aisle. I flipped open the tin, took a deep breath, and was transported back to the stoop of your cottage, and there you were, smiling that special smile and telling me again that you loved me.

When you left, things weren't going well for me, and I was too young to understand why. I was angry with you, and that anger chased away so many good things, including the lovely thick smell of lavender furniture wax.

But all it took was a tin of old-fashioned polish to bring you back. If only I'd known. I hadn't seen polish like this in years. In my new North American home, all I'd been able to find had been that thoroughly modern spray stuff. Spray and wipe, spray and wipe. A job quickly done and on to something else. And what was I saving the time for? To rush on to the next thing? Certainly not to sit out in the softness of the evening–for all those years my little front porch was a place for old rubber boots, drooping plants, and very little more as I moved through my life in a blur. No time to feel the smooth wood beneath the cloth, no time to appreciate the glow of polished wood. And if sometimes my fingers wished for the thick waxy feel of the polish block and the simple, mind-freeing task of rubbing, stroking, and coaxing a shine from the wood, it was a longing I never quite identified. Just as I never identified how much I missed you.

You were the one who taught me, as a very little girl, the simple joy of bringing order and comfort to the places we lived. You taught me the pleasant fulfillment of rubbing a rag across the perfumed wax and slowly teasing the big old solid furniture of your youth into a mellow shine. You were the one who taught a lesson I didn't understand until later—that the bits at the back should still be bright and clean, even if nobody can see them.

You wanted me to understand that there was no point putting on a bright façade if deep down inside your soul was crying out for the nourishment of a bit of polish and attention. It was a lesson it took me many years to come to without your guiding hand.

And in the evening, the day's work done and the tools put away, the bread dough already rising and filling the kitchen with the soft tang of yeast, there was the reward of a cool glass of your homemade dandelion and burdock pop outside on the stoop as the sky turned pink and gray.

I remember playing around your feet as you read in the shade of the cottage wall, the terrace flagstones still warm in the fading evening sun. Bees would dance in the lavender bush giving the flower spikes one last sip before bedtime. Your love of books remained with me, the memory of how you turned to the printed page for refuge when you faced so much alone—a refuge I still hold to.

Oh, but even now I remember the glorious houses that you took me to. You loved beautiful things—your eyes would light up at the sight of a lovely garden, a mass of wildflowers, the sun spreading soft light through gleaming windows and billowing white lace curtains. Remember the doll collection I could see but never touch? And the deep, thick pile of the carpets our feet sank into, something neither of us had experienced before—real wool, the tufts so fine and light between my toes! And the expensive furniture—sometimes lean and modern, sometimes staid, elegant, and old—all of it rich and beautiful.

None of it was yours, yet you loved it and cared for it all the same. Perhaps if your life had gone differently, you would have been able to have a home like the lovely places you took me to. But you were just the cleaner, there for a few hours each week.

Yet you used the beauty of these homes to help me look beyond the things I knew into an existence you knew was within my grasp. You showed me a world way beyond anything I could have imagined. Horizons opened out at a wave of your hand, and I became someone who could aspire to things untold. Your love of beautiful things became a part of me, just as much as your gentle touch when I was sick became my own gentle touch when my children ailed.

I'm sad to say that somewhere along the way, in North America, in Europe, in the wastelands of problems and loss, the faith you'd instilled in me slipped away. The faith that kept you going through a life that glowed as warmly as your polished table tops, ebbed and slipped away from the girl I was when you left. But it was to be resurrected again by the simple act of opening a tin of wax polish, by breathing in the fragrance of the lavender that I rub softly onto the bits of furniture we have collected and loved over the years.

Funny to think that I am now the age you were when I was born. My children never had a grandmother, but some day I hope to teach my own grandchildren the things you taught me—starting by plopping a soft duster into chubby baby hands and taking the lid off a tin of lavender polish.

I wonder if it was just an accident that I chose to make a new life in a place you'd never been but always wanted to visit—a place just miles from where your husband was born? Or did I come here so that you could see it through my eyes that we might come full circle? And that I might learn again the simple joy of slowing down, of sitting out in the sun, seeing the world pass my porch, and watching the garden grow?

Once, as we sat out in the evening all those years ago, you told me about your own grandmother. You said she still visited you, even though she'd been gone years long before. I thought it was just the ramblings of an old woman, until I found that you were still here in my heart, waiting to visit again as I polish the furniture or place a jar of wildflowers on the little wicker table outside my front door—wildflowers whose names you taught me, so long ago.

For here was yet another object lesson in love, for love never dies if you keep the memories bright and polished. It was no matter to you that a bullet took Granddad's life in France in 1918—for you he was always just a thought or dream away throughout the years, the memories taken out and lovingly polished and preserved. Just before you left us, you smiled that glorious smile and told us he was waiting for you.

Now I have a big pot of lavender on my porch. On sunny days, it's a delight for the honeybees, and the flower spikes are truly a sight for sore eyes. I sit here and rub a leaf between my fingers to release the perfume, happy with the sun on my face, pulling out memories I thought were lost forever and polishing them until they glow.

Gifts on a Porch Swing

By Barbara Deming
San Marcos, California, United States

Swinging with my grandfather on the front porch is one of the fondest memories from my childhood. Most East Texas houses in those days had a wraparound porch, each blessed with a swing. They were usually made of hardwood, often clear-varnished oak. This particular one was painted white like the gingerbread trim on the house and was tucked around the corner from the main entrance—for a bit of privacy, I imagine.

Today if we had a swing and a front porch and tried to apply the same use, I suppose it would be called "hanging out." Back then it was the center of family get-togethers. But no matter how many other relatives gathered with tall glasses of sweet tea in the high-backed wooden rockers and straight chairs brought out from the dining room, Daddy Joe and I always claimed the swing.

The aunts engaged in discussions of their children's progress in school, summer vacation plans, and the latest family gossip—voices lowered, of course, because as they said, "Little pitchers have big ears." Uncles talked about their jobs in Houston, the new Pontiac someone purchased, and deer season beginning in October.

I was Daddy Joe's first granddaughter. Maybe that's why we could talk about things that the other adults didn't seem to be interested in. Maybe it was because we both shared a love of fishing. Or maybe it was just that we enjoyed being together. The talk around us could be funny or serious, but we ignored most of it. Daddy Joe and I spoke of more important matters—such as work.

On Saturday visits, I worked for Daddy Joe in his country grocery store. First he taught me how to properly sack groceries for his customers. That was fun for a few years, but I soon wanted a promotion. It was more fun putting penny candy (always more than a penny's worth as per Daddy Joe's instructions) into a small brown paper sack and into a child's hand or to wrap up the sliced bacon in pink meat paper. Later I graduated to listing charges and payments in a daily ledger while seated in the chair on rollers at his big oak roll-top desk at the back of the store. On those Sundays seated together on the swing, we talked about sales, the cat chasing mice in the feed room, folks slowly moving their mule-driven wagons, or old beat-up trucks up the alley. And we always spoke of fishing.

That porch swing was the staging area for those week-end trips to White Rock Creek where we camped and fished. It was at the water's edge that Daddy Joe taught me to put a wiggly worm on a hook, cast out the line on a cane pole, and land sun perch on the sandy bank. Looking back, I think he received as much pleasure from watching me fish as he did with his own catch.

At Daddy Joe's, sunny mornings or rainy afternoons, the fun was on the front porch.

When I was a child, you created your own entertain-ment. Girl-cousins set up imaginary houses for their store-bought paper dolls. The boys flew their folded-paper air-planes with appropriate whining sounds of prop engines and the kaboom of bombs falling. The swing, that important piece of outdoor furniture, had been there for generations whatever the games. It had once served as the cockpit of our uncle's Navy Avenger as we reenacted the Battle of Midway. Or you could just sit there—reading, writing, thinking—or just talking.

There are things you can say in a porch swing that you can't speak of anywhere else. I remember Daddy Joe listening to me, offering advice that I could somehow find a way to accept when I was growing up. Parental discipline, sibling disagreements, boy troubles—Daddy Joe would hear me out, nod or shake his head, seeming to always know the right words to steer me along life's proper path.

There were times when we just sat in silence, enjoying the sound of mockingbirds perched in the pecan trees. Maybe Daddy Joe would be reading the Sunday newspaper while I paged through his collection of *Life* or *National Geographic*, lost in another world, one foot tucked beneath me, the other on the floor to keep the swing in slow motion. As the eldest of five children, I looked forward to these quiet times when neither of us felt we had to speak in order to be the center of attention. The stillness, the lack of words, in some mysterious way drew us closer.

When I was 20, it was on the porch swing that Daddy Joe talked to me about his future. Looking at the dark sky, he shared his thoughts. "I've spent many a night out here, BJ, looking at the millions of stars up there. Wondering, hoping there really is a God in the hereafter." He laughed, a little shaky sound like none other I could remember hearing from him. "I reckon this old swing has saved me many a dollar not spent on doctors, psychiatrists, or lawyers. It was here I made the hardest decision I guess I've ever had to make."

With my head on his shoulder, hugging him for what turned out to be the last time, I cried as he went on to explain that the store must be sold and how he'd be making a move to Uncle John's in Houston for his last days.

"BJ, it bothers me that I have nothing…no money, no property, nothing of value…for you to inherit."

I tried to reassure him. But how could I make him understand that his legacy would be the love and wisdom gladly dispensed for so many years to a gangly grand-girl-child? There on that porch swing he had given me peaceful security, taught a work ethic that I carried into the working world throughout the years, and instilled in me the courage to face life's ups and downs.

It was a precious gift.

Even now I can close my eyes and hear the creak of the chains, feel the sway as feet set it in motion. I hear the eager voice sharing the excitement of the day's happening. I feel the warmth of arms hugging me close as I nap, dreaming of the fish to be caught and pan-fried. And my hope as I dream of those days from my past is that somewhere there are other little girls sharing their secrets on a porch swing with a special grandfather.

Lullaby

By Kimberly Ripley
Portsmouth, New Hampshire, United States

"By-low, my baby," the old lady sang to the little girl on her lap.

Although the child wasn't a baby, she relished the comfort of the familiar tune. There was security in the warmth of the arms that brought her joy; taught her letters, numbers, and rhymes; and on rare occasions scolded her.

In the kitchen it was warm, heat radiating from the old coal and wood fired stove. Together they made pies, sifting flour from the great oak Hoosier. The girl took scraps of crust and made miniature pies. The aroma filled the house with a sweet, inviting scent.

Later they might cut paper dolls or scraps of cloth for quilt squares. "Idle hands do the work of the devil," the woman said. But on Sunday their hands remained idle. "Sunday is the Lord's day," she said, as she sat quietly in her rocking chair and gazed out at her garden.

Raised by her great-grandmother, and home-schooled, the little girl had no playmates. How she longed to run and play and make noise like the children she saw in the schoolyards when they made their trek to the A & P.

"Please can't we stop?" she begged her great-grandmother.

"Those children have diseases," her great-grandmother replied. "Some of them are lousy."

The girl didn't understand it was merely a tired old woman's attempt to protect the child she loved from perils beyond her grasp.

Twisted and bent with arthritis, at nearly 80 it was painful to make the trip for groceries. Hauling the child to and from school each day would have been impossible. But her strong faith prevailed. The Lord had given this innocent child to her care, and she would let neither of them down. Serving as parent, teacher, mentor, and friend proved tedious at times, but her love for the child girded her will.

Together they spent hours tending the small garden in the yard. The woman recited the names of plants and flowers to the child and explained how she planted them from seedlings, bulbs, or shoots. The child loved the moist crumbly dirt. Lifting it to her face, she smelled and sometimes tasted the damp earth.

The hens and chickens were the little girl's favorites. Fat and stubby with green pointed leaves, they mesmerized her. Listening to their history, she imagined they were animals and had been sold from one farm to the next. Tracing their heritage, they became more intriguing, and before long they had names and long lists of descendents. When the weather turned cold, they lovingly dug the hens and chickens from their flowerbed and brought them in for safekeeping from the winter.

Many afternoons the pair walked to the church where the Friendly Circle met. There the group of withered ladies pondered lists of needy families and assembled quilts and knit mittens to donate. Most days the little girl became bored with cutting the bits of colored cloth and wandered instead throughout the sanctuary and around the maze of classrooms. Closing her eyes and dreaming rooms filled with children, she imagined they were her friends and might say, "Come play at my house this afternoon." But that was just a daydream.

When her mother left her to live with her great-grandmother, she had told her, "Do what you will with the child, but don't drag her to church where she'll be brainwashed by the likes of Pastor Woodbury and his prissy wife!" So the child came only on afternoons when old ladies sat drinking their tea, doing their handy work, and chatting about daughters and sons and beautiful grandchildren.

Warm afternoons at home were spent on the piazza. That's what her great-grandmother called the large expanse of porch that was glassed in during the winter and screened against flies and mosquitoes in spring and summer. There they sat, peeling potatoes, shelling peas, or coring apples for a pie.

Setting the table was the little girl's chore, and she set their places at the long narrow table with care. The dishes, chipped and worn with age, and the tumblers, faded patterns in plastic, wore scars from many years of washing. A dusty bowl of plastic fruit served as the centerpiece. Not an ethereal setting, but one from which consistent praise and unconditional love had flourished. Holding hands, feeling power in the prayer they shared, the child was transformed. Unable to understand the feeling, she basked in its comfort and serenity. Lost in the innocence of childhood, she was oblivious to the significance of these mundane rituals.

But when the end of oblivion surprises us, we awaken to find reality has taken its place. Such was the chain of events that wrote the epilogue to those simpler times. I was the little girl. Each day I spent with my great-grandmother was an example of the finest of God's blessings. To feel that love and learn from her wisdom were gifts more gracious than any I'd received.

As a little girl, I balked at predictability. I grew weary of quilting and knitting and of supper at precisely five. I wondered what the point was in helping people you didn't know. Church seemed positively absurd. Why believe in things you can't see?

As an adult, I'm astonished at life's ironies. The child with no playmates has been blessed with lasting, meaningful friendships. Annoyances are now labors of love.

I established a relationship with an elderly woman in Mississippi. Though we have never met, through The Box Project we communicate with letters and cards. Each month our family sends a box of necessities and goodies to her. I also attend church regularly and am active in the congregation.

But I miss great-grandmother's lullaby. Mostly I miss her love and reassurance when I flounder in raising children or making decisions. She has been gone now for 23 years, and not a day goes by that I don't think about her.

One day last spring when I was undergoing health problems and stress was taking its toll, I was sitting by our flowerbed when I noticed a small cluster of hens and chickens. They weren't there the day before. Logic tells me they were planted by a kind neighbor. My heart says they were a gift from a stooped and weary old woman with hands that worked miracles and a heart overflowing with love and grace.

The Sanctuary

By Dorothy Thompson
Eastern Shore of Virginia, United States

My grandfather is gone now and has been for 44 years, but how well I remember him. A living icon on our little peninsula, the Eastern Shore of Virginia, but no one knew him more fondly than I.

I remember him as being tall, yet gentle and firm. In fact, I don't remember him ever scolding me. He didn't have the heart.

I used to climb into his lap while he was reading the Sunday paper on our little porch in the country and listen to the rain pounding on our tin roof. Its rhythmic poetry lulled my little body to sleep.

In fact, my grandfather had an affinity for sitting on our little wooden porch during rainstorms. I'd peek out the door and see him sitting there, pipe in mouth, humming to the beat of the thunder as it pounded above us.

"Daddy," I would ask, "aren't you scared?"

I called him Daddy because he was the closest thing to a daddy I had since my own father walked out on my mother and me when I was a baby. I never saw my real father after that.

"Hey, girl," he'd say, flashing his warm toothy smile. "Come here, and I'll tell you a story."

I so wanted to join him. Being four years old at the time, I was scared of everything from boogiemen hanging out by the outhouse to Uncle Cecil who loved to torment me by chasing me around the house with his dentures.

Sensing my hesitancy, he walked over and picked me up. Giving him the biggest monkey hug I could muster, he carried me over to the rocker and continued to rock to the rhythm of the storm, never missing a beat.

"Did I ever tell you about the time when I made the first plastic coat hanger?" he asked.

I laughed. "Daddy, coat hangers aren't made out of plastic!"

"They sure are!" he said. "I thought that clothes could hang better on plastic hangers instead of wire. I was getting tired of your grandmother complaining that her clothes weren't hanging right. She said if there was a way to make them not have creases at the top, it would make her life so much better."

"What happened?" I asked, oblivious to the pit-pats of raindrops hitting the tin roof.

"Well, I applied for a patent, and they told me I needed more money than I had. It seems the word got out," he continued, "and some guy beat me to it."

He looked off into the distance, almost mournfully. "We'd be rich right now, little girl," he said. "And we'd have a new house with a bathroom inside and all the food you could ever eat."

"But, Daddy? That's not fair. How could he do that?"

"Money talks, Sweetheart," he said. "But you know what?"

"What?"

"He may have taken my idea, but he didn't take my dreams."

I cuddled closer to Daddy, feeling his warmth and compassion with every breath. I didn't think much about dreams back then. I was more concerned with catching fireflies on a warm summer evening and watching them glow in Grandma's pickling jars.

As I matured, I forgot about those years as a poor, country child and strived for the material things we all yearn for: a house in the suburbs, a pool in the backyard, 2.5 children.

However, none of them became a reality for me. After my husband left me to care for my two children, the house in the suburbs became one rental after another. Losing myself in my quest to put food on the table, I lost my sense of peace and tranquility. I became a basket case of nerves, waiting to explode over one setback after another.

One day, I met a man through the Internet, 30 years my senior. It wasn't a romantic interlude by any means, but because of him, a very significant change occurred in my life. In fact, this man reminded me of the one male figure that meant so much to me—my grandfather.

This man sensed my raging insides, churning like a relentless storm, pounding upon the land with incredible force, destroying everything in its path.

"My child," he said, "you are like a raging inferno. It's time you found a sanctuary to collect your thoughts and discover your dreams."

He was right. But in order to do that, I knew I must return to the beginning—my roots. I started my car and made my way back to my childhood home. The little town had not changed much in 44 years, except for the occasional convenience store on the outskirts of town.

I parked my car in the parking lot of the same store where my grandmother had bought my first two-wheeler. It had not changed a bit.

I walked the same sidewalk I walked as a child, past neighbor's houses that were now inhabited by new faces.

Bicycles had become a thing of the past; in fact, I could not see a single one on my soul's sojourn to my past.

Finally, I reached my destination and stopped. My grandparent's house no longer sat by the side of the road.

Everything was gone.

I climbed onto the grassy knoll and sat under the mimosa trees that were still standing after all these years. The rusty railroad tracks lay dormant where, once upon a time, freight trains chugged slowly by, rattling everything in sight. The outhouse had long since been gone, but the spot remained etched in my mind. The garden leading to my neighbor's yard, where I had walked each morning to play with the neighbor's kids, was also gone.

And then the most remarkable thing happened. My grandfather appeared and spoke to me. He said that in order to have peace in this life, I must remember what he told me that rainy night sitting on the front porch with the rain hitting our tin roof.

Never lose sight of your dreams.

I stood and made my way back to the car, sitting there in the deserted parking lot. On the way home, I realized what had just occurred.

I had found my sanctuary.

Broom-Swinging Grandma

By Janet Elaine Smith
East Grand Forks, Minnesota, United States

It didn't matter what the weather was like, at 3:20 in the afternoon every weekday, Grandma Bowen was out on her front porch wielding her broom as she softly hummed a tune.

Grandma Bowen was a little bitty thing, just 4'8" tall. Yes, she had a name. It was Alice Matilda Bowen, but everybody called her Grandma Bowen. Even the local paper, once a year—in May—would announce on the front page "Grandma Bowen celebrates 80th birthday" or "Grandma Bowen is guest at her 92nd birthday." Every year Grandma Bowen's birthday was about the biggest news Lake City, Minnesota, had seen all year long. Oh—except the year half the town burned to the ground. But even such an event as that knew better than to mess with Grandma Bowen, so the fire was in a different part of the year.

Grandma Bowen's front porch had an old-fashioned swing on it. As little children, we often sat on it with her and listened to her spin yarns about "the old country." Grandma Bowen was Irish. We all knew it, because she told us so many times. And there was not a cleaner front porch in all of Lake City. Come rain or come shine, come wind or come snow, that front porch got the licking of a lifetime with Grandma Bowen's withered old broom.

She would take the watch she wore hanging from a chain around her neck and check it. When it was almost 3:30, she would sweep more furiously than before.

She pretended not to hear the snickers of the children on the way home from school. It was a ritual, just like Christmas and Easter. One of the children would stoop down in front of the old railing on the front porch and would eventually start to giggle. Every day was the same.

"Get out of my Johnny-jump-ups!" Grandma Bowen would yell, her voice booming much too large for her size. "Those little faces are going to jump up and bite you!" Then she would shake her broom at the children, pretending to be furious with them.

Then the children would scamper away from the garden and scurry up onto the porch with Grandma Bowen. They'd crowd onto the swing, and Grandma Bowen would disappear into the house. In a few minutes, she'd come back out onto the porch, a plateful of freshly baked round white sugar cookies in one hand and a pitcher of milk and a few small glasses somehow tucked into the other hand. Her hands were so tiny—it was always a matter of great speculation how she could carry so much at once.

The pitcher was a brown ceramic creation, and it was the most fascinating piece of pottery I have ever seen. It had two rows of trees encircling it and a path between the trees. If you studied it carefully, you could almost feel yourself walking on the path, feeling the gentle breeze on your face. And it always contained thick, fresh yellow milk.

Years later, long after Grandma Bowen had died at the age of 98, I began to do our family genealogy. As I searched through the personal scrapbook she had willed to me, I learned that Grandma Bowen, who had claimed to be Irish through and through, was actually born in Rossi, New York. While her older brothers were born in Ireland and came to New York with their parents during the potato famine, Grandma Bowen never saw the Emerald Isle.

Was she a liar? Never! She was as pure as the driven snow. I came up with two possible explanations: I believe she had heard her parents and brothers talk about "the old country" so much that she actually believed she had been born there; or, as my mother said, her mother had kissed the blarney stone so many times that none of the family knew fact from fiction.

The second surprise came when I discovered my husband's Keith family had not lived in Wisconsin, as we had been led to believe, but lived just across the way a bit from Grandma Bowen right there in Lake City, Minnesota. In fact, there were articles from the newspaper in Grandma Bowen's scrapbook that had been written by the Keith family. These articles talked about several incidents which involved both the Bowen family and the Keith clan.

I located one of the older generation of Keiths, a retired schoolteacher named Mabel, living in Illinois. I hurried to call her, and we had a delightful exchange. She told me about life in Lake City when she was a child.

I told Mabel that my family was from Lake City, as well. She asked what their name was, and I told her they were Merrills, Websters, and Bowens.

"Grandma Bowen?" she exclaimed excitedly. "You are related to Grandma Bowen?"

It was with great pride and glee that I told her Grandma Bowen was my real great-grandmother. And then she began to relate the story of the Johnny-jump-ups and Grandma Bowen sweeping that front porch so much that the paint was worn right off of it and the platefuls of sugar cookies and the brown pitcher full of milk.

"It was the most amazing pitcher," she said. "It had trees on it, and you could almost walk on the path around it." Oh, yes, I knew exactly what she meant! "I wonder what ever happened to that pitcher?" she asked.

I smiled. "I have it sitting on my kitchen table. I have artificial flowers in it."

I thought I was going to go deaf, she screamed so loud.

"That pitcher was meant to have milk in it! It was never made for flowers! You take those flowers out of it right now! And don't you ever put anything but milk in it again!"

The flowers were tossed aside. I poured a pitcher of milk and had a cookie (it was a "store-bought" one, not a homemade sugar cookie) as soon as I hung up the phone. Since then, I have never put anything but milk in my special little brown pitcher.

If I close my eyes, I can imagine I am sitting on the swing on Grandma Bowen's front porch. I hear the children giggle and Grandma Bowen yell at them to, "Get out of the Johnny-jump-ups or their little faces will bite you."

Grandma Bowen and I had a special bond. I felt it all of the years we spent together.

She died when I was a sophomore in high school, and it somehow seemed fitting that her funeral was on my birthday. It was as if she was telling me one last time that we were together.

As I sat on the swing the day of her funeral, a cool October day, I closed my eyes and still felt her presence. Oh, how I loved that front porch—and Grandma Bowen!

The Road Trip

By Heather V. Long
Sterling, Virginia, United States

Everything I needed to know, I learned in the backseat of my grandmother's car.

The Road Trip was the ultimate rush at the end of every school year. Once or twice, the year ended early as my grandmother informed the school that my brother and I were leaving on X date and that was that. We raced home on the last day, leaving behind the school bus, the books, and the endless hours staring at ugly yellow walls while the teachers droned on about some subjects that I had long since grasped.

We were wired for the trip that was waiting for us as soon as we burst in the front door. My grandmother sat at the dining room table, and a grin lit up her face at our breathless rush through the door. Backpacks were flung into the hall closet as we hurried over to join her. On the table was a map. We pressed in eagerly as she spread it out so we could see it in its entirety.

"Where do we want to go this time?" She asked.

The destination was always her question. Would we like to drive to the Grand Canyon? What about to the battle-fields in Tennessee? There was always Galveston Island and South Padre beyond that. We clambered up onto the chairs and leaned hard over the table as her finger drew the magical line from our city to these faraway places.

"I want to see Niagara Falls!" I announced imperiously.

"I'd rather see the horses in Kentucky," my brother countered.

"You always want to see the horses in Kentucky!" Not that I minded. I loved horses, but after all the pictures of the beautiful waterfall on television, I really wanted to see Niagara.

Sometimes we took planes, like when we went to visit England, but every other time it was always the car. I loved our beat up old station wagon with its wood board siding. The tales it could tell of our many adventures.

"So our options are the Kentucky Races or Niagara Falls?" My grandmother intervened before the argument could get out of hand. Her decisions were always final, weighing in on the argument with a great deal of gravity. She only took two weeks of vacation every year, so the destination needed to fit into that realm of possibility.

"Yeah!" We chorused.

"All right then," she smiled at both of us as she withdrew a Kennedy half-dollar from her change purse. "Heads Kentucky, tails Niagara. Agreed?"

Our heads bobbed enthusiastically. Coin tosses were the best way to settle a difference of opinion when both destinations suited everyone involved just fine. The coin flipped into the air and landed with a tinkle on the table, spinning for a moment before settling definitively heads up.

This year Kentucky, next year Niagara.

Once the decision was made, the house broke out into organized chaos as my grandmother directed us towards the packing of clothes, sandwiches, and other supplies necessary for car traveling. We loaded up one bag each with tapes, books, and games. The car could only hold so much! There was always eagerness in my grandmother's eyes as she helped us load up the car. We needed blankets and pillows for the back so that one or both of us could sleep while she drove.

There were rules to these trips, rules we observed with religious fervor. The car must be packed and loaded. Then back into the apartment we would rocket. Showers for both of us, our rooms to be cleaned, all the household garbage shuffled out, and finally a well-made dinner. My grandmother watched the rabid activity with fondness, helping out now and then if requested. We attacked the house, and our mother arrived home in the midst of the blitz. She watched us with a funny, little smile as we dashed about our chores with an eagerness rarely ever displayed. Once everything was done, we fell like ravenous beasts on the roast beef and potatoes Grandmother had prepared.

"Looking forward to the trip?" Mother asked, her amusement clear.

"Uh-huh," I answered around a mouthful of food. "We're going to Kentucky!"

"To see the horses!" My brother added.

"Don't talk with your mouth full," Mother laughed. "Want more?"

Two heads bobbed with absolute enthusiasm. We ate like it was our last meal. There were no arguments over vegetables at the table, because the grand adventure was only a few hours away! Dishes washed and tucked into the dish-washer, we deposited kisses on the cheeks of the two women who were so thoroughly enjoying themselves at our expense and trotted off to bed.

The night before was the hardest. I couldn't sleep. I tossed and turned, my mind filled with images of Stuckey's along the roadside, of treasures discovered in rest stops, and of course, horses. I tossed and turned until exhaustion finally worked its magic and sent me off into the land of sleep. Shortly after four in the morning, while the rest of the world still slept, a light tap on the door woke me. My grandmother peered inside and called out my name.

"Come along, Luv," she whispered into the darkened bedroom, "time to up and at 'em!"

The rush and tumble of excitement rebounded through me once more, and I flew out of the bed. I dived into the clothes that were laid out and as always, or so it seemed, I dashed out of the room before remembering to rush back and make the bed. Our footsteps sounded clunky as my brother and I jostled for position going down the stairs. Arriving on the first level, we found our mother waiting with our grandmother for hugs and kisses goodbye.

There were the usual admonishments of being on our best behavior as well as to try *not* to drive our grandmother *too* crazy. I only half-heard as my brother and I argued over who would get to sit in the first seat. My grandmother quelled the arguments quickly with another deft coin toss (I always seemed to lose that one), and into the back seat I clambered.

As my grandmother turned the key and coaxed the engine to life, my eyes invariably traveled back to the front porch. My mother stood in the doorway, illuminated by the porch light. She wore a sweater, wrapped tightly. One arm hugged itself to her and the other lifted in the wave goodbye. In my mind, a snapshot was taken—a captured moment carried with me until we returned home. The porch light would stay on during our absence, a light to guide us home again. It was the family tradition.

The dark was always the best time to leave, with the new day waiting just down the highway and our mother behind us, waiting patiently for our return. There would be stories to tell of our adventures and new knowledge to share. She had heard all about out trips to Carlsbad Caverns, the Grand Canyon, and Pike's Peak in Colorado.

"Are we ready?" My grandmother asked as she started to set the car into reverse. It was time to pull out of the parking spot and to begin our adventure for real.

"Oh yeah!" I shouted from the backseat, easily drowning out my brother's deeper voice in the front. The car lurched backwards, then smoothly turned. With a shift of the gears, it lurched forward, and off we went.

On every trip we left the mundane world behind and donned the caps of explorers. There was no finer way to spend a vacation than in the backseat of my grandmother's car on the road to adventure!

Porch Swing Cocktails

By Rusty Fischer
Orlando, Florida, United States

What kind of grandmother would give her grandson a cocktail every Saturday evening while he was growing up? As you'll see in the following story, only the best kind.

My grandmother, or "Nonny" as I called her, babysat me every Saturday night. You see, Saturday was the only night my busy parents were free to go out and have some fun for themselves. (Little did they know, my grandmother and I were the ones having all the fun!)

Dad always wore some gaudy red and yellow shirt with a very 1960's ruffle-collar and puffy sleeves and always had neatly trimmed sideburns that never seemed clean. Mom dressed in a mini-skirt, sunglasses, and shiny white go-go boots with an oversized purse that matched perfectly.

But I knew I had just as much fun as they did, if not more.

Nonny went all out for my weekly visits. Shortly after Mom and Dad dropped me off, she served dinner at the tiny dinette set in her equally tiny "dining room." I loved her carrots. Sliced thick and never mushy, they swam in a sea of butter and salt and melted in my mouth like vegetable candy, if ever there were such a thing. "Orange wheels," I called them, which always made her laugh.

Nonny's other specialty was a steaming platter heaped high with succulent chicken and rice. I was too young to know that since Nonny was approaching her mid-70's, this was the only meal of the week she actually cooked anymore. With her arthritis, it was all she could do just to open the can of Campbell's mushroom soup she stirred in the rice to give it that special "oomph." And skinning and de-boning the chicken breasts (they were cheaper that way) was a nearly Herculean effort for the little old lady who spent the rest of the week zapping Lean Cuisine dinners and sipping tea with blueberry muffins for dessert.

Nonny had a special set of dishes she'd purchased, one dish a week, at the local grocery store. They were white and covered with blue windmills and those little wooden shoes and called "Dutch" something or other. Nonny told me that she had bought them just for our special dinners and that she only brought them out for me. This always made me feel 10' tall. (It was years later before she finally confessed that the real reason she only used them with me—and me alone—was that she'd skipped a few weeks down at the grocery store and the set was incomplete.)

Dinner was usually over by the time *The Lawrence Welk Show* came on, and even though it was her favorite TV program, Nonny said she preferred spending time with her "little man." Instead of watching TV, we'd retire to the creaky wooden porch swing just outside the rickety sliding glass doors.

Nonny's husband, my grandfather, had died many years earlier. The two of them had spent countless hours in this very porch swing, rocking back and forth and admiring the Florida sunset while the neighbor children played, dogs barked, and flowers bloomed. And now it was my turn to sit next to Nonny and while away her lonely Saturday evenings. But it never felt creepy taking my grandfather's place in that creaky old porch swing. To me, it just felt right.

"Do you ever miss Pa Pa?" I asked Nonny one balmy Saturday night, watching the neighbors shoo the bugs away with a giant citronella candle.

"Sure I do," said Nonny in her no-nonsense, mid-western, I-grew-up-in-the-depression scoff. "Same way you'd miss me if I was gone. But I know he's up there looking out for me right now, and every other day, the same way I'll be up there looking out for you when you and your wife sit in the good old porch swing and while away a long, leisurely Saturday night."

"No way," I argued. "I'm **never** getting married. Gross! And besides, wherever you go, I'm going with you!"

"Don't worry, little man," she reassured me with a hug that smelled like talcum powder and the jug of Jovan Musk my mom helped me buy her every Christmas. "I don't plan on going anywhere for a long, long time. At least, not until you're married, that is."

"Gross," I repeated, with a case of the shivers just for luck.

As champagne music from the TV set bubbled through the screen door, Nonny and I would sit and swing, swing and sit. Sometimes I'd draw and she'd sew. Other times, we just talked about the neighbors or what each of us had done that day. She shared stories about growing up in the Great Depression until the closing strains of champagne music were corked for yet another week.

Then it was time for dessert, which in the best of all grandmotherly traditions, was something my Mom would never give me at home: a bottle of Coca-Cola, the short kind that fit perfectly into a young boy's hand, and a can of fancy mixed nuts. Nonny showed me how to drop the salty Spanish peanuts inside the bottle and watch the soda fizz and foam, then take a sip, chomping the slimy nuts and tasting the salty sweetness of the fizzy soda all at the same time like some great kid cacophony of bittersweet flavors and eye-watering goodness.

Nonny called this cola concoction our "Porch Swing Cocktail." Not only were they delicious, but they made me feel grown up. Imagine, a seven-year-old drinking a "cocktail" on a Saturday night!

When the Cokes were gone, we'd chomp on cashews and almonds to our hearts' content and listen to dogs bark in the distance. Nonny would light a citronella candle of her own to ward off the incoming mosquitoes, so big and plentiful that she called them "Florida's State Bird!" (It was years before I learned that Nonny hadn't actually coined this popular southern term.)

As the night grew darker, the tempo of our rocking gradually slowed down until finally our feet simply dangled in the warm air above Nonny's postage-sized porch. We hardly moved at all except for the smooth ocean breeze crawling over us from the beach. Living half a block from the Atlantic Ocean, there wasn't a night of her life that Nonny didn't enjoy falling asleep to the sound of ocean breakers crashing against the sandy beach. She said she wouldn't trade that sound for anything in the world.

Eventually, she did have to trade those breakers in. As the years passed and I grew older, my parents divorced, and Mom had nowhere to go on Saturday nights herself, so I took off with Mom where I left off with Nonny. Then school started, and before long ended, and I went off to college and started a life of my own.

Nonny grew older and older, and living at home became too much of a chore for her arthritic hands and creeping cataracts. Lean Cuisine dinners gave way to cups of blueberry yogurt, and with the decline in balanced meals, so declined Nonny's health. One living room fall turned into two, and it became too much for my single, working mother to handle on her own.

One weekend, Mom and I finally moved Nonny to a beautiful assisted living facility that became her new home. No more back yard, no more citronella candles, no more porch swing.

It has been quite a while since I've stopped by Nonny's. And although I am old enough now to enjoy the real alcoholic drink, I sure could go for a Porch Swing Cocktail, (minus the porch swing, of course). I doubt I could find two real, honest-to-goodness glass "bottles" of Coke in this re-cycle-crazy world, but I could easily swing by the gas station up the street and grab two of those 16-ounce plastic bottles on the way to the home. Of course, with the way I've been packing on the pounds lately, I'd probably go for a DIET Coke. Better grab Nonny one, too. (All that sugar might give her gas, don't ya know.)

And those nuts aren't all that good for you, I hear, with the fat and the salt and the preservatives. I may even have to smuggle them past the receptionist at the front.

But maybe just this once.

Bubble Gum in Disguise

By Georgiann Baldino
Naperville, Illinois, United States

Grandpa Blom didn't belong inside the house. He'd rather be outside.

Even when confined to an easy chair, his hands and eyes kept working. He was an elfin man, small stature and twinkling eyes. By the time I knew him, he could no longer stand up straight. Years of hard labor had perpetually bent him over. His legs formed a pronounced arch. To walk, his body twisted at the hips throwing one leg, then the other, rather like forcing a wishbone to amble across a table.

I have one treasured photograph of him taken near the end of his life that shows him seated on someone's front porch. The barrel-shaped chair swallows him up, but his smile couldn't be more complete. His whole face is involved. Hard to imagine how he could keep smiling like that after life had broken his body down. Even his grin shows wear and tear, for the teeth that remained were only nubs. But though he smiled readily and often, I distrusted him. Baby teeth seemed out of place on someone his age.

Grandpa Blom died in 1955 when I was a preschooler, but over the years I have often thought about this picturesque man. He provided my earliest childhood memory, and I've reconstructed the rest, building up his legend by talking to people who knew him. My mother reinforced my toddler images of him by laughing about my confrontations with

Grandpa. He made light of everything, you see, and even at age four, I took myself seriously. Even then, I doubted his veracity. The shakiness of his gait didn't fool me; here was a man eager to make trouble.

When I was older and asked questions about him, Mother fleshed out his beginnings. She told me how he emigrated from Norway, then fought with the woods to clear 40 acres of Wisconsin farmland on which he somehow managed to support his wife and 13 children, supplementing his income by working for the lumber company. As a teenager, I saw their house. I recall three rooms downstairs, two upstairs. The first floor consisted of a large kitchen, small bedroom for Grandma and Grandpa, and a parlor. The second floor under exposed rafters housed all the children. They still had no indoor bathroom. They used the privy, or at night, the chamber pot.

One of the stories my mother told seemed to make her very proud, as though proving his mettle. To get an even better picture of what kind of man this shadow figure was, I asked my aunt what she remembered of her father, and she confirmed the story my mother told. Grandpa never went to a doctor, ever, and he certainly never went to a dentist. One time when he was alone in the woods and a tooth pained him, he pulled it himself with a nail.

My aunt also told me the story of his Saturday night entertainment. How in the days before they had electricity, his prized possession was a battery-powered radio. It must have been a cumbersome receiver compared to what we use today, because Grandpa had to go into town on Saturday to get the batteries charged. He rarely took time for himself, working every available hour on the farm. The one exception was Saturday night when he put his freshly charged battery into his radio, settled into his rocking chair, and listened to

Barn Dance. On a really rare occasion, he also treated himself to a cigar.

But that was years before I knew him. When as an old man he stayed at our house, Grandpa Blom had more time. And time on his hands meant trouble, for he chose to fill it with mischief. To prove he didn't belong in a winter-warmed house, he'd pester one of his grandchildren. My mother told me that I was very often his target, because I got the maddest. The man with the childish smile knew exactly how to rile me. I can still remember his voice when he yelled at me, "You're a Blom!"

I was old enough to know my last name and proud enough to defend it. "I'm a Grever—"

"You're a Blom!"

"Grever!"

We yelled back and forth for a while, each of us getting more stubborn with each volley.

Then suddenly he upped the ante. "You're a Bum!"

I can still feel the exasperation I felt. Perhaps that's because I see the scene replayed in any preschool child who loses patience. A tiny foot stomps. Irate fists clench.

But Grandpa never gave me a chance to recover. He changed the rules constantly and did his best to keep the assault coming from all angles like a precursor of today's music videos and the rapid fire of images and information. Another curve. Before I could convince him I really did know my name, he motioned me to come closer, luring me with some hidden treasure in his pocket. The twinkle in his eye said I'd want it—whatever it was. A grizzled hand slid in and pulled out what looked like burnt taffy. Conciliatory, he leaned close. "Have a bite—"

In my memory I feel myself taking a half step backward.

"It's bubble gum." He savored the sound of his lie by smacking his lips.

The ugly wad he held out was too big for bubble gum. It had no wrapper, and a few bits of lint came with it and lay in his palm. His wrongly idle hand inched forward, tempting me to take it. The crevasses of his face spread into a smile. What teeth remained, those funny stubs, looked even more out of place.

Raising the disgusting wad to my lips, Grandpa Blom said, "It's good."

I picked up the doubtful looks my Grandma and my mother gave and stomped off in the opposite direction.

For years and years afterward, I felt that chewing gum would wear away my teeth, like Grandpa's, down to the nubs. To this day I don't chew gum; it always seems to upset my stomach the way tobacco would. Why is that? A physical process or a mental one, I can't say. But I can say that I wish I were more like Grandpa, able to face the harshness life dishes out and never lose a sense of humor. I wish that God had given me a talent for mischief—and to not fear pain, but to face it and move on—to enjoy simple pleasures and treasure scant moments stolen for myself. How I wish that I'd taken a bite of his chaw. If I had, the smile he'd have given me would have been one more precious, life-defining memory.

What Grandpa Taught

By C. C. Hammond
Georgia, United States

Air, playing at being a breeze, brushed against me.

Becoming as small as possible on the porch steps, I hunched over my knees and sat watching Grandpa buy vegetables from Eliza. He turned from the blue painted school bus carrying a basket of dull green husks and sparkling gold hair—fresh corn. I watched the bus rumble a little way down the street.

Children waved from the bus's back windows. They worked with their mother on her farm. It was her bus. I wanted to go with them, but I couldn't. I waved back anyway.

Grandpa put the basket down and sat beside me. My feet rested on the first step; his rested on the path beyond the fourth one.

"Kinda hot out here," he said.

I pushed my blunt cut bangs out of my face; they fell back where they had been. "I'm in the shade."

"Attic fan's on inside."

I knew it was. I'd pushed a chair over to climb up and turn it on. When you're seven, you use a lot of chairs to reach the world.

A caterpillar climbed up the stairs. Grandpa pulled a strip of corn husk loose and held it for the caterpillar. When the long bug climbed on, Grandpa carried him over to the hydrangea. "God created all life. Why did he create us the way he did?" he asked.

I didn't like bugs very much, but I knew the answer. "To help the ones who need us."

Coming back, Grandpa eased onto the porch. "You mad about something?"

"It's too hot to be mad," I said. That was something he and Grandma said all summer. In the winter it was too cold to be mad, in the spring and fall it was too nice. There were only a few hours when it was the right weather to be mad. So far I hadn't found them.

"But not to be disappointed?"

"Disappointed?"

"Something not the way you want it to be?"

"Yeah." I focused on my knee. A humming pushed into my mind, and terror ripped through the whole of me. I shrieked, "Bee! Bee!"

Grandpa slipped his arm around my shoulder. "Hush now—God's creature, same as the others. Don't you scare her."

Stiffly, I nodded.

"Bumbly, tumbly, humbly bee, fly away from my honey and me," he said. Then he blew on the bee. The bee floated away. "Better?"

"Yes." I rubbed my knee.

"When you're afraid, it draws them."

"Why?"

"'Cause they can't image what could possibly scare somebody as big as you."

I giggled.

A curled petal fell off the Rose of Sharon, a lavender splash on the gray porch floor.

"You got too much disappointment going around in you for pound cake to cure?"

"Uh-huh." I was seven, not five.

"Even with ice cream?"

"Uh-huh."

"Too much for going to the drug store?"

The store with the penguin painted on its screen door and its air conditioning was tempting. The trip had cured a lot of things, especially with the possibility of getting a comic book. Sighing, I had to be honest. "Uh-huh."

"Then it must be your ma."

"My legs itch."

"Sun moved." He stood and swung me up and onto the metal porch glider. My feet didn't reach the porch, but his did. As he pushed us back and forth, the glider squeak-squealed. I leaned against him. He smelled like soap, Old Spice, and himself.

Across the street, Miss Pat brought her canaries onto her porch. She hung their cage so they could watch the birds in her yard.

"She doesn't like me," I said.

"Who, Miss Pat?"

"No. Mama."

"Ah. Why do you think that?" Sunlight skittered along his police boots.

"She's gonna kill me."

"She's kept you a long time to up and kill you now. If she was gonna do that, why would she have kept you this long?"

I shrugged. How was I supposed to know why grown ups did the things they did?

"How is she gonna do it?" he asked.

"Well, you know how sometimes you go to visit someone, but you don't take your body with you?"

He nodded.

"And sometimes you go to be with someone, and sometimes you just go to explore."

He nodded.

"But you have to be the one to decide to go. I have to decide when to go, so I can decide to come back."

"You have trouble getting back in your body?"

I shrugged.

"What's your ma got to do with this?"

"She's gonna take me to the hospital, and they're gonna put me to sleep, and then I won't be able to get back in my body, and I won't be here any more."

"You been here long enough to know how to get back here from anywhere."

"I get lost pretty easy."

"You get lost easy walking around in your body. All you're gonna do at the hospital is take a nap. You take naps all the time, and you wake up in your body."

"When something pushes you out, it's different."

"When has something pushed you out?" he asked.

"When stuff scares me."

"You know all you have to do is think *body mine* and you're back."

"Are you sure?"

"Uh-huh." He pushed the glider. "Anyway, if you stay out of your body too long, a voice reminds you to get back in it."

"God's voice?"

"Probably."

I watched the light dance along his black boots. Then I looked at my short, bare feet. It was hot for boots.

"There's a bee on your shoulder," he said.

Before I could breathe, I was standing beside Miss Pat's canaries. Across the street I saw myself slumped against Grandpa. A stray splash of sunlight glinted on his thick, silver hair, and he looked up.

"Bee's gone. Think it!"

Body mine! With a jolt I was back in my body.

"Okay?" he asked.

"Okay." I looked at my toes. "Grandpa?"

"Right here."

"What are tonsils?"

"They're something you don't need any more."

"If I don't need 'em, how come I got 'em in the first place?"

"You used to have bibs, didn't you?"

"Yes."

"Well, tonsils are bibs for your insides. You don't need any bibs anymore."

"Okay."

"Not your fault or your ma's. You just outgrew them, same as you do your shoes."

"Like shoes."

"Your ma doesn't even know you take trips without yourself. See, she's not trying to kill you; she's helping you grow up."

The blue school bus rumbled back up the street.

"I wish I lived on a farm."

He put his arm around me. "You'd still have to have your tonsils out."

The porch glider at the farm would go squeak-squeal just like his did. And Grandpa would still smell like soap, Old Spice, and himself.

4

Special Memories

Where would we be without our memories? They tie our present to our past and help us put all the pieces together. Those memories made us who we are today. In writing them down, we can share them with future generations, and they will be immortalized forever.

Walks Through the Woods

By Kristin Dreyer Kramer
Andover, Massachusetts, United States

I spent a lot of time walking through the woods behind our house when I was growing up. It was thick and wild, perfect for hiding during evening games of hide 'n seek. It was also home to a racetrack my older brothers and their friends had cleared in the middle of the trees back when they were my age, and the boys in the neighborhood often left bike tracks in Dad's neatly-trimmed lawn on their way back there to race. But I didn't spend too much time in the woods. I usually just walked through—on my way to see Elsie.

Elsie was a smiling, silver-haired woman who lived alone in a little red house on the street beyond the woods. She'd been a widow for years—and she and her husband, Red, had never had children—so all she had left was her three dogs, an indefinite number of cats, and us.

And she had her garden. Actually, that's how we met Elsie—because of her garden. She had over an acre of property—more than anyone else in our little suburban neighborhood. Her house was hidden on the far side of the property—and the rest of the yard was covered in every kind of plant imaginable and the most beautiful and fragrant sunflowers and gladiolas and roses I'd ever seen. She grew fruit, too—blueberries and raspberries and strawberries.

But she was an old woman, and the gardening was getting out of hand. So when my brother, Kurt, stopped by one day and asked if she was looking for some help in her yard, she didn't hesitate to hire him. When she hired my brother, though, she got the rest of the family, too.

Kurt spent his summers in Elsie's garden, and I spent mine in a director's chair in her driveway, sipping lemonade and petting the dogs. Mom would often send me through the woods to Elsie's house with a plate full of warm muffins or a fresh loaf of banana bread. When Elsie spotted me on the road, she'd declare it break time. She'd take off her green rubber gardening gloves and set up the table and chairs—and the three of us would dine on Mom's baked goods, washing it down with a tall glass of Elsie's ice-cold lemonade.

I'd spend my time in the shade of her driveway, giggling and playing with her two well-fed dachshunds and Joshua, the cocker spaniel that she'd rescued from the pound, until it was time to go home. Then came my favorite part. Elsie would get her knife from inside her garage, and she'd stutter, "Let's pick some flowers for your m-m-m-mother, Dear." And I'd trot after her as she wandered through row after row of her scented rainbow, carefully selecting the brightest, most perfect flowers, quickly cutting each stem with her wrinkled yet agile hand.

Sometimes, she'd lead me to the gate toward the fenced-in backyard where she kept her favorite flowers—the roses. I could smell them as we approached, and once we were inside, I felt like a fairy tale princess, choosing my favorites from Elsie's collection of rose bushes and breathing in the heavy, sweet perfume. Elsie's roses were the most perfectly beautiful flowers I'd ever seen. They were red and white and purple and peach and speckled. And as she picked them, I walked up to each bush and took a deep, euphoric breath. Then Elsie tenderly removed the thorns and wrapped the stems in damp paper towels for the trip home.

I'd carefully step back home through the woods, my hands full of flowers, breathing in the different scents as I tried to hold them all. Then I'd run inside and help Mom arrange them in a vase and place them in the middle of the kitchen. I always loved the smell of the kitchen in the summer—Elsie's flowers mixed with Mom's freshly baked bran muffins.

But even when the flowers wilted and the leaves turned colors—and I went back to school—we still went through the woods to Elsie's house. Then we'd go in the evening—after dinner, while Dad raked leaves. Mom would hand me a fresh loaf of warm bread to carry, and she and I would go swishing through the fallen leaves on the trail to visit Elsie. When we got to the little red house, we'd see the light on in her living room window. I'd ring the doorbell—a deafening buzzer that summoned a choir of barking dogs and often called a curious cat to stroll past the window.

"Oh!" Elsie would exclaim, her face brightening when she came to the door and found us standing there on the front porch. "Oh, m-m-my! Thank you, Dear!" she'd add when I presented her with the bread. "Come in!" She'd lead us into the tiny living room where we took our usual seats on her afghan-covered old couch.

I never really liked those school-year visits. Her house had a lonely, musty, old-house smell. It was quiet and dark—and I always missed the summertime visits, when it was bright and sunny (even when Mom and I visited after dinner) and I could run with the dogs and drink lemonade and pick flowers and eat fresh strawberries. But I always went anyway.

While Mom and Elsie caught up on the family news and the latest on Elsie's friends, I'd pet the dogs, who always hopped up beside me, and I'd play hide 'n seek with Patches, the more daring of Elsie's anti-social cats. And as it got later, Elsie would start to tell stories about how she and Red met—and about his days in the war. When it was time to go home, it was always dark, so we'd have to navigate the trail by moonlight and instinct.

I was in my teens when the light in Elsie's living room window no longer came on at night to welcome us. She spent her last years in a nursing home miles away—near her nephew, her only real family. But sometimes Mom and I would still walk through the woods. Though I missed Elsie and her dogs and the pitcher of lemonade, the thing that saddened me the most was the lonely garden that had been left untouched, dried out, and wildly overgrown.

Last spring, I decided to take my husband to visit Elsie's. I tried to walk through the woods behind Mom and Dad's house, but the path had grown over, so we had to take the long way. When we turned onto Elsie's street, a light once again lit up the living room window, but the garden was gone. I could have sworn, though, that the street still smelled like roses.

And every time I breathe in the perfume of a rose or see a straight-and-tall sunflower, I'm reminded of those childhood summers, of Elsie and her garden and my walks through the woods.

Miss Fitchett's House

By Jozette Aaron
Ontario, Canada

"No more pencils, no more books…no more teachers dirty looks! Kick the tables, kick the chairs…kick the teacher down the stairs!" This was the chorus sung by the children as they raced along the dimly lit corridor, old hardwood floors groaning under their weight.

High-pitched squeals of delight accompanied the scurry of several hundred kids as they burst through the doors of their brick and mortar prison. They squinted in the glare of the sun, the heat unbearable as it rose from the cracked concrete and patches of sticky asphalt that formed the grounds of the schoolyard. None of this mattered…it was the last day of school, and summer vacation had finally arrived.

Running around to the side entrance of the school, I waited patiently for my best friend's class to come through the doors. We had promised to meet here to say goodbye. We were going to be separated for most of the summer and wanted to exchange addresses so we could send postcards. We both knew what that meant. We would write the cards out and exchange them when we saw each other in school after summer break. We were too poor for stamps, and besides—who wanted to lick yucky old glue anyway?

Mom's voice drifted through my mind as I waited. "Make sure you come straight home today. We have to get an early start if we're to beat the traffic." I watched as the door was shoved open by the vice-principal and then, like a roll of thunder, the students came roaring through.

"Bye Mr. Tate!" some of the kids hollered as they scampered across the schoolyard and disappeared in several directions. The vice-principal waved goodbye and then retreated into the school, now silent and empty. The loud "click" of the closing door reverberated for a moment and then was silent.

"C'mon. Let's go. Aren't cha excited 'cause school's over?" My friend asked as she skipped and hopped excitedly at my side.

"Yeah…I guess so. Where ya goin' for the summer?" I asked.

"Mom's sendin' us to sleepover camp. Never stayed at camp before."

"Think ya gonna be scared?"

"Nah…my brother's goin' too and a couple of my cousins, so I won't be afraid."

"Yeah, but what about at night? S'pose somethin' crawls on ya? They got all kinds o' crawly things at camp, ya know."

My friend was quiet as she contemplated this new information. We walked in silence for a bit.

"So…where're you goin'?"

"Oh…we're goin' to Miss Fitchett's house."

"Who's Miss Fitchett?"

"Some lady…I don't know. But when my Dad's workin' in the club near there, she lets us use her house for the summer. Anyway…I'll tell you about it in the postcards, okay?"

We hugged and then walked the last half block arm-in-arm. When we reached the corner, we hugged again before continuing on in separate directions.

Careful not to let the door slam, I entered the small, cramped apartment that I shared with a sister, four brothers, Mom, and Dad.

I dropped my empty satchel onto the bare worn linoleum of the kitchen floor. Mom was at the sink washing out her coffee cup.

"Hi Mom," I whispered as I stood on tiptoe to place a kiss on her soft cheek. "What's for dinner?"

"My favorite and yours—spaghetti," she replied with a sigh sounding somewhere between tired and sad.

We ate a lot of spaghetti in our house. It filled a lot of bellies, was cheap, and it tasted good! No one ever grumbled when it was spaghetti day. Even the neighborhood kids lined up for Mom's spaghetti, which she shared with all who happened by at suppertime.

"Remember now—we have to leave in a few hours, so go wash up and let's eat. There's still some packing to do. Call your brothers and sister, and tell them to get washed up."

"Kids!" I yelled at the top of my lungs. "Mom said get washed for supper." I was still standing in the kitchen as my voice resounded throughout the apartment.

"I could have yelled," Mom scolded.

"Sorry…"

Excitement coated the conversation as we slurped spaghetti in long strands into our mouths. We laughed at the spots of sauce we all wore on our faces and all over our clothes.

"You kids behave. Eat right." That was all Mom could manage before she burst out laughing at our antics, which made us laugh all the more.

With dinner over, the dishes washed, and the kitchen cleaned, we set about packing the rest of our belongings and had everything neatly piled at the front door. Dad would be home soon, and we had to be ready to go.

It was much later before we were finally on the road. We climbed into the cavern of our midnight blue Chrysler, the smell of leather instantly nauseating me. I could not understand why I wasn't allowed to make the trip while standing on the wide running board on the side of the car. Surely, if I held on tight enough… This was a constant query every time I had to endure a trip in the car. I climbed inside anyway and had to fight to keep down the contents of my stomach as I positioned myself closest to the door with the window lowered.

"You just want to sit near the window all the time, that's all," one of the boys grumbled as Dad set the car in motion. He was wedged in between two other siblings with hardly any room for his legs.

"Mom…tell him to leave me alone." I whined. When Dad said he'd turn the car around and we could all go home, there was instant silence, lasting the remainder of the three-hour trip.

I watched the darkness descend and saw the lights of the city loom large as we crossed the Brooklyn-Queens Expressway into Manhattan. Winding through the countless trails of the concrete jungle, we arrived at the mouth of the Holland Tunnel that would take us under the Hudson River and deposit us on the other side—New Jersey.

My ears fluttered with the drone of car engines as the sound of hundreds of vehicles bounced off the tunnel walls. A sprinkling of fear snaked its way through my body, thinking of all that water above us. What would happen if the tunnel started to leak? My eyes hurt with the effort of looking for cracks in the tunnel walls.

I glanced at my siblings, using the glare from the tunnel lights to see. I realized that all of them, except my older brother, were sleeping.

"Don't cha hate this part?" he whispered.

"I know. It takes too long, and I don't like the sound the tunnel makes."

"Don't worry. It'll be over soon," he said as he reached across the sleeping kids and took my hand. He held it, knowing I was afraid.

Shrouded in the darkness of night, it was only the smells permeating the air through the open windows that told us we had left the city and were now somewhere in the countryside. Before too long, we turned off the main road into what appeared to be a black abyss. *How could anyone see in this darkness?*

Dad drove the car through the old battered, weather worn wooden gate and slowly crawled up the long roadway to the house. It was a large, old farmhouse set on several acres of neglected land. It stood tall and proud, basking in the rays of light from the moon as the car came to a crunching halt near the front porch. Memories started to filter through my mind…memories of another summer spent here. I was too young to appreciate its uniqueness then…but not now. After all, now I was eight—practically a teenager.

Nausea long since forgotten, I scrambled out of the car and took a deep breath. The essence of cow manure hung heavy on the air as the others, now wide-awake, held their noses in disdain.

"Eewww…what's that smell?" the baby of the bunch yelled at the top of his lungs.

"That's cow doodee," chimed in another.

"C'mon kids. Grab a bag, and let's get this stuff inside. It's off to bed with you all—no nonsense now. We had a long trip, and tomorrow is another day," Mother announced.

"Can't I sit out here for a bit Mom…pleeease? I just want to swing a bit," I begged and whined. "I just love this swing. Please, Mom?" I begged some more, looking longingly at the faded, chintz covered pillows that lay haphazardly across the padded seat.

"No. You've been up since early this morning—" She began in the now famous litany. "C'mon upstairs and I'll get you settled. You boys head for the bathroom; brush your teeth, wash your faces. I'll be in to check in a minute."

Miss Fitchett's house was always ready for company. It was dusted and kept clean by the neighbor women. Miss Fitchett was away visiting her sister and had left instructions with the neighbors to expect our arrival. The fridge was well stocked, the beds laid with fresh linen. All we had to do was decide which rooms to sleep in.

My sister and I settled in a large, airy room. When the lights came on, we were delighted to see yellow and white gingham curtains fluttering at tall windows and a matching bed ensemble. Mom and I unpacked the one suitcase holding our clothes, and by then my sister was asleep across the bed. Mom quickly changed her into pajamas and tucked her in for the night. I wiggled into my pajamas and sat near the window, still wondering how anyone could see in such darkness.

By the time it was my turn in the bathroom, I was barely able to crawl into bed. I found it more inviting than I thought I would. I planned to lie awake and watch the stars through the window. The first night of a summer vacation was always the greatest. That thought was my last as sleep claimed me as soon as my head hit the pillow.

Bright and early the next morning, I slipped on my yellow satin halter-neck bathing suit and tiptoed downstairs to re-acquaint myself with the rickety wooden porch swing. It screamed in protest when I sat down, sending it into motion with my toe. Back and forth it swayed as the heat of the rising sun gradually warmed the morning dew.

From my perch, I looked at the vastness of property that was Fitchett land. It extended for as far as the eye could see in either direction. Large weeping willow trees bent their tears to shelter the earth from the sun's relentless intrusion. There was a pond somewhere off to the side of the house. I would swim today. My brothers would catch tadpoles and make my life miserable. They know how much I hate those things.

Before long, the sounds of breakfast being prepared traveled through the screen door, and the scent of brewing coffee permeated the air. Most of our meals would be eaten on this porch, and afterwards, we would play board games, go for a swim, or I'd sit and watch as my brothers played ball with Dad.

The weeks lazed past, and each day brought new delights. Mom and I sat and broke off the tips of green beans picked from the small garden at the rear of the house, which would be great additions to the dinner table. I watched the porch floor as an army of ants disappeared through the cracks, wondering where their journey led.

My favorite time was when the storms hit with great flashes of lightening and loud claps of thunder. Sheets of rain fell, hitting the railing and spreading wet patches near my feet. I would scramble to pull the swing further under the overhang before my seat got wet. Once the rain gentled and the lightening and thunder abated, my siblings and I sloshed through the wet grass on our way to the pond, the heat soon rising as the sun reclaimed the sky.

I spent the evenings writing my postcards and making entries in my diary. I hoped my best friend was having as much fun as I. Mom allowed me to stay up late, and I'd sit and watch the fireflies as they sent coded messages. Moths encircled the porch light as they danced to the beat from my pocket radio. The stars seemed especially bright, as though they were shining just for me.

We were allowed to camp out on the porch, its vastness making it large enough for the six of us. We'd get a bunch of old blankets and, draping them over chairs and other porch furniture, create an enormous tunnel-like tent. Inside we covered the floor with more old blankets and bedding, threw in our pillows, and then crawled inside. We'd shine flashlights through the dividing flaps that separated the girls from the boys and use our hands to form images against the light.

Days turned into weeks, and all too soon, it was time to return home. I planted some seeds that I saved from my watermelon, hoping that when we returned next year, there would be tons to eat while I swayed on the swing. I beat the dust from the old chintz cushions and placed them lovingly in their place on the swing. I swept the porch and threw boiling water over the floorboards to make sure it was good and clean when Miss Fitchett returned.

We barbecued that night, and a few friends of my parents stopped by. Much as I wanted, I didn't get to sit and swing. We had to leave early the next morning. We sang songs, played games, and ate until we were so full we thought out bellies would burst. The next morning, dressed and ready to go, I sat on the swing while I waited for my parents to close up the house. I let my hands trail over the railing as I made my way to the car.

Before climbing inside, I looked at Mom with that same question in my eyes.

"Get in. Just sit near the window."

With a chorus of farewell to the now empty house, we watched through the rear window as it disappeared from view. My swing looked especially lonely as I said a silent farewell.

"Goodbye 'til next time."

It's All About Yellow

By Rita Tubbs
Vanderbilt, Michigan, United States

Racing heart, weak knees, and sweaty palms were constant companions the summer before I stepped foot on a school bus for the first time.

All summer my parents had reminded me, "You'll soon be a big girl, Rita, going to school with your sister." The first day of kindergarten had arrived, but I didn't think about the actual school day. I fixed my thoughts on the transportation that would get me there.

Just the idea of getting on the huge, yellow monstrosity that picked up my older sister each morning of the school year drove deep abiding fear into my soul. I was much more than just scared. My every waking moment, along with each dream that worked its way into my slumbering thoughts, became entangled with the apprehension of what my parents had deemed a good thing.

"You'll love it," Daddy said. But I imagined a wicked school bus running down the road with huge teeth, gobbling up innocent little boys and girls while they raced to kindergarten class.

That particular morning, much too early in my opinion, my mother combed and pulled my long, knotted hair while I stared at my reflection in the full length mirror on the back of the door in the sewing room.

In 1967, all young girls wore long hair and gritted their teeth in pain, while their parents transformed them into gorgeous, little princesses. Brushing my thick mane was nearly as bad as thinking about getting on the bus! "Ouch!" I yelled. No amount of screaming and fussing was going to stop my mom, though. I would have to get on that school bus looking as regal as she could possibly make me.

I looked again at my reflection and stared into the big, brown eyes peering back at me. What would happen if the other kids on the bus teased me? I knew I was small for my age, so it was only natural that I would be easy prey for them. What if Susie didn't stand up for me when the others were mean? So many what if's, and I hadn't even begun to think of the actual kindergarten class yet. I was still hung up on that school bus waiting to take me to the huge elementary school my parents had taken me to visit the week before.

Funny, public school hadn't seemed so terrible when Mommy and Daddy held my hands and did all of the talking—when we'd met the teacher.

Finally, with my hair groomed to perfection, my mother proclaimed me presentable, or at least good enough for school. With her hands on her hips, Mom said, "Don't want to miss the bus." I glanced at Susie, who had just finished her breakfast of corn flakes, and forced a quick smile. Inwardly, I trembled. Outside, I was ready to conquer the world!

"Be good girls," mother warned as she patted us firmly on the heads. Then she sent Susie and me outside to walk down our extremely long driveway. Normal, everyday visitors were afraid to travel down our winding driveway, which passed over a creek, so it was to be expected that the school bus driver would never try it. We had to wait for the bus beside the busy state road.

Those five minutes or so of waiting for the bus, while we counted red cars going by, began to wear on my young nerves—if five-year-olds have such things. My heart beat in quick, loud thumps while Susie calmly sang the silly songs she had learned the previous year in her third grade class. She clearly enjoyed riding the school bus, but I dreaded it more and more with each ridiculously long moment. When Susie said, "You may have to sit in the back, you know," I worried all the more.

Trying to think of other things, I glanced back at the front porch of our ancient, white farmhouse. It was larger than most porches—wrapping around a good third of the house. How I wished I were there now, sitting with my mom, sipping lemonade on the swing. Back in the old days, we always spent our mornings that way after Susie boarded the school bus. Although I did occasionally fall off and hit my head, that swing had to be a lot safer than the dreaded bus!

I figured there would no longer be lazy mornings on the porch alone with Mom now that I had grown up. Her words echoed in my head: "You have to go to school now, Rita."

I'd tried to wiggle my way out of the bus ride. "Susie could go on the bus, and you could bring me to school." I'd flashed Mom one of my best grins, but she wouldn't budge.

Mom had finished her glass of lemonade and took my hand in hers. "We all have to do things we don't like to do sometimes," she said softly. "After you ride the school bus just once, you'll want to do it over and over, just like your sister." She rose to her feet, opened the screen door, and went into the house.

I had stayed on the porch for some time, pouting. Nothing would change my mind.

I jerked back to the present when a bright, yellow bus with a full load of children came to a screeching halt at the end of our drive. Susie waved to her friends, and I froze in my tracks, but the school bus driver peeked down from her perch behind the steering wheel. "Come on up," she invited. Her friendly face bore a warm smile, so I really had no clear excuse not to enter.

I climbed up one big step, then two. As Susie had warned, no seats were available in the front. Great. I had to walk all the way to the back and sit with an older kid—just what I had been afraid would happen. Right away Susie plopped down in a seat beside her friend, Peggy, who had been gracious enough to save her a spot. The big kid I ended up with, probably a fifth-grader, was a boy, and a mean looking one, too. He looked at me with squinted eyes, and then he turned away without saying a word. I sighed heavily with relief and waited for the rest of the adventure to begin.

The ride to our elementary school can only be described as a noisy one, with the radio blasting pop music, children laughing and yelling, and a boy constantly tapping his foot near my seat. It couldn't have been more than 10 minutes to the school from my house, but it sure seemed like longer to me. "Puff the Magic Dragon" blared on the radio, and some of the kids sang along, swaying back and forth in a strange, rhythmic motion. Susie chatted easily with Peggy, but I just stared up at the gray ceiling and hoped that I was only dreaming.

Suddenly my worst fears were realized. Two boys got into a nasty fist fight—right there on the bus! They were in the seat directly in front of me and that big boy, and I was so afraid they would accidentally hit me that I panicked. I screamed and put my hands over my face, ready to shield any wayward fists. But a word of warning from the bus driver brought the skirmish to a quick end.

Soon after, the bus pulled up in line behind two others at the school, and the children filed off. As I climbed down the steps on very shaky legs, my eyes caught Susie waiting for me with a big smile spreading across her freckled face.

At least she had done that much! I looked up at the massive, brick building, and I exhaled all of the air I had been holding. One adventure had ended, but another one was already beginning.

I Feel So Free

By Bette Milleson James
Hoxie, Kansas, United States

I stood alone in the shelter of a long, covered porch at the front of our country home as a thunderstorm raged, on an evening that had changed suddenly, in typical Kansas fashion, from mellow moonlight to lightning-crossed brilliance. In the distance, I saw the lights of our small town come and go as the flashes obliterated and the darkness redeemed their sparkle. Out there in the damp windy air, I thought of other porches, other storms, other times, and of all the homes where these things have been a part of my life.

In our part of the Midwest, the far western ends of Nebraska and Kansas, rain is scarce enough to be celebrated no matter how it comes. It is important and noteworthy, and I have always been unable to take it for granted. As a child, I played rainy day tag with my brothers and the neighbor children on the front porch of a concrete-block duplex where we lived in North Platte, Nebraska, during the '40s. Sometimes the moms made popcorn or fudge, and often the games settled into story times or playing "house" or "school." The old porch seemed a big place to me then, as many places do when we are children, though on returning years later, I found a rather small house with a covered concrete porch along one side. Standing in the yard among old lilac bushes and cottonwood trees, I still felt those early days all around me.

World War II was raging when we lived in the duplex, and we had, right there in unlikely Nebraska, air-raid drills and "blackouts." At designated times all over town, the mothers turned out all but the dimmest lights and pulled down the "blackout shades," the city officials and businesses darkened street lights and neon signs, and the cars pulled over, lights out. We all went outside and waited under the stars for the airplanes from the base at Omaha to fly over, looking for lights on earth from the night sky above. I had no idea of the purpose then, but I remember being lifted up by my father as we waited, and watching the lights of airplanes moving steadily among the stars. Afterward children and parents sat on the porch or on the block steps talking quietly in an eerie darkness, and I felt safe and permanent. It seemed no more unusual an event to me than mothers making big trays of sandwiches to take to the Union Pacific Depot, where Red Cross volunteers maintained a coffee-and-sandwich canteen for soldiers who passed through constantly on troop trains that whistled from time to time both day and night and spoke to me of faraway places.

Many years later, describing this, I was told indignantly by a young man in a college class that there were air raid blackouts only on the two coasts. But my hometown is a railroad town with a large installation there, and the railroads, absolutely essential for the movement of troops across the country, were considered to be at risk. I knew I was right, and I still cherish the memory of those dark and quiet nights when someone very wise seemed to be hovering over us.

Time moved on in my life, and there were letters sent by a soldier brother and a cousin from France, from Korea, and in time from Army bases and diplomatic posts all over the world. Through the years, a series of dorm rooms and apartments finally gave way to another small house with a covered front porch. Like my mother, I couldn't resist being outside on the porch when it rained, especially with thunder and lightning.

My own children, grown and gone now, have their own memories of wrapping up in an afghan in a chair on that little porch, of popcorn or fudge, of books and storytelling, and of sometimes just watching the rain as it fell. I still see their small figures, cuddled in their blankets in a chilly spring, or running into the rain and back to the porch on warm summer days, splashing and giggling at the change in routine brought by weather. Their innocence was unaware that another war was raging, an uncle gone to Vietnam, and it seemed to me that time was revolving and renewing old experiences both tragic and true.

In those days, there were toys on the porch—a wagon, a tricycle, and a very important rocking horse with squeaky springs. Our middle child so loved the horse that she rocked long and contentedly every day, inevitably growing sleepy. When the squeak of the springs slowed down, I dropped what I was doing and went to the porch where a sleepy two-year-old was beginning to sway ominously on the back of her pony. She never once awoke when I caught her limp little body and carried her off to bed.

A few years later, home was an old Victorian farm-house with wraparound porches front and back. Older and more sophisticated, the children didn't cuddle much on the porch any more, though they still loved the novelty of rain and thunderstorms and would sometimes drag a rocking chair outside to watch the weather. Mainly, those porches were home to numerous pets on the farm—a dog always, some-times two, and large, long haired gray cats with inevitable litters of kittens brought up from the barn. We still have photos of Tippy sleeping by the back door with four or five kittens on top of him, warming their paws and noses in the big dog's thick coat of winter fur.

Eventually, we made a final move to a new house with the essential big front porch, this time of brick, with arches defining the front and wide eaves giving added protection from the weather. It is there that I go now to watch the flashes of distant lightning and hear the rolling of thunder that seems to come from every direction, as I have done for more than 25 years. It is there that our family finished growing up and prepared to leave home, there that we went at times to escape the noise or activity in the house, there that we grew to share confidences and problems and to seek solutions. In the quiet shelter of the porch, I sat uncounted times waiting for a teen-aged son to come home, for some critical piece of mail to arrive, for carloads of friends or family or returning college students to drive into the yard.

One summer, our eighth-grade daughter wanted desperately to go to a particular dance in town. We sat sadly on the front porch looking at the lights in the distance, she wishing she could go and I wishing the dance were appropriate for her. Somehow that front porch kept us centered that night and held at bay the feelings of anger that can arise when "No" is the only possible answer.

Recently, we welcomed friends from Central America whose home in Guatemala is surrounded by a 10' solid stone wall with barbed wire rolled along the top. After a celebratory meal, the crowd of people naturally gravitated to the porch and spilled over onto the lawn. Etched into my memory is a picture of the father standing on the grass in front of our house looking at the stars, his arms raised into the wind, saying, "This is paradise. I feel so free!" A gentle man from a distant, difficult land, he redefined "home" more broadly for me—as a house, a country, a state of the heart, and a gift from the past. How I loved home that day.

Now the front porch is frequented by grandchildren who love the red glider seat and the wide yard and cuddle into a blanket when it rains, believing their popcorn and snacks and stories are necessary parts of a rainy day. For their mother, the porch is part of the identity of "home," and when she seems to have disappeared, that is where we find her.

Somehow those early experiences of popcorn and candy-making, of lilacs and cottonwoods, and of books and comfort and safety have defined my life and extended to those of my descendants as, I suppose, our early experiences always do. We cannot escape ourselves, nor can our children escape our influences. Time out of mind, old generations have lived on through young ones, and in our family we tend to realize who we are and to nurture the traditions that have helped us to prevail. Now I sit on the porch in summer and remember the darkened streets of the war years and the great gift of freedom those years bought so dearly for us all. I see again the little house in the rain, the wraparound porch of later years, the wide brick arches defining the flashes of light, and the wind-tossed trees in the distance. I remember once more the words of our friend whose life is so different from ours, and I know that his truth is also mine: "This is paradise. I feel so free."

A Pitch in Time

By Gloria MacKay
Camano Island, Washington, United States

Edna, my genteel friend and longtime mentor—who I always picture with a crochet hook in one hand, rings on her fingers, and beads on her blouse—sat straight up in her high backed white (as white as her hair) plastic chair and asked, with just a trace of an ingenuous frown, "Dear, why do you like to watch all those baseball games on television with the men?"

I remember fumbling for a flip retort, but I had no answer at all. I felt strangely guilty, as though I were caught in some sort of indiscretion. I was annoyed. Not at Edna, but at myself. She was right. Now that she mentioned it, I would rather be sitting in the stuffy living room watching the Seattle Mariners with all the men even though they wouldn't want me. I would rather not be sitting on my friend's breezy front porch with a cup of fresh coffee having a chat, but I wasn't sure why.

I didn't know what to say. It frustrates me when I can't figure something out no matter how carefully I think it through, no matter how deep inside me I go. I should have been able to tell Edna—right off the bat as we lovers of the game like to say—why baseball is one of my favorite things, but instead I mumbled disclaimers. "I don't even know all the rules," I admitted. How high is an infield fly? How big is a strike zone? How far is a bunt? And who makes up the ground rules anyway?

Edna went inside and poured us more coffee, clearly sorry she had brought the subject up.

But I was glad. It got me thinking. Baseball is not just a game to me—it is part of my life. The neighborhood where I grew up was within walking distance of Sick's Seattle Stadium hillside, home of the Seattle Rainiers. At least it was then, in the safe, slow moving days of the 1940's. At that time in Seattle, you couldn't get more professional than that. The stadium, painted creamy beige, hunkered into its site on Rainier Avenue and McClellan Street like a giant squash that could never be moved. Actually, all sorts of vegetables were planted, thrived, and harvested on the hillside which sprawled above left field, the same hillside where frugal fans spread blankets and watched the game free of charge.

When the Rainiers played at home, I could stand in my front yard and let the roar of the crowd wash over me in the grandest stereophonic sound you could imagine. Cheers and groans flew out of the stadium and bounced along the rooftops, and at the same time, the same sounds spewed from radios lined up on almost every front porch in the neighborhood.

While grown-ups clustered together intent on every play, we kids met at the corner and played—what else but baseball? How could a kid, even a girl, grow up on a street like this and not love this game for the rest of her life? This is what I should have said to Edna.

And when I paused for breath and she rose from her chair like a jack-in-the-box, I should have pulled her back down and kept talking even if a breeze rustled the clematis and cooled our coffee and the roast in the oven smelled a tad more than medium well done. I should have taken her back to my high school days—one particular class—taught by Mr. Wettleson, the journalism teacher. He was most relaxed in our little newspaper office next to the classroom, but he knew how to teach with a capital T in the traditional manner, demanding we stay on the subject, use quiet voices, and raise our hands.

One afternoon he stood before us—jacket off, shirt unbuttoned, and tie awry—and tossed out an hour of proverbs, platitudes, clichés and old-fashioned sayings like he was giving us batting practice. Our task was to tell him what these figures of speech really meant.

"The pen is mightier than the sword." No problem for us. After all, we were journalism students.

"A stitch in time saves nine." Slam dunk.

"A little learning is a dangerous thing." Our hands waved high in the air.

"Two wrongs don't make a right." We got it, first try.

"Birds of a feather flock together."

"You can lead a horse to water..."

"The grass is always greener..."

"Two many cooks spoil the broth."

We polished off one after another.

Next, Mr. Wettleson barked, "A friend to all is a friend to none." We grappled with this a bit longer.

"Some rise by sin and some by virtue fall." Our hands were not quite as jumpy as the clock ticked toward the end of the hour.

"Condemn the fault but not the actor of it." What was Shakespeare trying to say, we argued back and forth?

Finally, but not in time to be saved by the bell, Mr. Wettleson did us in with, "The child is father of the man." Our hands remained in our laps while we pondered, but we just couldn't get it. The bell rang. Students were milling around in the hallway, but Mr. Wettleson did not open the door until he dragged the meaning out of us with the help of a short nature versus nurture dissertation, one final allusion to little acorns and mighty oaks and a wry little smile which brought us out of our seats and on to the next class.

That child stayed for years in the back of my mind, only coming out at night. In all respect to the best teacher I ever had, something wasn't quite right. You know how it is when you can't sleep, but you don't have to think of things to think about, because your mind is cracking bats faster than you can throw the balls? I finally figured out what Mr. Wettleson must have been thinking as he opened the door. The child is the mother of the woman, as well.

This is what I should have told Edna, with a wry little smile and perhaps just a touch of an ingenuous frown. As for watching baseball on television, a picture is worth a thousand words so goes another old saying. As a one-time journalism student, I might opt for the thousand words. But a picture will do when I can't hear the roar of the crowd floating over the rooftops above the clamor of the radios on every front porch in the neighborhood where I grew up.

When Fairies Danced

By Carole Bellacera
Manassas, Virginia, United States

When I was a child, fairies danced on the lawn at my grandparents' farm in Kentucky. It happened in the early morning hours of summer, around four o'clock. As the last of the moon's light glimmered out of a pearl gray sky, the trees came alive with a sigh, and the fairies danced under their boughs to the music of rustling leaves.

I never actually *saw* this happen, but Pa Pa Larl claimed it did. "You're just not quick enough to catch them," he said, his blue eyes twinkling. But I believed him because I knew my grandparents' farm was enchanted.

The summers I spent there brimmed with enchantment—especially if my cousin, Paula, happened to be there at the same time. Paula and I loved playing "dress-up" with Grandma Ina's old clothes and shoes. After making up our faces with leftover cosmetics, we'd totter through the farmhouse, pretending to be fashionable ladies going out to lunch. If we were in a generous mood, we'd allow Paula's younger brother, Jeff, and my younger sister, Kathy, to play the parts of the waiter and cook—always, of course, bossing them around as fashionable ladies are wont to do.

When Grandma Ina grew tired of trying to do her daily chores around our "restaurant," we'd end up outside—rather unceremoniously, I might add. Then it was off to the front lawn where Pa Pa Larl kept a row of used cars for sale—a side business to his farming.

Each of us picked out the vehicle of our choice and climbed behind the wheel. Soon our cars were humming down the road, our lips providing the motor and our hands fixed on the steering wheels. My motor trip came to an abrupt halt one day when I casually glanced over to wave at Paula in the next car and instead of seeing her, found myself staring into the beady eyes of a small green snake curled up on the seat next to me. The screams that erupted from my mouth brought both grandparents running—Grandma Ina from the house and Pa Pa Larl from the garage. They were white-faced and trembling, thinking, I'm sure, their eldest granddaughter was being murdered in their own front yard.

Grandma Ina was usually a pretty patient woman, but there were times when her beloved first grandchild got on her nerves. Like the time when she'd just finished styling my hair in bouncy pin curls, and I went right out on the front porch during a thunderstorm and stuck my head into the pouring rain. I must've had a mean streak running through me back then. For years prior to this event, I'd heard my mother talk about conniption fits. Well, after that little incident with the rain ruining my pin curls, I found out exactly what a conniption fit looked like.

On rainy days when we were forced indoors, we'd play in the haunted room. The grown-ups thought we were silly to think it was haunted. It was just a room used for storage off Grandma Ina's bedroom. But *we* knew something wasn't right about this scary place. Dark and musty, the unused room provided fodder for our active imaginations. Surely such a place held deep, dark secrets—like maybe a murder had been committed there! How else to explain the cold dank air and shadowy corners? Of course, it had *nothing* to do with Pa Pa's collection of gory detective magazines that we spent hours poring over with shuddering fascination.

Apparently Uncle Fred, a boisterous 16-year-old, encouraged our fantasies by scratching at the boarded door leading outside and peering through the grimy window at twilight, sending us screaming into the bright comfort of the kitchen where Grandma Ina was cooking dinner. At the time, I didn't understand why Grandma Ina fussed at Uncle Fred. What did *he* have to do with the boogieman lurking outside?

As the summers passed, inevitable changes took place. Uncle Fred graduated from high school and joined the Marines. Paula and I became teenagers, and our play habits changed, too. *16 Magazine* and records took the place of dress up, and instead of dreaming up scary stories, boys and romance became the object of our fantasies. A new kind of magic filled our summers.

One summer in particular stands out in my mind—the one when I was 15. Paula and I were both in love with Mark Lindsay, the lead singer of the pop group, Paul Revere and the Raiders. At night, we'd talk for hours, much to the annoyance of everyone else in the house who preferred to sleep. We made up elaborate stories about how Mark Lindsay and the other Raiders would be driving down the road in their tour bus and it would just *happen* to break down in front of the farmhouse. We'd have to put them up while Pa Pa Larl took several weeks to repair their bus. Of course, Mark would fall madly in love with one of us. It was always a point of contention as to which would get *him* and which would be relegated to Freddy Weller, the lead guitarist—a point that was never resolved to our satisfaction. As it turned out, ironically enough, years later in real life, my younger sister, Kathy—the same sister Paula and I often excluded from our play—would actually date Freddy Weller, whom she met while working in public relations in Nashville. Did I mention she was a *little brat*?

One morning after a night of story telling, Paula and I crept out of the house and waited for sunrise in rocking chairs on the front porch. Of course, neither of us admitted we were waiting to catch fairies dancing on the lawn, but even as teenagers, we hadn't totally dismissed the possibility of magic. I guess we were too young to realize what is now obvious.

Magic had been there all along. We'd been surrounded by it. Perhaps we'd even created it.

I returned to Kentucky last summer. My husband and I drove by the place where I'd spent so many enchanting days and nights. The old homestead is gone now, burned to the ground years ago. My grandparents moved to a newer house after I'd grown up and left home—a place that held no memories for me. When they died, it was as if the final tie with my childhood had disappeared.

Yet, my memories of that special place live on. And I'm convinced that in the early morning hours, the fairies still dance in that childhood land of enchantment.

Our World

By Helen Kay Polaski
Milan, Michigan, United States

Everything my siblings and I saw, and everything we touched in the little hamlet we grew up in, is etched on the walls, ceiling, and floors of our souls—artists' renderings of things not to be forgotten. Through the clear eyes of childhood, we tackled each moment and absorbed our world, breath by breath.

The land, its creatures, and everything found in and along our paths became part of our very essence. We were like spilled wine spreading across the land, saturating the ground. We added the spice, enriched the soil. We were the buffer zone between harsh reality and gentle fantasy. With the flip of a hand or the nod of a head, we changed never to maybe and sometime to now.

Though we didn't realize it at the time, our parents provided a security blanket that spanned the 40 years it took for all of us to reach maturity and fend for ourselves. Daddy kept a roof over our heads, and Momma kept the real world at bay.

Maybe it was because of the love shared and the magic created, or maybe because kids don't care about things such as contracts, but the village of Metz was there for the taking, and we gobbled it up. All of it.

Our world extended as far as our little feet could carry us in any direction and as deep as our imaginations could dip and swirl and tangle with one another. We were the clouds, the buzzing bees, the singing birds, and the whispering pines. We understood and became one with the soft wetness of the meadow and the rushing electric iciness of the wild running water. We smelled and tasted the different scents on the rising winds and scurried along well-worn paths like small animals, content in our environment, completely at peace in our space. Our world was bright and sunny, and rose-colored just like Momma said.

Metz was a small hamlet, huddled against an east to west railroad track in Michigan's northern lower peninsula. The train came on a regular basis, and there was two of everything in Metz: beer gardens, churches, and stores. Seven streetlights flickered liked lightning bugs when the older kids played pranks by shining flashlights on the meter or when a severe thunderstorm showered the world with brightness and fooled the meter into thinking it was daytime. Other than those few moments of darkness, our world was lighted, bright, and attainable.

Each day was born without worry or hassle. We were queens, kings, and conquerors of our space, and we utilized every inch of our kingdom. Our world consisted of everything we could see, both inside and outside of our house. And though there were several scary places in our kingdom, the worst, and ultimately most compelling, was our own basement.

There were shelves along the wall for Momma's canning, a potato bin and a place for a crate or two of apples in the far back, and plenty of nails in the rafters to hold Daddy's pelts when it was trapping time. Coal was dumped onto the floor through a side window, and tiny black salamanders with yellow spots made their home in the dampness, peeking from behind pieces of coal. Sometimes toads and snakes lived in and around the coal, too. The creatures called to us, but the basement flooded—especially in the summer—and stepping into a dark flooded basement with no idea what manner of creature also occupied water space was down right horrifying.

Daddy installed a sump pump, and most of the time it worked, but when it didn't, the basement was a mess. I don't know where all the water came from, or where it all went when the pump was humming, but I was glad it usually worked. When the water didn't go away, it stared you in the face and wiggled and slurped around your feet with every step. Because the basement was dimly lit and black from coal dust, it was hard to tell if something else besides your foot was making the water move. Canning jars, pieces of wood, Daddy's spare boots, an ice skate or two, and sometimes apples floated in the water along the walls.

My imagination conjured up other things, things that couldn't be seen. Horrible things. But the basement was part of our world and special attention was lavished on it. Scary or not, we spent a good deal of time in that basement searching for salamanders or toads and hiding from one another.

The basement was the scariest part of our world, and the front porch was the most peaceful. Sometimes, after a day of exploration when my feet were stumbly and my legs hurt, it was such a relief to see the front porch come into view!

The porch was small and made out of cement. There were three brick and wood pillars holding the porch roof up and five magical steps that led to the outside world or accepted a child back into its fold at the end of a busy day. A screen door creaked and slammed, willing to swing either way. Over the years, Doodles, Jack, Queenie, Mariah, and Butsy—and many other dogs—found a place on the porch. Tongue hanging out, anxious to join the group, the dog would jump up, muddy paws dragging great brown streaks across our faces and shirts.

During the summer, the front porch was the best place to be the first thing in the morning and the last thing in the evening. In the morning sun, we blinked away sleep while eating Momma's pancakes with sugar syrup spilling down our chins or sugar crystals clinging to our cheeks as we planned the day's adventures. In the evening, we watched while Daddy showed the big kids how to pick night crawlers and squealed when they waved the fat worms at us.

An old lilac bush grew at the corner of the house to the left of the porch; so did hollyhocks of various colors. The old-fashioned single petal rose bush always grew in the same place, but hollyhocks grew when and where they wanted—a fact that never failed to make Daddy smile. Sometimes a stray seed would plant itself right smack dab in front of the porch, growing wildly for a few days before one of the babies pulled it out, not understanding its importance.

That upset Daddy. "Well," he'd say with a sad shake of his head. "It lasted almost two days longer than I expected—that's pretty good, considering."

Momma loved the lilac bush. Butterflies and bumblebees swarmed in circles around the flowers, drunk on nectar and bumping into each other. Most ended up as angry prisoners inside mayonnaise jars whose lids were riddled with nail holes and screwed on tightly to ensure no escapees. Momma made us let them go again so they could find their way back home before dark and *their* Momma's wouldn't worry.

For a brief two weeks, handfuls of lilacs graced every windowsill and table inside our house as individual youngsters added their daily bounty of token gifts for Momma. Even if Momma was busy, she was always happy to stop and put flowers into cups or jars before they wilted.

But each year, long before we were ready to give up the fragrant flowers, they turned brown and the butterflies chased one another into the meadow where more interesting smells beckoned. Then, for a short while, it was time to chase our dreams in other corners of our world.

Still, at the end of each day, we set our sights on a small cement porch with red brick pillars, and before long we were home again—safe from everything, especially thunderstorms that blasted the sky with lightning and drenched us with raindrops the size of elephant tears.

Sometimes when it rained, we holed up on the porch with Daddy and listened to Momma clatter away in the kitchen, the smell of strawberry and raspberry jam or simmering peaches filling the air.

After each clap of thunder, a handful of little voices chirped, "One thousand one, one thousand two, one thousand three..." As soon as the lightning flashed, we squealed and pressed tighter into one another's arms. The storm was one mile away for each one thousand we counted, and the closer it drew, the more excited we became.

When the storm got too close, Daddy opened the screen door with one hand as he balanced one or two kids on his lap. "Windy! Get these kids. Storm's coming."

When he was in a playful mood, he called Momma Windy. Her name was Stella, but he liked to call everyone different names. He had a nickname for each one of us, too. Momma frowned at the name Windy, and on occasion shook a rolling pin or spatula at him, but she didn't really seem to mind.

Once when he called her a Big Bag of Wind, we watched with enormous eyes as she wadded up the dish towel that was always slung over one shoulder and threw it at him. It hit him in the face, hard. He just grinned at us, his eyes twinkling, and she shook her head as we dissolved into giggles. She grabbed the towel back and tossed it over her shoulder and returned to the mountain of dishes in the sink, a satisfied smile on her lips.

But even if Daddy was in a playful mood, when a storm was brewing, he shooed us all into the house.

"Nooo!" We wailed bravely. But Daddy was adamant. If there was no lightning and no thunder, we were allowed to stay as long as we wanted, but with the hint of either of those mighty forces of nature, we were banned to the living room.

"Go in now," he'd say gruffly.

Then, of course, one of us would be brave enough, or foolhardy enough, to ask the burning question. "How come you don't have to go in?"

He'd frown, spit a stream of tobacco juice into the Maxwell House coffee can at his feet, and point toward his shoes. There was our answer. Daddy always wore shoes and we never did. That was the difference between staying on the cement porch in a thunderstorm or being sent back inside.

"Because! I'm grounded."

Apparently our looks of incomprehension were enough to make any father think he was raising a bunch of dim-witted children. Pointing at our feet, he emphasized the obvious. "How many times do I have to tell yous what happens when lightning strikes and you aren't grounded? Even the layers of dirt won't save yous!" His arms waved in a big circle. "You'll disappear in a puff of smoke!"

Suddenly Momma would appear at the door, shaking her head. "Oh, Harry," she'd sigh, clucking her tongue against the roof of her mouth. "You're worse than the kids."

That would bring back Daddy's smile. "Windy! 'Bout time you got out here."

Motioning like a mother hen busy collecting her chicks, Momma got us all back inside. "Come on kids. Get back in here."

Though we normally held out until another clap of thunder shook our world, we always ended up screeching in unison and racing back to the safety of the living room and Momma's arms.

A Faithful Friend

By Nanette Thorsen-Snipes
Buford, Georgia, United States

For years I had wanted a Bassett Hound. When I told Jim, my new husband, he searched everywhere for one. Finally, he found a dog at an adoptive home that was part Bassett.

But Susie was the drab color of red Georgia clay, not the cute tri-colored Bassett Hound with large droopy ears that I envisioned.

"Why did you bring that dog home?" I asked when I first saw her. "She's ugly. Not only that, she's not the puppy I wanted. She's old." I couldn't believe my husband thought I would like Susie. She was the plainest dog I'd ever seen.

"But the lady said she was a good dog," Jim kept saying. "She's only a year old, Nan. Just give her a chance."

I turned away from both of them and began washing dishes. "She's old, Jim," I repeated. I fussed out loud about this new animal taking up room in our house.

Jim had agreed to take Susie for a week and we couldn't take her back before that. To add insult to my perceived injuries, I couldn't believe I had to suffer through a week with a dog I didn't like. However, before the week was half over, I began to fall in love with this unassuming dog because of her smiling, liquid-brown eyes. Susie eventually became our ultimate protector and diligently watched over my family. Because she was older, she came when I called and understood the word "No."

Her best trait though, was that she seemed to instinctively understand my moods. She became my close friend and confidant. She even liked my cat.

When we moved from a small house to a larger one on the other side of the railroad tracks, I remember Susie wandering back to the old house. One day, the woman who had moved into it phoned and frantically begged us to come get Susie. It seemed that she had stationed herself outside of "her" house and refused to let the new people in. For several days, Susie created a commotion by not letting them go in or out of their newly purchased home. In time, however, Susie realized we had moved and let the people live in peace.

When our children went to school, Susie followed them to the school building, and whenever she could, she'd sneak in with them. I laughed when I learned how often the janitors had to shoo her out.

There were days when I'd sit down in front of Susie and pat her silky head. I'd look into those deep brown eyes and absorb the unspoken feelings that passed between us. How do you explain those times with an animal? Those times when an animal is your best friend in the entire world? It was times like that when I liked to pick up her favorite ball and toss it. She'd race after it and, with her tail wagging wildly, bring the ball back.

Once Susie followed the whole family to a regional football game not far from our house. During the first half of the game, I saw her racing beneath the bleachers playing tag with another dog. But as soon as the second half began, I noticed Susie ambling down the sidelines. When I saw the kickoff ball cartwheel into the air, I knew what Susie was thinking. I gasped as she raced after the ball. The whole game came to an abrupt halt until the referees physically lifted her and put her outside the fence.

Several years passed, and Susie's reddish face began turning white, but she still loved to roam and stayed gone for days at a time chasing neighbor cats, butterflies, or anything that moved.

One mid-summer day with butter-yellow Jonquils blooming by mailboxes, a boy from the old neighborhood called. There was sadness in his voice as he said, "Please come over right away. It's Susie. She's not moving." The boy's voice broke as he added, "I think she's dead."

I swallowed over the growing lump in my throat. "Come on kids—something's happened to Susie!" I loaded my four children into the station wagon and headed to the old homestead. As I drove down the street, I heard sniffling coming from my kids in the back seat.

Across the street from our old house, Susie lay in the grass. I leaned out the car window and yelled, "Susie!" My old friend didn't move. The sniffling in the back seat grew louder. "It's all right kids. She's just asleep," I said. Then I prayed, *Lord, please let her be asleep.*

"Susie!" I called again. But Susie lay perfectly still.

"I think she may be dead," I whispered. I walked slowly over to the motionless body in the crabgrass. One lazy ear perked up as I approached.

Choking back tears, I said, "I think she's still alive, kids." I heard the car doors quietly open behind me. About the time I leaned down to see how badly she was hurt, Susie looked at me with those smiling eyes. Then she bounced to her feet and gave me her yuckiest dog-kiss ever. I squatted down so I was eye-level with her and wrapped my arms around my funny friend.

Several years later, my mother died of lung cancer. The dogwoods were in full bloom as Susie and I sat outside on a wooden front porch swing, and I told her about the pain and anguish I felt. In empathy, she placed her large paws in my lap and after awhile laid her head down. We rocked back and forth to the rhythm of tears flowing down my face. I relived my life that day, and Susie dreamed of hers. I thanked God for the unconditional love He and this dog gave me.

The years passed, and one unbearably hot, summer day when Susie was nearing 12, she took off toward the woods and never returned. My heart ached, because I never had a chance to say goodbye to my best friend.

I told God how much I loved and missed Susie. I asked Him to take care of her and my broken heart. God was faithful; He reserved a special place in my memory for my dog. I've finally been healed of the loss of the most beautiful dog I've ever known.

I keep a color photo of Susie on my desk. From time to time, I look at the fading picture and remember the good days. When I think about my old friend, instead of crying, I picture her smiling eyes looking up at me in unconditional love—just like God's. And I smile.

The View from the Porch

By Maureen Beaman
Newhall, California, United States

August of 1979 was a hot one in the small town at the base of the Rocky Mountains where my family had recently moved. Our new house was large and had a wide front porch running across its entire length. The best part of the porch was a low brick wall built at the front edge, perfect for hiding and watching the unfamiliar neighborhood.

The summer had been spent sitting on that front porch with my sister, trying to figure out where we fit in. We got to know our neighbors through watching their daily comings and goings.

Being a young animal lover, I associated people with their animals. There was Rocky, the rambunctious black lab, and Holly, the fat, little mutt. But my favorite was Suzy, the red wiener dog.

Suzy was always outside with her family while they were mowing the lawn or washing the car or just lying in the cool grass watching the world go by.

Eventually my sister and I ventured beyond the front porch to explore the neighborhood. Suzy always ran over to make sure we had enough kisses and she had enough petting. Soon we were taking walks just to play with Suzy.

One morning my sister and I took up our usual post on the front porch, this time playing a game of Slap Jack. For once, I was winning, but we stopped when the mailman arrived in his truck to deliver our mail. As soon as he drove off, we pushed and tripped our way to the mailbox. A streak of red flying after the truck stopped us cold in our tracks. Suzy was chasing the mailman!

The truck hit Suzy and sent her flying to the side of the road, where she landed howling in pain, unable to get up.

To our horror, the mailman continued on as if nothing had happened, turned the corner, and drove out of sight. People rushed out of their houses to see what had caused the commotion, among them two young girls from the house across the street.

As Suzy's family frantically scooped her up and rushed her to the vet, the two girls asked us what happened.

"Did you see what happened?" cried Heather, the younger of the two.

"The mailman ran her over—we saw the whole thing!" My hands flew as I recounted the story. "He ran her over and then drove away!" My sister and I told and retold the story, growing angrier at every telling and yet enjoying the spotlight.

The two girls were also sisters. Heidi was one year younger than my sister, Mary, and Heather was one year older than me. They were the owners of Holly, the fat little mutt. Heidi and Heather invited us to their house for lunch and filled us in on the workings of the neighborhood.

Apparently we had been missing out on quite a bit that was not visible from the porch. There was the afternoon game of kickball at least three times a week and the neighborhood hide and seek event going on nightly.

We sat and chatted all day until the sun had set and the streetlights came on, our signal to head home. I lay awake that night thinking of Suzy and how scared she must have been. My eight-year-old mind couldn't fathom injuring a dog and then driving away as it screamed in pain. By the next morning, I had come up with a plan. Recruiting the help of my sister and the girls across the street, I set out to write the offensive mailman a strongly worded letter.

Dear Mailman,

Yesterday you ran over Suzy. She screamed and screamed, and you didn't even stop. She has a broken leg and has to have a cast, so she can't come out and play. You should have stopped.

I folded the letter and put it in my mailbox. The four of us sat on the front porch and waited for the mailman to come. We talked about how we would stand up to him and demand an explanation. We would make him say he was sorry to Suzy's family. One way or another, we were going to make him pay for what he had done to our beloved wiener dog.

We must have all seen the mail truck round the corner at the same time, because we all ran for the shelter of the brick wall in one big pack.

So much for standing up to the monster and stamping out injustice—instead we hid and watched him take the letter from the mailbox and read it. When he was finished, he shook his head and looked up at the house.

"Girls," he groaned in his big monster voice.

We stared at one another in pure terror, wondering which one would respond. After several frantic hand signals and facial expressions passed between us, we all stepped out at once.

"I didn't know I hit the dog."

My knees were ready to give out on me; unfortunately, so was my mouth. As much as I wanted to come back with a biting comment, I couldn't say a word. We all just stood there and stared at him. Eventually he tucked the letter into his pocket and drove off to the next house. Within a few weeks, Suzy's leg was healed and her cast was removed.

While I'm sure the experience was traumatic for her, she never showed it. Her heart and her spirit made it through unscathed, and her body showed only a slight limp as evidence that it had happened at all.

Throughout the years, I have often thought about that mailman. I wonder if he has regrets for not stopping either on the day it happened or in the days following to see how Suzy was doing. Although Suzy was the one who had to suffer the physical pain, I imagine the mailman suffered, as well. I always hope the courageous acts of four young children made him stop for a minute and take a look at himself and his priorities.

Today I am a Veterinary Technician dedicated to helping the Suzy's of the world. Although I no longer live in that small foothill town, I have never lost touch with the girls from across the street. I found lifelong friends and a lifelong career from the front porch on a hot August afternoon.

5

Growing Up

Growing up isn't always an easy process, but somehow, despite the difficulties, we get through it. And isn't it funny how hindsight is 20/20? We never seem to mind those troubles so much looking back on them years later. In fact, the good times and the bad, our growing up years often create some of our most treasured memories.

Porch Swing Memories

By Fran Finney
Independence, Kansas, United States

Back and forth, back and forth...the white painted oak swing sailed back and forth every summer day and evening when I was growing up in the 1940's and 50's.

We lived in a small town in southeast Kansas, dwelling in four houses in those years, and many of my strongest memories include that swing.

Actually, the first house of the four didn't have a porch, and that is the primary thing I remember about it. There was a tiny brick stoop that didn't even have space for a single chair, let alone a glider or a swing! I had to sit on a hard brick step to play with my dollies and to decorate my color books. Fortunately, we moved from that house when I was five, just in time for lasting memories to be made.

Our second house, made of brick, had a side porch with a concrete floor. The swing was purchased and installed soon after moving into this house. I cannot remember it ever being the natural oak color, so I'm guessing it was purchased at an estate auction. Pennies were watched during those years following the Great Depression. Mother made a padded cushion from an old quilt my grandmother had pieced.

That swing became my imaginary train, transporting me to places familiar as the homes of friends or relatives or to strange and exotic locales I read about or saw in the newsreels at the movie theater. I read all of Laura Ingalls Wilder's *Little*

House books in the swing on that porch, as well as many Cherry Ames, Nurse and Nancy Drew mysteries.

This was also the porch that gave me refuge when my older sister, Janis, contracted polio. Seated there on the swing, "out of the way," I watched while the family doctor telephoned and made arrangements for her to be admitted to a large city hospital where skilled medical staff could care for her. The ambulance, owned by a local mortuary, came in the night, and I watched from the safety of the swing as she was carried from the house. My mother accompanied her in the ambulance, and my father followed in the family's 1940 Chevrolet. I, however, was quarantined to the house and its property. I could not leave for several weeks, and no one was allowed to visit. An elderly neighbor couple cared for me during my parents' absence. They gladly accepted the doctor's expanded quarantine that included their house. Imagine volunteering to be housebound for several weeks! Groceries and other necessaries were delivered to their front steps.

After the quarantine had expired, two aunts decided to alternate weeks "taking care of Martha."

The swing's steady back and forth comforted and consoled me while I waited for updates on Janis's condition. This information came via long-distance telephone calls made late at night when the rates were cheaper. Whatever adult was staying with me would forward the message to me the next morning, and I would go to the haven of my swing to contemplate the import of the words delivered to me.

After 13 weeks, Janis came home and joined me on the swing, sharing the warmth of a late Indian summer November day.

By the next summer, we had moved again—to a house just a half block away from the fire station and two blocks from downtown. This house had a view of the highway that ran north to south through town. The swing made the move with us and had a front-of-the-house location. The porch ran across the entire width of the house, was wooden floored, and was completely covered with a roof extending a good foot or more beyond the supporting porch posts. Unless there was a strong east wind, the porch remained dry, even in the heaviest of rains.

It was in this location that I learned, by spying on Janis, that a porch swing could be used for courting. More than once I was asked to play out back or go upstairs and read in order for her to entertain her boyfriend-of-the-moment in private. Of course, if I went to the backyard, I would sneak around the side of the house to see why I had been excluded. If I went upstairs, my bedroom window was directly above the porch, so I could listen in.

That was a glorious porch. People drove past it on their way to the semi-pro baseball games in the park where Mickey Mantle played several times during his first season as a professional baseball player. When his team, the Independence [Kansas] Yankees, played our local team, we were always in attendance. Even then we knew "that new kid from Commerce [Oklahoma]" was going on to the majors. His powerful switch-hitting abilities, coupled with his big friendly grin, made those games extra special. He never sat on our porch, but quite a few of our local "boys of summer" did. Most had rooming house accommodations, so they truly enjoyed watching the town's activities from our porch.

Fire trucks could be observed dashing off on life-saving missions. Cars going to and from downtown shops and businesses seemed to swing past, the occupants waving cheery hellos. And up on the highway, there were cars, trucks, and busses to watch and we often speculated on their destinations.

The swing stayed in that location only three years. As much as we girls loved being at the hub of the town's activities, our parents desired a more quiet, less trafficked location.

There was much discussion as to where the swing would be hung at the new house on the far west edge of town. There were three possible sites for it. My father's choice was in the back yard, hanging from a sturdy branch of a huge elm tree. Mother opted for putting it in an arbor back by the unattached garage. But, in the end, we sisters won, and the swing's final location was on a magnificent brick and concrete-floored, east-facing front porch. It hung in a covered recess where there was always a cooling southerly breeze.

Mother made a festive sunflower print cover for the quilt pad, and the swing was the prime choice of seating. Whoever was first out on the porch got the swing—unless our father pre-empted us with the words, "Girls, let your mother swing for a bit. It's hers, too, you know." Father never sat in the swing. He would check the chains every spring, changing them when he deemed them worn. But to swing back and forth—I think he never did. The swing was for "his girls."

The swing was where I discovered the worlds of fashion magazines, movie magazines, crossword puzzles, and "honeymoon bridge." There was just enough room on the swing if two occupants scooched real close to the armrests, for the cards to be played. We also sang the latest songs, as well as show tunes and the old standards. Mother often accompanied us on her 1920's ukulele.

Ironically, the quiet locale didn't last. During our second year at the house, the county built a new hospital four blocks south. Soon after, the local community college relocated its campus about 10 blocks south. Traffic again was whizzing past the swing. Friends and even strangers waved, and we responded. Father usually queried mid-wave, "Who on earth is that crazy fellow?"

Often family friends out for a drive to get relief from the heat would stop and spend the evening on our porch, as would teenaged friends with new drivers' licenses or the unexpected treat of getting the family car for the evening—who usually had a mileage limitation accompanying the privilege so they couldn't actually drive around all evening. They would park in the driveway and come up on the porch to visit and watch the world go by.

Mother always had some kind of beverage and cookies to serve these guests—iced tea, colas, root beer floats. Our porch was a social hub on warm summer evenings—and the swing never ceased going back and forth.

Janis and I graduated from high school and then college. We both took jobs away from our hometown. But whenever we visited our parents, we still opted to sit a while in the swing if the weather was cooperative. When we married, neither of our husbands had grown up with swings, so the allure eluded them—and we didn't have to vie with them for our coveted swing seat.

Our father died, and eventually Mother sold the house. The new owners wanted the swing, so it went with the house. The last thing I did before ownership was transferred was to sit out on the porch in the swing one last time.

On Mother's Day a few years ago, I received the ultimate gift. A porch swing! It isn't white painted oak, and the pad I made for it isn't from an old quilt, but it has the power.

That power is to transport me, not to geographic places, but to transport me back in time. I remember all of those special times spent in the old swing and how much it was enjoyed!

Someday My Kiss Will Come

By Kathryn Jones
West Valley, Utah, United States

I still remember the moonlit night. Actually, it might not have been a full moon but it could have been—I was on fire. And so was he. We were sitting real close—he at the wheel, me next to him on that little bump between the passenger side and the driver's.

Doug put his arm around me. His dark brown hair, worn longer than most of the high school graduates his age, was slicked back. Though not long enough for a ponytail, I imagined running my fingers through the thick strands and speaking "sweet nothings" in his ear.

I can still feel the chills traveling to Bermuda and back when he said, "May I kiss you?" His face was real close. I could see the fine lines between his eyebrows. My lips were ready. They quivered instinctively. And then suddenly—they stopped.

Was Doug really asking if he could kiss me?

All the guys previous to the prince were more of the "take and grab the kiss when you can get it type." What should I do? What would he say if I told him, "No?"

So I made up this line, right then and there—a line, by the way, that I'd never had to use on any other guy before. I said, "I don't kiss until the fifth date."

...The fifth date? The FIFTH DATE?

But I had said it.

He was looking at me with his puppy brown eyes, and they seemed to be saying, "That's a joke, right?"

...Why DID the chicken cross the road? What is black and white and red all over?

My face. My face. My face.

Fortunately, this guy was smart. "Can you go out tomorrow night?" he asked.

Man, he wanted to kiss me bad. And well, I wanted to kiss him, too, so what was the problem? More directly, what was my problem?

My oldest brother promised me it would happen. He'd watched me from the kitchen window at the end of the first date, the second date, the third and the fourth date. After being mad at him for spying, he'd simply said, "Don't worry, you'll marry him!"

Marry the guy? Was he nuts?

Still, after a few minutes in Doug's car, this being the fifth date and receiving nothing but a good-bye, I found myself walking into the house crying, "He doesn't like me! He hates me! On the fifth date he was supposed to kiss me!"

I knew then that the prince of my dreams would never call again.

I was wrong.

The next day he called, and we went on the sixth date...but nothing, and I mean *nothing* happened. Not even a kiss on the cheek. Unbelievable! Maybe I reminded him of his sister.

I had met his sister the previous week. Although attractive, she was tall, big boned, and had so much boundless energy that I thought the floor was going to sink in when she spoke.

No, it couldn't be that. Maybe...maybe...with a swish of my arm, I took a quick smell.

Oh, glory!

I smelled like the old leftover spaghetti from the refrigerator! Actually, not exactly like the spaghetti. My mom was still getting after me for putting the leftovers in the cupboard by mistake. We were looking for that meal for days!

"Is anything wrong?" ...Oh, the sad, puppy eyes. His inquisitive eyes searched my own as I clamped my arms to my sides and shook my head—a definite, "No."

"Well then, can you go out tomorrow?"

Tomorrow?

The next day I cleaned my pits especially well and waited somewhat impatiently for my prince to come. Maybe he was just nervous about kissing me...maybe he wanted to, but because he'd never done it before...maybe this was a huge joke initiated by my "supposed" friends in school.

I hadn't yet forgiven my friends for the orange peel incident. Four years later it was still running through my mind like a slow motion picture movie—the tray with my hot lunch...potatoes...gravy...chicken fried steak...feeling hungry...smiling...my stomach groaning...walking down the aisle to sit...receiving strange looks...some private joke? Losing my balance...slipping...slipping...clank! Silverware flying...crud in my hair...faces...too many faces laughing...

Maybe...maybe he WAS afraid...

I went back to the bathroom and re-brushed my teeth and looked into the mirror for that all-too-common zit that always made its appearance at just the wrong time. I smiled at myself, trying to let "the inner glow" that my mother said I had, shine through. But all I saw was frightened eyes. Okay, frightened eyes and a large zit trying to break forth on my chin.

The doorbell rang. I could picture my beloved standing on the front porch waiting for me.

My heart skipped. I turned from the bathroom mirror. He was down the hall in the living room. My dad was giving him the old "now take care of my daughter," routine, which was really, "if you lay a hand on my daughter, you are dead, Buddy," lecture. My stomach rolled over once, then twice, before I entered the room and our eyes met.

He smiled, his eyes walking into my own with silent words I could only imagine meant, "Don't worry, the kiss is coming later."

"Hi," I said.

"Hi," he answered. "Ready to go?"

I was more than ready. The movie was fine, too. You could hold hands and kiss in the dark. The screen glittered like so many lips—what was this movie about anyway? I just couldn't guess. *The kiss, where was the kiss?*

And then the movie was over, and his hand was in mine, and he was walking me to the car. *This has to be it*, I thought as the door opened and he walked to the other side. Or was it?

"Did you like the movie?" he asked. The car sputtered its famous start.

"Yeah," I lied. Well, I *could* have liked it. "You?"

"It was great! I loved that cool part when—"

I was no longer with him. Sure, my body was in the car, but my soul was thinking of what was to come.

What would it be like? Smooth? Swift? Wet? Tender?

The car stopped. I was waiting. And sweating.

"Sooo…"

"So, do you want to go out to dinner tomorrow?"

After the kiss, Buddy…

"Sure."

Doug opened the door and walked around to my side. The door creaked open like a great gate. I stood in the cool evening breeze ignoring the heat of my thundering heart.

"Sooo….I guess I should go inside…"

"Okay."

Okay?

"See you around seven?" He winked and walked me to the front porch.

Well, what was that supposed to mean?

Later that night on my bed, I reflected on my lack of charisma or my great "smelling" body—whatever it was that was keeping him from kissing me. Why hadn't I just allowed him to kiss me on the first date? Why?

On the seventh date, Doug and I spent an entire day together, beginning at the city zoo. As animals of all sizes and shapes stared back at me behind wire fencing, I couldn't help thinking about how different this dating experience had been for me. I had dated various men—boys, I think now, and had allowed them to kiss me even before I knew if I really liked them. It was the kiss, always the kiss I wanted, with no thought about what it all meant.

Symbolically speaking, I had dated lions, tigers, bears, monkeys, birds—even frogs, but never a prince.

As the evening became a misty gray, we left the zoo, talking and laughing. Doug and I held hands, and he told me about his family, his job and how much he enjoyed being with me. Somehow I forgot all about the kiss.

When it came, we were in the car as before. The sky was dark, the moon shining within the window like truth. And yes, the kiss was grand, kind of like a dairy smooth ice-cream cone, chocolate, only warmer. We finished some minutes later—I'm not sure when. All I could think about was how much I liked him.

P.S. You know why my husband didn't kiss me until the seventh date? Just to get me back.

The 1967 World Series

By Eileen Sateriale
Bowie, Maryland, United States

Having a younger sibling can be both a nuisance and a blessing. Growing up in the 1960's, I had a seven-year-old brother who followed baseball religiously. It was a passion for him and his friends. When the newspaper was delivered to our house, the first thing Eddie did was run out to the front porch and grab the sports page. The rest of the paper became a disheveled mess, abandoned on the porch. Anything about baseball, he read avidly. He knew everything there was to know about baseball, especially the hometown team, the Boston Red Sox.

One time I asked him, "Why are you so interested in baseball?"

"It's fun."

"Fun?"

"Yastrzemski's on the way to winning the Triple Crown."

"Is he a horse?"

He shook his head and said, "Being a girl, you don't understand." He folded the sports page and hid it under his bed.

I accepted the explanation, but I thought his obsession was silly. He was in the third grade, and I was a sophisticated sixth grader who knew better than to care about baseball.

In 1967, the Boston Red Sox won the American League Pennant. It was hard fought and well earned. Political events around Boston were temporarily tossed aside as the whole six-state New England region rallied around the Red Sox. The event transformed people like me, who didn't care much for baseball, into avid fans. It was especially thrilling for my brother who had been a fan during the season. I even felt guilty about my comment earlier that summer that Yastrzemski was a horse.

The Red Sox now had the task of facing the National League St. Louis Cardinals. Could the Red Sox bring home a World Series victory? On paper, the Cardinals were the better team; they had won more games during the regular season and secured the National League pennant long before our team secured the American League pennant. The Red Sox had a few good players and a lot of talent, but they were plagued by injuries late in the season. Many predicted that the Cardinals would sweep Boston four games to none and the series would be quickly forgotten.

I said to Eddie, "Are you upset because everyone's predicting St. Louis to win?"

He answered, "Boston can win."

To Eddie and his third grade friends, the odds didn't mean a thing. They had their hearts and minds set on a Boston victory. But they were not alone; many Bostonians optimistically prepared for the possibility of a World Series victory.

I tried to pretend that I followed the series for my brother, but I must admit, I got a dose of Series Fever at the end of the regular season when the Sox were vying for the pennant. When I asked him questions, he acted glad that I was interested. He even showed me the sports page and explained the strengths and weaknesses of the two teams.

Of course, I cheered for the Red Sox hoping that they might win a few games, but not expecting the Series to go all the way. I thought it was an honor to win the pennant, as the Red Sox had only won it a few times in the history of the franchise, and they'd only won the World Series once or twice.

St. Louis won the first game at Boston's Fenway Park. The next day, Boston tied it up. The third and fourth games were won by St. Louis in their home stadium. The fifth game was played in St. Louis, and Boston won, bringing the sixth game to Boston and a possible seventh game, only if Boston could win the sixth. With the entire New England region solidly behind them, the Red Sox won the sixth game.

The score was tied three games apiece, and we were facing the seventh and deciding game. Now we were all on the edge of our seats. Could the Sox do it? Could they defy the odds and go all the way? If they won this one game, they'd win the Series!

My wise teacher assigned one thing for homework that weekend: root for the Red Sox. That was one assignment everyone happily complied with.

The day finally came. It was a Sunday in October. The final game at Fenway Park had been sold out for weeks. I knew my brother and his friends would have liked to go. Actually, I would have liked to go, too, but I was really trying to pretend that I was in this for my brother.

We decided to do the next best thing. The neighborhood kids held a kickball game in front of our house because it sat on the flattest part of the hill. It was a makeshift field on an asphalt, potholed street. A telephone pole served as first base, second base was a rag in the middle of the street, third base was a crooked tree, and home plate was on the crest of the hill. Whenever a ball was thrown to home plate, it generally meant that the catcher had to chase it down the street. We even had a prickly bush in left field that served as the green monster of Fenway Park. One of the rules was that if a ball landed in the green monster, it was an automatic homer. (I thought that was really clever.)

We chose up sides, making sure that each team had some good players and some weak players. Some people like me, who played kickball occasionally—usually when the boys couldn't get enough players—were swept into the game.

Everyone who had a transistor radio brought it along or ran into their house to get one. We positioned the transistors at equal distances along the sidelines, tuned to the same AM station, and turned each one of them up, full volume. That way anyone could hear the game from wherever they were standing. Anyone who had to run down the hill to retrieve the ball was quickly filled in on the action they missed. When the series game got tense, the kickball game was put on hold, and we all gathered around the radios to listen. When they took breaks for commercials or to change players, we resumed the kickball game. I remember the continuous Dr. Pepper advertisements on the radio and joking that Dr. Pepper was probably the team physician for the Red Sox. One of my neighbors ran into their house and brought out some cans of soda for all of us.

The kickball game was going full guns. The Sox were powerful with pitcher Jim Lonberg giving a strong performance. Then St. Louis slugger Julian Javier hit his three-run homer and broke all of our hearts. It wrapped up the series for St. Louis. We were the defeated team, and the baseball season was over. Of course, we all wished it had gone our way. One by one the transistors were turned off and the kickball game disbanded. We picked up the empty soda cans littered on the side of the street and threw them in the trash. Within a few minutes, everyone went home.

I looked at my brother. I knew Eddie and his friends were bitterly disappointed. I felt sad for them that the home team didn't win. I thought it best not to say anything, as I might say the wrong thing. Eddie didn't say anything. He walked up our walk, onto our front porch, and into the house.

Eddie grew up, his friends moved away, and the Red Sox players retired or got traded, but he never lost his passion for baseball. I think it was because of Eddie and his passion for the game that I became a baseball fan.

A few years ago, I toured Cooperstown and saw the Baseball Hall of Fame. I enjoyed seeing the players who were inducted into the hall, including Carl Yastrzemski who won the Triple Crown in 1967. When I looked at the exhibit, I remembered that first baseball conversation with my brother and how I became a fan.

Behind the Tractor

By Karla Jensen
Beaver Dam, Wisconsin

The road of hard knocks that led to a positive learning experience occurred behind the tractor on the family farm when I was little older than my now nine-year-old son. Today, as we head to the front porch for a chat, we maturely discuss the reasons none of us should smoke. As the conversation continues, I envision my past sins and then proceed telling my own growing experience that took place behind the tractor.

As the youngest of four children, I followed in the footsteps of and sometimes on—often times off—the straight and narrow path of my three older siblings.

Both my father and my grandfather enjoyed smoking. My father chose the lesser of two evils, clinching his polished pretty pipe between his teeth no matter if he gardened, cheered for the Iowa Hawkeyes, or shaved wood from two by fours on the saw in his shed. He let me puff on the tip of the well-worn stem and smell the aromatic flavor of his favorite brand, Velvet tobacco. Even now, nearly two years after his death, I've squirreled away a box of his old Velvet tobacco in my cupboard and sniff it as a reminder that his memory is never too far away. My father also entertained his children by blowing smoke rings, but I never considered taking up the less than healthy past time in order to accomplish the same tricks.

As fond as we were of dad's pipe, we didn't receive the same privileges with my grandfather's cigarettes. Since we marched to his small bungalow after school nearly every day and even spent time there on weekends, we couldn't help but notice his stash of hand-rolled cigs in the bureau situated on his own front porch. Our curiosity peaked on a dull day after school as my conniving brother suggested we pocket some of the smokes and save them for a more convenient time at our farm, out of Grandpa's site. We stepped out onto his porch, making certain the coast was clear.

"You guard the door, Karla," my siblings nodded to me as I rigidly stood on the outskirts of the interior screen door that led into the bungalow's dining room.

"Hurry up," I demanded as Karen and Wayne rifled through the first couple drawers, then finally hit pay dirt as they discovered the tiny white rolls of tobacco. "We're gonna get killed if Grandpa finds us stealing his cigs," I cautioned feeling sweat roll down the back of my neck in the summer heat.

Once we returned home, our deceitful trio gathered on the front porch of my farmhouse. Like a squadron of spies, we synchronized our watches and disseminated for a few minutes to deflect suspicion prior to converging at the appropriate time. Well before supper, my older brother, one older sister, and I—the three of us small enough to be hidden by one gigantic tractor tire—squatted near the tractor spokes facing away from the two-story farmhouse. We each took turns peeking around the tractor's rear and eyeing the front porch, just in case Mom or our older sister decided to venture out the front door and wonder where we had gone.

With wooden matches for furnace fires and pipe smoking prevalent inside the country farm dwelling, my bold brother, Wayne, had managed to snatch a hefty handful of matches adequate for this devious drama. We'd witnessed our father on many occasions scrape the wooden match across his work boots seeing fire instantly blaze atop the match. Although I, too, longed to feel the rough wooden matches against the smooth surface of my young fingers, Wayne decided for us that he would do the match lighting.

"I'll light the matches for all of us," Wayne announced as he lectured us on the hazards of playing with fire.

We each selected one of the cigarettes, awaited our brother to light the correct end, and gazed at the white casing burning before our wide eyes to reveal the tobacco innards.

"This reminds me of a campfire," I offered, mostly to ease the tension among us. When my turn came to puff on the tobacco-packed stick, my mind raced ahead to hours or even minutes into the future when someone, perhaps my mother, would detect the strange aroma of tobacco breath upon my lips. *"Why in the world does your breath reek of tobacco, young lady?"* I could hear my mother question. Even worse, perhaps someone, again most likely my stern mother, would read guilt in my shifty eyes at the dinner table. *"Karla, is there something you'd like to tell me tonight about the events of the afternoon?"* I heard her voice echo in my mind like a song stuck in my head that just wouldn't disappear.

What if someone, surely my overly critical mother, discovered our terrible deed of smoking? I closed my eyes, praying that the act I was about to commit would not haunt me in years to come or any time more immediate than that.

"Do you think we'll get a spanking for this if someone finds out?" Karen asked quietly.

When I opened my eyes, I tasted what I surely believed to be dirt. Puff, puff, puff, cough, cough, cough, spit, spat, sputter. *How could smokers get hooked on something so revolting?*

"This is awful," I choked. "I'm going back to the porch to pet the kittens," I added.

My sister grabbed my arm and held me there, her intent not to be the only girl partaking of this rebellious act. I vaguely recall a discussion about how to correctly inhale the contents of what I held in my shaking hand, but blew the notion off as easily as I had decided to blow out the distinct, yet dirty taste of my first cigarette. Certainly I inhaled, I claimed to my observing siblings, but inwardly and truthfully, I made the decision in that instance to never smoke the repulsive things again.

In the midst of huffing, my eldest sister, who had not been invited mostly due to her snobbery, hollered from the front porch, just as we had anticipated, to high tail our carcasses to dinner.

"Where are you guys?" Jennifer wailed. "It's time for supper. Get in here now!"

We rushed to conceal the contents of burned matches and partially utilized smokes. The three of us scattered the evidence under piles of lumber near our father's shed. I wonder if he ever found them.

I also wonder why no adult ever bothered to discuss with us the pitfalls of smoking. As an adult today who lives in a generation bombarded with Surgeon General's warnings, I grimace in knowing that my parents' generation lacked the knowledge or warnings of which we are well aware. If I had been forewarned of cancer, emphysema, and the surmounting costs associated with this atrocious habit, surely I wouldn't have bothered meeting my siblings behind the tractor.

The only smoking I've partaken in as a youth or adult since the day behind the tractor came in celebration of adulthood just after my husband and I moved into our first house. In honor of independence and marriage, and due simply to the fact that my spouse wielded a fresh cigar or two from a friend's announcement of a new baby, I held my first cigar. We padded out into the summer breeze to enjoy our new front porch and lawn chairs. Dusk had fallen and cicadas served as our evening orchestra.

We lit the bulky stogies, and as I held the broadness of the cigar between my thumb and fingers, I recognized that 15 years had swiftly passed. Although I wasn't hiding behind the tractor wheel, I recalled the sibling rendezvous like it was yesterday and momentarily wondered if I sat in the midst of making a ridiculous choice.

"This reminds me of my very first smoke," I told my handsome husband. "You'll never believe what my brother and sister and I did behind the tractor." He smiled as if he, too, held a story about his first smoke close to his heart.

The stub tasted worse than cigarettes, I determined immediately, and only puffed a couple of times for rebellion's sake. I wondered how men could stand such sogginess between their teeth and gums. I preferred my father's hard, smooth pipe to the pliable, soggy consistency of a cigarette or cigar. We toasted that evening, my spouse and I, to making good decisions about never getting hooked on the habit of smoking. In fact, I followed up those first couple of puffs by telling him this story of the memory behind the tractor.

How one childhood memory could surface so many times throughout my life is remarkable and surprising. The minutes I shared in my initial puff of a cigarette have followed me like a stray dog that refuses to return home no matter how many times you yell at the beast. At a Christmas gathering a decade or so ago, when a safe amount of time had passed and mother wasn't about to allow anger to overtake her in her old age, my siblings and I shared the story of smoking behind the tractor. She swore she hadn't a clue of that afternoon when we meet on the porch first and reconnected behind the tractor.

Although I have made the good choice not to smoke, I still prefer the strong wooden matches to a book of the weaker version that never seem to light as crisply as the former. I also enjoy caressing the smooth surface of dad's wooden pipes that sit timelessly on a shelf in our old farmhouse to jog memories of my childhood.

My Kingdom for a Book

By Helen Kay Polaski
Milan, Michigan, United States

Books have always been one of my passions.

Almost from the first moment I held a book in my hands, I fell deeply and madly in love. Not just with the written word, but also with the creative process that coerces and cajoles the mind until said word is preserved on paper. Words being so important to me, I couldn't help but wonder how many pictures a thousand words could paint, if indeed a picture painted a thousand words.

It was a private quest.

King Arthur searched for the Holy Grail; I searched for an answer to my question. How many pictures could a thousand words paint? How many more pictures could a million words paint?

Like the Knights of the Round Table, my faith was strong, and I marched forward day after day, reading whatever I could get my hands on and reaching for the answer. Each week, I patiently waited for the Book Mobile to arrive at my one-room school so I could exchange my book for another. The Book Mobile was a big van filled with shelves and shelves of books. I never questioned where the Book Mobile Lady got the books—only reveled in the fact that she stopped at my school. While I waited for her return each week, I read my siblings' books, the books on the exchange table in the classroom, and whatever else I could get my hands on. My favorite tales always included dragons and knights, elves and fairies, and the ever-elusive unicorn.

With each story, my vast knowledge of words and their importance grew, and I fervently wished I could paint what I read, for my own Camelot, vivid and oh, so real, sprouted before my eyes. My imagination danced to tunes no one but I understood or heard as I moved within the murals and tapestries in my mind, created through the magical realm of books. The world inside my head was filled with the elusive, the unbelievable, the perfectly unpredictable, and the extraordinary, yet the world I walked around inside of was totally ordinary.

I was normal, I suppose, for all children believe in magic.

The year I turned 10 was perhaps the most eventful for me—certainly the year I would mark as my biggest eye-opener. For one thing, one-room schoolhouses were done away with and country kids were shipped to the city 13 miles to the north. For another, a bakery with dozens and dozens of scrumptious jelly donuts was only a few blocks from school.

The idea that Mom would never know I spent my nickel on a donut instead of milk was a revelation that still makes me smile.

But more important, all on my own and quite by accident, I discovered something that flooded my mind with endless possibilities and more than trivial wonder.

At the same time, 10 is that devastating age when a child begins to realize she must grow up. Tearfully, I realized King Arthur and Lancelot had begun to disappear in the mist, their quest less important, my own quest nearly forgotten.

One day as I marched to the bakery, my nickel clenched tightly in the palm of my hand, my eyes focused on something other than the girl in front of me. We were about a block from the school when I noticed a sign partially hidden by two rows of overgrown hedges. The sign read: Public Library. Intrigued by the word "library" and captivated by the magical lure of the hedges, grown so close an adult could not enter without brushing both shoulders in the narrow passage, I ventured onto the sidewalk. At that moment, Lancelot, my champion, erupted from the mists and moved before me, his sword glittering in the sunlight, and my heart leapt with joy as the magic resurfaced.

I was tall for my age and thin as a reed, but still the branches reached for me—hurrying me along as I moved through a type of hedge maze that led to a small fieldstone house. When I reached the end of the sidewalk, I turned around in amazement. The hedges grew right up to the building on both sides. It was as if I was in an inner sanctuary. Only muffled street sounds reached my ears. Time seemed to stand still, and I swear I saw the air shimmer as fairies glided past. I would not have been surprised to see Excalibur jammed into one of the massive fieldstones of the cottage sized house or a unicorn nibbling on the dark green hedge.

I took a quick breath and slowly walked up the three steps and stopped on the small front porch. The sign on the door read: Open, Come In. I peeked inside the screen door and froze. Books lined every wall! Awestruck, I opened the door and moved inside.

From across the room, a tiny gray-haired lady lifted her head from the book she was reading. With sharp little bird eyes, she followed my movements as she hopped from her chair and quickly moved toward me. I started to back away, convinced I had traversed sacred ground, but she motioned for me to come closer.

"Please, come on in," she said, her mouth forming a cheery pink bow. "Are you looking for a book?"

I nodded, my tongue glued to the roof of my mouth.

She leaned forward and peered into my eyes. "What kind of book are you looking for—a mystery?"

I shook my head again and whispered. "About unico—about horses."

Her smile widened, and she winked. "I should have known! You young girls always like the horse books." Pivoting on one heel, she moved quickly toward a section marked Easy Reading. "Let's see...I think we have...ah-ha, there it is." She reached for a thick book and pulled it out with a smile on her face. "Here you go. How 'bout Black Velvet?"

She must have recognized my stunned silence for what it was, for she smiled again and patted me on the shoulder. "Do you already have a library card?"

When I didn't answer right away, she motioned for me to follow her to her desk. Once there, she pulled a pink sweater up over her shoulders and buttoned the top button. Suddenly, she was all business. "You do not have a card, right? And you'd like one? Are you 10 years old?"

I nodded yes to every question. Finally she sat back and looked at me.

"Cat got your tongue?"

"No, ma'am."

"Well, that's a relief! For a minute there, I thought you were never going to speak. I guess children with library cards don't need to speak," she winked again. "They can read, instead."

I quickly agreed, and within five minutes she had issued me my first library card. I wandered down the aisles and checked the titles, then walked back out the door. I closed the screen door behind me carefully so it wouldn't disturb the librarian—the gray-haired Keeper of the Books—and sat down on the porch. The sun beat down on me, the wind blocked by the hedges on either side, and I stared at the library card in my lap.

There, as the world continued to spin on its axis, as cars beeped and braked 20 feet away and school children rushed on their way back to school, jelly smeared on their faces, I basked in the glory of my treasure and felt King Arthur's hand on my shoulder. I smiled up at him. With this card, surely hope for fulfilling my quest had returned.

I no longer cared about donuts. I'd found something far more delicious. For the remainder of that school year, I spent every lunch hour in the library. Hours later, ravenous, I wolfed down bits of bologna sandwich on the bus on the way home.

Though I had my library card tucked safely inside my pocket, it was well over a month before I checked out a book. Instead, in the quiet confines of that solemn, beautiful building, I read Black Beauty from cover to cover.

When I started to read it a second time, Keeper of the Books tapped me gently on the shoulder and explained I could, in fact, take the book home. By then, I had gained enough courage to actually check out a book, and that day, before the cover on Black Beauty had firmly closed, I walked out the door with several horse books in my arms and visions of unicorns in my head.

I never shared the library with anyone. It was my Camelot, and in order to keep the magic, I had to keep it as my own precious secret. I imagined the hedges were sentinels keeping my special world hidden until I returned again.

The Keeper of the Books surely had been bound by a wizard, caught in the elixir of an aging spell. Surely she was a young princess of extraordinary beauty merely hiding from a bad knight. She could count on me to keep her secret.

I fully intended to remain in that magical place forever. But life moves on. Soon the teenage years caught up with me and I did what comes naturally to young girls. I dropped my books on the floor of my bedroom and raced out the door after every boy in the neighborhood. Then it was time for the real world—with jobs and marriage and children of my own.

But nothing can take Lancelot and King Arthur away permanently.

They are still my steady companions when I read, or daydream...or breathe. Since I found my sanctuary on that tiny stone porch, no matter what stage of life I'm in, I eventually drift back to a library, and regardless if the building is made of brick or wood, in my eyes it is fieldstone from top to bottom. As my feet touch the sidewalk, I rediscover the magic I found one brisk autumn afternoon so long ago.

My Own Personal Lifeguard

By Dale Davies
United Kingdom

It was a hot summer afternoon, and I was fuming.

How dare my own family upset me like this? Yet again they had said that I couldn't do it. Like the time I was going to go on television for a cooking competition. They told me that I couldn't do it—I'd lose.

I can do it! I will do it!

This time I said I was going to pass my exams with flying colors—all A's, maybe A+'s if I was to work really hard.

But I didn't, of course.

I sat on my great-grandmother's bench on her back porch and thought about how horrible the world was to me. Of course, it was! How could I be wrong? I'm a teenager—I'm **never** wrong. Or am I?

No, I was right, and they were pure evil.

I heard them all laughing at something in the front room, so I guessed, being self centered, that it was about me. I felt a tear start to creep out to say "hi." But I couldn't cry, because I'm a big strong boy, so I gave it a quick fistfight and it went to hide.

I was feeling rotten and by now had forgotten why I was annoyed and had moved onto the question: Why does everyone hate me? I thought about people at school and my friends. Did they really like me, or was I a last resort or possibly someone they couldn't seem to shake off?

Does my mother really love me?

Why are my friends my friends?

Did I have some kind of power over them all?

Before I could totally destroy myself from the inside to the out, my mother opened the back door and came to speak with me. I couldn't help but be happy to see the person who had pulled me through the worst times of the little time I've spent alive on the planet.

I turned my head away from her and tried to look annoyed and upset, which wasn't too hard because I was already the first part.

My mother walked across the porch and sat down on the bench next to me. In her best mothering voice, she asked, "What's wrong?"

I pretended to blank her off but couldn't help but smile.

"What's wrong?" She repeated.

"Nothing," I responded. The sound of joy blended with anger in my voice. I always felt better when my mother came to make sure I was all right. At least *she* didn't hate me.

"Then why not come back inside and stop being moody?"

"No."

"Suit yourself." She stood up and started to go to the door.

"Wait!" I shouted. I needed comforting or at least a kiss and a quick cuddle since no friends were in sight.

"So you want to talk then?"

"I suppose so," I grunted.

She took a seat next to me, and we started to talk.

"I don't care! They still shouldn't have said that about me."

"We were only playing. You know they don't mean it."

"Yeah, they did! It's not nice. It was mean!"

She tried to reassure me and, as usual, she did.

"Why don't you come inside?" She asked again.

"They'll be mean again."

As soon as those words left my mouth, I felt my emotions escaping through my face. My throat began to dry out, and at the same time the tears started to roll—one droplet at first making its way down my face clearing the way for a tidal wave of tears showing me up in front of my mother.

I'm a big baby.

With tears flowing, I tried to say something to my mother so I didn't look like a big baby, but I couldn't. I merely swallowed the wave of tears streaming down my face. My mother, being as caring as she always is, let me rest my head on her shoulder while I felt like a loony.

"It's okay now. They didn't mean it."

I guessed she was right, but I still cried.

As always, my mother comforted me through it again like the many times before and the many times afterwards. She was my lifeline, she was my counselor, and she kept me sane. Well, most of the time anyway. Her hugs could cure everything—a bad mood, someone upset, even someone with a cold or flu. It was a warm motherly hug, and when you felt it, you knew everything was good again.

"It's okay," she said. "You want to come inside now?"

Not with them horrid people.

"Want to come and sit with me?"

I felt like I had gone back in time and I was five years old or something, still a child.

"No. I'm going to sit here for a while and get some fresh air."

I liked fresh air. It had a nice taste to it—better than the mothball flavored stuff they had at school, the taste of chalk. We didn't use chalk anymore but it was still there—dust and things that had been lying in state for about 50 years.

"Okay, I'll see you in a bit."

My mom gave me a huge hug—trying to kill me—and gave me a kiss.

"Thanks, Mom."

"It's okay. See you in a bit then."

My mother stood up slowly from the bench, being careful because of her bad back.

My poor mother—crippled at the age of 33. She was in pain all the time. I'm not really sure what it was that made it bad—perhaps carrying me for nine months and many years. I felt sorry for her, because even if you were to tap her shoulder lightly, it caused her pain. Could you imagine giving her a cuddle? Ouch! You'd think she would crumple into a pile of ash. It must have hurt, but she always gave me big bear hugs when I needed them.

I stood up swift and fast and took in a huge gulp of air. Now that tasted really good, unlike the fly that flew down my throat the last time I took in a great gulp of air! They say you swallow eight spiders during your sleep in a lifetime. Me, I swallow flies while I'm awake. It's happened before; they fly in my ears, as well. I should install some wire mesh, or something, over my mouth.

Maybe it says something about my breath?

Hope not.

I stood around for a second and tried as hard as I could to mop up the lake that had started as a few tears in my mother's arms a few moments ago. I dragged myself around my great-grandmother's wonderful garden and tried to prepare to re-enter the house of horrors. I went to the bottom of the garden and back again feeling the breeze on my tear-stained face.

I stopped next to the hole where the old metal air raid shelter had been. There were flowers there now. The hole had been turned into a pond sort of thing—not used anymore, but a memory of my great-grandmother's children who used to play around it entered my head. Once used as a shelter from the bombs dropped by the German air force, now used as a play area and place of beauty.

Like many children before me, I stepped down into the dry hole and sat looking at the house. Memories came back of old times from when I was a child playing with other kids in the family—the time we were doing cartwheels on the grass, playing hide 'n seek with no places to hide, and just having fun playing and getting into mischief.

That's what I would like to be doing now, but life had changed, and so had I. I was supposed to be grown up now—at least that was what I was told by my elders. I didn't want to be a grown up. I wanted to have fun, and being an adult wasn't fun at all. I didn't want to grow up. I wanted to be a child and have fun, just like Peter Pan!

Looking back, I did have fun as a child, and that has affected my life more than I thought it would. There was the time when we all came out at summer time and sat on deck chairs and chatted away like madness. The grown-ups were on the porch because that was where they ruled over us. I remember trying to get in on the conversation but failing. I'd sit near and listen in, laugh when it was right, and look sad when something horrid was said about somebody's week.

It was listening in on those conversations that made me grow as a person and help me become more mature for my age—when it suited me most, of course. After all, I was a teenager.

I wanted to be a child again, but time travel isn't possible. So what if I was supposed to be grown up? You only live once, so why waste it? I was going to have fun while I still could, and if things went wrong, my lifesaver would help me through.

With a determined look on my face and my courage on standby, I stood to attention, not quite as swift as before, but to attention at least. Clenching my clammy hands and then wiping them on my jeans, I leapt up to the path from the hole and made my way towards the back door. With my hand on the doorknob I looked back on what had happened, and a grin turned up the corners of my mouth. I opened the door and stepped into the house. Everything was fine again, because my mother helped me through.

6

Family Ties

Memories are the ties that bind us to family. They are our "forget-me-knots," and they keep us moving forward while still retaining our connection to the past and those that came and went before us. Our families—and our most precious memories of our families—should never be forgotten.

The Simple Things

By Gwen Morrison
Canada

Growing up we never did have a front porch, though I always dreamt that one day I would sit on my own front porch and sip iced tea in the hot summer sun while rocking in an old chair. Instead, we had a back porch.

Our back porch was a cement patio with a makeshift roof that Dad constructed out of wooden beams and covered with those colored plastic shingles. It sounds tacky today as I write about it, but back then it was all the rage!

Though we did not have an ideal childhood, the memories that we shared on our back patio are forever etched in my mind. They were the good times. They were the times when we escaped the chaos in the house and just enjoyed the outdoors and being together. My sister, Michelle, and I—though she was years younger than me—spent a lot of time together. Sometimes we did nothing—sometimes that was the most fun of all.

When we were very young, my sister and I spent hours listening to the radio on hot summer days—singing along to our favorite tunes. We were convinced that one day we would travel the roads together and sing in those smoky night clubs—maybe even record a hit single. We enjoyed making our dreams come alive with our little radio outside on that back patio. Using whatever we could find as microphones, we put on our own little show.

Michelle and I shared a bond that was so strong. It got us through some of the rough years—we often turned to each other in those days. We always had each other. It was an unspoken bond that spanned many years. In later years, I would need her again, and she would be there.

There was a great swing just past the patio in our yard that Michelle and I often sat on for hours—chatting and laughing. We made up stories about what we would do when we grew up (after our music career took off), and it always felt so real, so exciting, as we kicked our legs back and forth to the rhythm of the swing.

"I will be the manager," Michelle would say.

"Well, I am the oldest, so maybe I should be the manager."

"Yeah, but they always think I am, so I should do it."

And I would always agree with her. She was wise beyond her eight years—so strong and determined. I always knew that no matter what she did, she would do it well.

As sisters go, I was the weaker one. I was the one afraid to cross the road or tell a lie. I was not the daredevil—Michelle was. She inspired me to try new things, to be less afraid, to take the next leap. It was always Michelle who took the huge dives off the swing set. She was full of adventure and spirit. I envied that in her.

I was the reader. I would sit on the patio in the big chair with the floral cushion and read my newest Nancy Drew novel. Michelle was always nearby practicing one sport or another. One day she coaxed me away from my book to help her practice her pitching. Thrusting a bat in my hand, she said, "Just swing at the ball!"

Sure, easy for her to say. She could run, hit, swing, slide and catch a fly ball all in one day. But she was my sister. So I stood sideways, held the bat in front of me, and as she threw the ball, I swung. I missed three times in a row, which frustrated Michelle, who decided I needed another bat-holding lesson. I didn't see her move closer and took a practice swing just as she was right in front of me. I knocked the wind right out of her! She dropped to the ground, doubled over in pain. Though it isn't a good memory for her, after that I always remembered to "look before I swung!"

On those really hot days in August, when the only thing you can do without sweating is watch the red juice of a Popsicle trickle down your arm, we always seemed to find something interesting to do. And sometimes it was the figuring out what to do next that got us in trouble.

The funniest thing my sister and I ever did had to be when we collected at least a hundred tadpoles from the creek across the road from our house. We carted them home in a big bucket and dumped them into the tiny swimming pool that our mom had filled for our baby sister. I guess in our hearts we were always jealous of our cute little sister, Paula. Paula was born five years after Michelle. She was born three months premature, and she was hooked up to all kinds of tubes when we first saw a picture of her. She was the tiniest thing that we had ever seen. Being so tiny and vulnerable, she got a lot of attention from our mother. Our little adventure with the tadpoles backfired on us—as did most of our adventures as sisters in crime.

Imagine our surprise when all those tiny tadpoles transformed into frogs—filling the patio and the yard with green hopping creatures. My dad was furious at us for our prank and even more upset when some of the poor frogs met an unfortunate demise with his lawnmower. Needless to say, it was not pretty.

But the patio was a place to play, to chat, and just to hang out with each other, and before long, the frog incident was behind us and new adventures called.

My mother, who was an avid sunbather and gardener in those days, loved the patio. Eventually they added the indoor/outdoor green carpeting that was popular in that era. It made it seem even more like an actual room.

As we got older, the patio was a great place to sit and entertain our new boyfriends. On a rainy day, it was the most romantic place in the world. The easy pitter-patter of the falling rain on the patio roof would fall in beat with the pitter-patter of my fluttering heart. Young love was the best. I would sit in the double seat patio chair, cuddled close to my boyfriend as we watched the storm. I loved watching the rainfall. I still do love it—the louder the better! There is just something so powerful about a storm. The flash of light—the crashing boom of thunder. Back in those days, I pretended I was scared— well, who wouldn't at the young age of 15 cuddled next to the cutest boy on the block?

Years later when Michelle got married, she had her wedding photos taken in the backyard. The perfectly manicured lawn was a beautiful backdrop as she stood in her gown looking so happy. I loved to see my sister happy. I vividly remember my two-year-old son sitting on the back patio in his white suit and tails waiting patiently for the group photo. Tears filled my eyes as my little son crept up in front of my sister and patted her big white dress.

He thought she was Cinderella—and so did I. She was the most beautiful bride I had ever seen.

Michelle bent down and swooped him up in her arms. She glanced at me. She didn't need to say a word; I knew what she was thinking. This was it—we were grown-ups now. The years of playing in the yard and laughing on the back patio were behind us. Our dreams of becoming music stars faded—but our love for each other remains strong. I love my sister and wish I had just one more day to play on the back patio with her. I would tell her about my hopes and dreams.

I'd tell her how much those days spent with her meant to me. How much she means to me still.

Michelle and I don't live close enough to do those things anymore—it all vanished too quickly. But the best thing about memories is that, with the blink of an eye, I can relive those carefree moments with her. The things that stay with me are the simple pleasures in life—the hot summer days just hanging out with my best friend, my sister, Michelle.

Our Memories Make Us What We Are

By Lynn Huggins-Cooper
County Durham, England

The garden of my childhood was always sunny; the drowsy drone of bees filled my ears with its comforting hum.

I drift back in my mind's eye to long afternoons spent in the shallow pool—blue as the Mediterranean. Blossoms fell in drifts from the honeysuckle to turn the water to perfume. My mum would sit in the sunshine making beautiful jewelry and tell me about the folks who had commissioned her.

I remember once an intricate collar of tiny, brightly colored beads. As she rewove the patterns, she told me the collar had once belonged to a great Shaman and legend had it that the pattern held the magic in the amulet. She laughed and said she had been warned of terrible curses if she failed.

My favorites were the pearls she strung into necklaces for great ladies. Her most famous piece was the pearl collar with a dazzling sapphire center, made for Diana, Princess of Wales. Funny to think of objects of such worth on a rickety table on our back porch!

My parents, sitting on the porch, would quietly read the paper while we played nearby. From time to time, they'd rise to pluck a fading bloom or pull a weed from the dark, crumbly soil. I spent afternoons watching huge, humpbacked snails rumble across the stone walls surrounding the garden. I followed their glistening trails for what seemed like miles.

Next to the porch, my sister and I dug a huge pit—who knows why? We dug until we hit sticky orange clay. Together we gathered huge tubs of clay and made all manner of thumb pots and relics.

In autumn, as the days shortened and the tang of wood smoke filled the air, I'd peer out from the cover of the porch as the tiger spiders wove their silken traps. On misty mornings, the webs would be spangled with jewels of moisture. My dad, a burly fireman, was scared of the spiders. He would negotiate a path through the bushes waving his hands in front of his face shouting and cursing. Close up, the spiders were a miracle of striped legs and a fat body embellished with a star.

Autumn, too, meant Halloween. My mum would help me sculpt a pumpkin lantern, our hands slick with earthy smelling juice. Out on the porch went the lantern to wait for our guests. Diminutive witches, miniature devils, and goblins soon filled the house. The table groaned with spider cakes, star cookies, and cauldrons of "witches brew." Candles flickered on the porch, adding their touch of magic.

My beautiful cats, old friends now long gone, used to circle the porch, soaking the sun into their furry bodies. I miss their soft touch and the weight of their bodies as they slumped on my lap.

The porch was my shelter and sanctuary. I sat and read for hours, listening to the yarns my dad told, watching his face avidly as he changed in the throes of the story from giant, to Jack, and then the goose.

In later years I sat and smooched in the same spot—until I heard Dad's voice calling.

When I go back today, the porch has gotten smaller somehow. Snails still paint the garden walls with filigree tracery; frogs still sing their rusty song in the pond. The pool has gone, as has the clay pit. The spiders still mass to torment my dad in the autumn, and new feline incumbents grace the suntrap the porch provides.

But the memories glow down the years, painting a pattern for my own life as a mother. My own porch is a day's drive away from that childhood haven. But today I have a garden full of the laughter of children as they play in the water or the sand, and a tribe of rescued feral cats stalk through my herb garden. As they pounce, ever hopeful, on butterflies and bees, the sharp scent of lavender fills the warm air.

Strangely, we have no snails, despite the dry stone walls that embrace the garden. Instead, huge, rubbery black slugs fill their niche, making intricate lacework of my cabbages. My youngest daughter tracks them in amazement as they climb the walls. Tiny shrews live there, too—"enraged squeakers," as my son dubbed them—tiny rodents with the hearts of lions.

I now sit on the porch making memories with my own children. We look out over the Pennines as the sun sets crimson and gold. Sometimes, sitting on the porch, I read the paper. From time to time, I rise to pluck a fading bloom or pull a stray weed from the soil. We watch the spiders as they gild the bushes and trees. The flowerbeds are a mass of butterflies all summer, and the croaking of frogs from the pond fills the air.

And in autumn, as frosts nip the garden back, I sit on the porch, carving pumpkins with my children. We fill the windows with flickering lanterns. Homemade phantoms waft on orange and black streamers as the door opens and closes. The table is full of treats, and the house, just like the house of my childhood, fills with gaily-dressed children.

It is no coincidence, I think, that I grew up to be a mum and a writer. Those warm porch memories stay round me like a cloak. I try to remember to weave memories for my own brood on our back porch. I write children's stories, and strangely—or perhaps not—they are filled with dragonflies, flowers, and wonderful parties…just like my childhood.

The Shopping Expedition

By Trish Gallagher
Victoria, Australia

Looking back to 1961, I don't envy my mother taking five children to a town where shops lined both sides of the longest main street in New Zealand.

Mum was too nervous to drive but loved the family to be smartly dressed, and Dad loved driving but hated shopping, so it seemed a fair exchange that he would take us to town and set Mum loose with the kids and the checkbook. The only downside was the time limit, as afternoon milking on our dairy farm always called us back by four o'clock. If we were late, cows with swollen udders would be mooing and queuing by the cowshed.

I remember the rigmarole of getting us all spit and polished for these outings. The polish was Dad's job, lining up all the leather shoes, scraping off the caked clay, and brushing life back into them with globs of black polish. The spit usually came later, in the car, when Mum would notice someone hadn't washed all the Vegemite off her mouth and out came her hankie, a bit of spit on the corner to clean up the evidence.

Mum shooed us out to the front porch while she went into her preparation frenzy. With us safely out the front, she hauled out the ironing blanket and sheet that she draped over one end of the kitchen table. The four girls had to be well turned out: frocks ironed, socks white, cardigans pastel, hair glossy, fingernails clean, teeth brushed. Our little brother, Ra, had to be forced into tailored shorts and ironed shirt after playing with his tractor in the dirt all morning.

"Can I help, Honey?" Dad would ask from his kitchen armchair.

"Um." Mum flipped and ironed. "Could you check the kids?"

So Dad would put down his newspaper and poke his head out the door only to find the front porch empty. We were all out in the garden collecting pussy willows, those silky gray buds that bloomed in profusion and made great toys. Hearing his call, we bounded back, shirts and skirts tucked up full of our bounty.

Dad glanced at his watch. "I thought Mum told you to get ready. Look at your dirty feet!"

"But she told us to stay out here so we were going to play cowsheds," I explained. "Look!" And I unloaded a skirt full of pussy willows on the porch floor and plopped down, cross-legged. I began arranging them in rows for the cowshed and herding groups of them as cows until I realized I was alone out there.

Unsure what to do next, Dad had gone inside to read the paper and await instructions, and my sisters had vanished. Without my playmates, I wandered in, too. The kitchen was inviting. I pulled out a chair, stood on it and clamped my ear next to the radio, turned up the knob, and listened to pop music while Mum finished ironing.

"Get to the bathroom now and have a wash and brush your teeth." I was back in half a minute. "I thought I told you to go to the bathroom."

"Can't. Snowball's in there with the door shut, and she won't let me in."

With an exasperated sigh, Mum called to her eldest daughter. "AJ! If you're dressed, come in here and put Turtle's hair in a ponytail."

Enter AJ and exit Mum, ready for her turn in the bathroom where her ritual was to take a shallow bath.

"Ow! Stop pulling!" I yelled as the rubber band caught my untamed hair.

"Sorry, Turtle," my 14-year-old sister said, trying to loosen the culprit strands. "What are you wearing today?"

"Huggy's old green frock, but Mum's going to buy some material for a new one just for me."

"Oh, that will be nice. There, I've finished. Come and have a look in the mirror."

"Why did Mum want me to have a ponytail?"

"Probably because your hair is getting so long. Look, isn't that nice?"

Huggy laughed. "Ha ha ha! Turtle's got a ponytail, Turtle's got a ponytail!"

In the mirror, I saw my face blush red.

AJ frowned. "Don't listen to her, Turtle. Get out, Huggy—go to your own room. She looks good, doesn't she, Snowball?"

Snowball, clean and sweet, turned her pretty blue eyes and blond curls to my straight black hair. "I suppose it's all right. How does mine look?"

AJ ignored her and took my hand. "Come on Turtle, I'll help you do up your buttons." We walked around the corner to my room as Mum left the bathroom in her dressing gown.

"Who left all these wet towels on the floor?" Mum demanded.

"Not me!" AJ said. "Must have been Snowball."

Mum sailed down to her room with a backward glance. "Thanks for doing Turtle's hair. Now take her in for a wash before she gets changed."

I stepped over soggy thin towels and wrung out a facecloth to wipe my face and neck. "That'll do," AJ said and went with me to the bedroom I shared with Huggy to help me dress. Ra was there on the floor, grubby knees under his chin, lips vibrating as he "brmmm-brmmm-brmmmed" a Tonka truck around the rug. Huggy was dressed, sitting on the bed watching him.

"Oh, Raro! Go and get Dad!" AJ exclaimed. "Huggy, you go with him. He's got to get ready."

Mum emerged from her bedroom in her carefully applied make-up, best dress, and high heels. While she worked up a sweat chasing the dressed Snowball and Huggy out to the front porch, Dad discarded his jeans, flannelette shirt, and woolly gumboot socks dotted with hayseeds. He collected his only boy and dunked them both under the shower to emerge clean. While Ra escaped naked to his room, Dad shaved and scented himself with Old Spice. Minutes later, transformed in shirt, tie, and dress pants, it was his job to ensure Ra was dressed and shoed, then whisked back into the bathroom to have a lump of Brylcreem massaged into his hair and combed into a peak at the front.

Flustered by the time Ra and I were dressed, Mum sent us back to the front porch with instructions to play with Huggy and stay clean.

"Oh, Huggy, you've wrecked my cowshed!" I cried.

"Didn't," she said, wiggling a hula hoop around her hips. "It was Snowball."

Dad appeared. "What's the matter? Where's Snow-ball?"

"Someone's wrecked my cowshed!" I wailed, sitting down to stroke the pile of pussy willows.

Huggy shouted again. "It was Snowball!"

"What was me?" Snowball yelled from the bedroom she shared with her elder sister and then counter-attacked. "AJ is lying on her bed reading a book instead of getting ready!"

Through the door we watched Mum stomp down the hallway to see what AJ was doing. "Oh, not another Angelique book. Get on the porch. You can read in the car."

"Can't read in the car—makes me feel sick," AJ relied.

Stomp stomp stomp. "Leo? Leo? There you are. Would you tell AJ to get a wriggle on?"

Dad left the porch, car key still in hand, and looked in the bedroom—tactical error on Snowball's part—and walked into a haze of hairspray that we could smell half a mile away.

"What the…? Snowball—you look like an owl! Wash that black stuff off your eyes or you're not coming to Thames."

Ra and I giggled when we heard the thwack of Snowball's plastic hairbrush on her dressing table. "But, Dad, all the girls in my class wear mascara."

"Well, they can't come to Thames with us either. Now, AJ, off your bed and get outside. Don't keep your mother waiting."

Finally ready, we were shooed down the front steps, warned to avoid the mud, and shuffled into the car. Ra jumped into the fold-down seat between Mum and Dad while we four girls squeezed into the back and drew patterns on the fuzzy seat fabric.

Dad usually had a roll-your-own cigarette smoldering on his bottom lip so the car smelt of smoke as we traveled the country roads to the town of Thames. I always opened one of the triangular windows in each side of the back seat and let my hair be sucked out by the wind.

"Mum, Turtle is messing up her hair," Huggy tattled.

"Pull your head back in," Mum snapped.

When we came to the long, one-way wooden bridge with slippery planks, I huddled close to my sisters rather than look through the flimsy wires at the frothing brown water below. It was the object of my nightmares.

Huggy gave me a push. "You're going to fall out the door!"

"Don't! Mum! Huggy's trying to kill me!"

"Leave Turtle alone, will you? You know she's scared of the river."

Amazingly, we always arrived safely and Dad drove up and down Pollen Street in the gray V8 looking for a parking spot right outside Mum's preferred shop. Sometimes he couldn't park that close but didn't object to a spot further down the street where he could look at "for sale" signs on cars with fins that twinkled temptingly out of reach of his income.

Dad settled down with a book and his yellow box of Pocket Edition tobacco while Mum launched her assault on the shops. We traipsed behind her into a drapery store where little eyes were fascinated by money jars whizzing overhead on wires to a cashier's den, high in a corner. Mum's fingers examined the fabric on display, but she was never ready to buy without shopping around.

In another store, the wide wooden counters were rubbed smooth by decades of fabrics being unrolled and cut on their surfaces. Mum pored over sewing pattern catalogs as she rested on a spindly wooden chair with a round seat and long legs, while ten tired legs shuffled around her.

Pollen Street, Thames, used to have a pub on every corner, remnants of a gold rush era, and we were always hustled past them. The occasional whiff of tobacco smoke and a stale beer bouquet would assault the back of my nostrils as a door flicked open to ingest or expel a customer from its forbidden interior.

Crossing the street was another dangerous enterprise. There was always one last shop we must visit to seek an elusive garment of choice—be it a petticoat or a cardigan in the latest synthetic. Mum clasped the smallest hands in her own as we braved the zebra stripes across the bitumen and piled in to another of an interminable range of shops.

Once over the road, it was logical to make the necessary toilet stop. In Thames, this meant a trip down a side street to the War Memorial Hall, a building that looked immense to us, neat in red brick with a tall desert cactus rising to the eaves. The Ladies Rest Room required spending a penny.

"It's my turn to put the penny in the slot!" Huggy said.

"No, I've never had a turn," I wailed.

"You're too young, you'll drop the penny!"

"None of you can have a turn—I'll do it myself," Mum said and settled the argument.

We took turns and had to make sure we held the door open for the next sibling so the one penny covered us all. Ra was in for a ribbing.

"Watch out, Ra, a lady might come in," Snowball teased.

"I'll stay in the toilet then," said the four-year-old.

"We'll leave you here all night! What if one lady after another comes in—what will you do then?"

"Mum! They're being mean to me!"

"Oh, shut up you girls. Now, has everyone been? You haven't, Turtle? Oh no, who let the door shut? Turtle, you'll have to crawl under the door—but don't get your frock dirty!"

Dad got a lot of reading done while we played follow the leader with Mum. Cocooned in the car, he would read and read until one by one, the kids filled the back seat, energy spent, curiosity used up. Mum added parcels to the car, stopping to open her powder compact, apply a dusting to her nose and cheeks, and re-stain her lips with Clear Clear Red before renewing her assault.

We wondered at her stamina as we watched her departing back, feet stepping out in shoes that matched the handbag slung over her forearm, gloves clutched nonchalantly in one hand, right arm pumping, hat holding permed curls in check. Not until we were older did we recognize the incentive of choosing something for herself without children tagging along.

The 12 miles home seemed an eternity. No one could enjoy trying on new clothes or draping new fabric over their shoulders until the best clothes were off, shoes discarded, and the kettle switched on for cups of tea or cocoa. This restorative was accompanied by crackers layered with butter and cheese.

While the kettle was boiling, I liked to drift into the mysteries of Mum's bedroom to watch her remove the toe-pinching shoes, the hat, the dress, the stockings and suspenders, and, oh, the relief, the easies. Why an elastic girdle was ever named "easies" I don't know—although I imagine whalebone corsets would have been much harder to take on and off.

With her bunions in a soft pair of slippers and her voluminous middle released in a loose dress, Mum was almost ready to relax over a hot cup of tea. Only one more task.

"Kids—get into your old clothes and go out and play on the front porch!"

Now that we all have children of our own, we realize what an ordeal shopping must have been for Mum. But as she nears 80, our sympathy is heightened. Dad died last year, and we miss him terribly, but not as much as she does. She still can't drive.

The Barn

By L. L. Rucker
Campbell County, Tennessee, United States

The world at large can be an awesome place when you are young. Common occurrences to adults can frighten or delight a child. One such happening took place the summer I was 10.

It was late evening, and my sister, baby brother, and I were out in the yard catching lightning bugs. We put them in a Mason jar as we caught them, determined to make a lantern to take fishing with us.

The sun had set perhaps 30 minutes or so prior, and we scrambled around chasing the bugs, giggling, and in general having a wonderful time. It was early summer, school was out, and we could stay up until 10 o'clock if we didn't bug Mom.

Suddenly my sister let out a frightened yelp, and the play came to an abrupt halt.

"What's the matter?" I asked, irritated that she had stopped the game so early.

"Look!" She pointed to the sky, her eyes round with fright.

I looked up and let out a squeal of my own. Our little brother then began screaming in earnest, and we all took off flying for the safety of the front porch, screaming every step. We were certain that the Martians were finally landing and we were being invaded. After all, we had seen the movies, and we knew what those Martians were up to.

Dad and Mom hurried outside to see what the commotion was about, certain from our screams that one of us had been murdered or kidnapped at the very least.

"What in the world is the matter?" Mom asked. Her voice was anxious, her eyes huge in the light of the porch.

Trying to calm my racing heart, I took a deep breath and pointed skyward. "Look, there's a flying saucer!" My breath was coming in gasps like a swimmer who has just surfaced from a deep dive.

Daddy looked up and began to grin. "Well, it certainly looks like a flying saucer," he said, his eyes twinkling.

Mom followed his gaze, and she too began to grin, and then the two of them began to laugh.

My siblings and I, however, didn't see anything the least bit amusing about an invasion from Mars.

My sister stamped her foot. "I don't think this is one bit funny!"

"Me neither!" I declared loudly. "We're all going to get zapped by those Martian ray guns and get disagrated!"

"Disintegrated," Mother corrected me through her laughter.

My little brother just stood there, looking from Daddy to Mom and back to Daddy again, his little face a mixture of fear and mirth. Finally Daddy stopped laughing and picked him up.

"Those lights are not Martians, so calm down," he said.

"Well, what are they?" I asked, somewhat miffed that he had laughed at our fear, certain that he was wrong.

"Those are the Northern Lights."

"What are those?" My sister wanted to know, and now that Daddy had stopped laughing at us and my pride was a bit less wounded, so did I.

"The Northern Lights are just the sun reflecting off the ice up in Alaska, and the light reflects back to earth, and this is what we get to see. It's beautiful isn't it?" Mom said in a hushed voice.

We turned back to the sky and looked. There was a swirling mass of twinkling colors—blues, yellows, pinks, and silver flashing across the night sky.

"This is not anything you're likely to ever see again." Mom said.

"Why?" I asked.

"Well, this doesn't happen that often. I'm not very smart about science, but I think that it has something to do with the alignment of the sun and the moon and earth," she explained.

"Really?" Now I was curious. I wanted to know the how, why, and what of this thing. Personally, I still half believed that Martians were invading us. That was a much more exciting possibility.

We all sat down on the front porch and for several minutes watched the light show Mother Nature provided. It was one of the most beautiful things I had ever seen.

Over the course of my life, I have seen many wondrous things, but the shared excitement of the Aurora Borealis viewed from our front porch that summer's eve is still one of my favorites.

Later that night, as we were getting ready for bed, I decided to play a prank on my little brother. He was so much fun to scare. His little eyes got huge and round, and his bottom lip trembled, and at the time it was so funny to me. What did I know? I was just a kid myself. And I would never do anything to hurt him, but scare him? Well, that was a different story altogether.

I waited until Mom had gone back downstairs, then slipped quietly from my bed, pulled the sheet off, and then draped it over my shoulders. I rummaged around in my closet until I found last year's Halloween mask. I had been a witch, and the mask had scared my little brother into tears. This was going to be delicious.

I tiptoed into his room and stood over his bed. In a quiet voice, I began to speak in Pig Latin. "Eyea amyay umfray eethay anetplay arsmay," I said in my best scary Martian voice.

He opened his eyes and began to scream. I flew back into my room and hopped into bed, barely getting there before Mom came flying up the steps.

She spent some minutes comforting my brother, then came to my room. I lay still trying to pretend I was asleep, but of course, she knew better.

"Young lady, if he cries one more time tonight, I am going to make you sleep in the barn!" The death threat! Oh, boy, I was in serious trouble. Nothing put the fear of God in my sister and me like the threat of the barn! It was by far the spookiest place we had ever seen. It was old, and the wood was dark and worn. There were millions of spider webs, and we knew that some horrible creature lived in the loft just waiting to grab some unsuspecting kid who was dumb enough to be in there at night. We wouldn't go near the place in daylight, keeping a respectable distance between it and ourselves even in the wildest of play.

Our mother had used it to her advantage for years to keep us in line, and it had always worked. Nothing could snap us into behaving like the threat of sleeping in the barn! And now that very threat was hanging over my head like a guillotine.

"I didn't do anything," I protested, sitting up in bed.

"Don't hand me that. I know you scared him again, and I am tired of it." Mom stood with her hands on her hips and her lips pursed in that all too familiar, *I will not tolerate any more of this nonsense*, way of hers. "If he cries one more time tonight, you are sleeping in the barn!" And with that, she switched off the light and left.

I lay there in the darkness praying. I knew the horrors that awaited me in the barn, and I also knew Mother meant every word. I could feel my heart racing as fear invaded my very pores. The barn!

I tried to listen, straining my ears for the slightest whimper from my brother. I knew that's all it would take to send me to the barn in the dark, where the un-named IT waited. I felt my skin crawl as goosebumps popped out on my arms and felt the hair on the back of my neck rise in fear.

"Please, God, don't let him cry anymore." I prayed in a hoarse whisper. And then it happened. What I had feared most—my brother began to whimper.

I flew out of my bed and into his room and lay down on the bed next to him. He lay there in his Superman pajamas, and he looked so tiny and helpless and so scared, and I felt like the meanest person in the world. Perhaps I deserved to be banished to the barn. Then I remembered what awaited me in the barn and panic set in. I cradled him in my arms and began to beg.

"Butchie, please don't cry anymore, okay? Please? It was just me in my Halloween mask. You remember that old mask, don't you? I was just playing. Please don't cry. There's no such thing as Martians." I was crying now. "Nothing is going to get you. Promise. I won't let anything get you, okay? Please don't cry anymore." Nothing. He was silent, but at least he wasn't crying.

I listened and heard his gentle snore. *Well good, he's asleep. No barn for Linda tonight!* I grinned in the darkness. "I wonder if he's afraid of worms?"

Christmas 1938

By Dave Huggins
Sussex, England

Looking back, I remember many childhood Christmases. One in particular really stands out. It was 1938, and I was 12. The planning for it began as the bonfires were dying and the last penny rocket hurtled skywards on November 5th. This might sound early, but times were hard, and Christmas was a bright spot on the horizon.

The first item on our list was how early dare we start our door-to-door caroling? All our plans depended on the success of this. We needed the money for decorations, a Christmas tree, and presents for each other and Mum and Dad. Left over money was used to buy groceries, which were then presented to Mum just before Christmas.

I think the earliest we started was December 10th. We used to dress in the warmest clothes we had and never ventured out without a hand warmer. This was an old cocoa tin with holes punched in it containing a piece of smoldering rag. Sometimes it got too hot—and by the end of the "carol singing season" we all had a good crop of blisters on our hands. It was dangerous, really—but people were less safety conscious in those days.

We used to go round in pairs, and my pal and I always picked a district of larger houses as we knew they would be more likely to have a little money to spare. At each house, we stood on the porch singing a carol without missing a verse; if the light came on in the hall, we knew they were listening, so we sang a second one. Then we politely knocked and waited. If the door was answered by a woman, we thought we might be lucky, as they were far friendlier and more generous to children than men.

Most people were generous and kind and gave us money and mince pies. If it was very cold, people sometimes gave us cocoa. This had to be drunk on the doorstep, as Mum had threatened me with a fate worse than death if we ever went into anybody's house.

As soon as we had some money, it was all systems go—first the paper chains had to be made to decorate the front room and kitchen. We couldn't afford already "made up" decorations, so we bought packets of colored paper. Paste was made from flour and water, and the job began. Each strip of paper was pasted at one end and formed into a loop. The next strip was threaded through this loop and the ends stuck together. Other garlands would be made by cutting crepe paper into strips, then twisting them. We brought home large twigs from trees, and my older sister used to dress them with small flowers she had made from colored and silver paper.

Nearer Christmas would be the time to collect holly. The place we got ours was a well-kept secret. Imagine what it would be like the weekend before Christmas with hundreds of boys and girls scouring the neighborhood for holly!

My pal and I had found a huge holly tree on the grounds of a large deserted house said to be haunted—all large empty houses as far as we kids were concerned had to be haunted. To keep the other kids away, we told of terrible moans we had heard from the house whenever we had ventured near by accident. I was so convincing, I nearly frightened myself!

We struggled through the overgrown grass and bushes until we reached the tree, then took turns standing on each other's shoulders to reach the desired branch. Why is the best holly, smothered in berries, always at the top of the tree and protected all the way up by those hideous thorns? Now and again, whoever was at the bottom would lose his balance, and we would fall against the tree. Yelps of pain would fill the air, and it was probably this noise that convinced other children that the place was haunted. Finally, with a huge bunch each, we crept away like ghosts and headed for home.

A few days before Christmas, carol singing became frenzied because present buying was upon us. For Mum and Dad, it was easy—Black Magic chocolates for Mum and a packet of Digger Flake pipe tobacco for Dad. We suffered all over Christmas for this present—the smell when he smoked was horrific. Years later when I was in the Fire Brigade, I endured the same smell when attending a farm fire involving 200 tons of smoldering manure. Nevertheless, Dad seemed to enjoy it.

Christmas Eve arrived, and that was the day for buying the meat we would eat for our Christmas dinner. Turkey in those days was for the very rich. Chicken on the table, which we all take for granted now, was beyond the reach of most working-class families. It was a choice of pork, beef, or lamb. It's funny to think now that these meats are more expensive than chicken or turkey. I suppose somebody found out that poor people liked them!

Mums in those days, who had little money to spend, were very canny. Late Christmas Eve, they went to the market knowing full well that the later it got, the more desperate the butcher would be to sell off the meat. Those were the days before freezers. The meat just hung in the shops on hooks. As it got later, the meat dropped in price. The butcher would hold up a piece of pork and offer it to the crowd at a low price.

If his offer wasn't taken, he would place a pound of sausages on top. If it still didn't go, he'd put a piece of suet on top, all for the original price! The trick was knowing when to say yes.

I used to go with my mum and stand under the gas flares that lit the market and get more and more desperate as she appeared to miss bargain after bargain. She knew exactly when to shout. She got so much for her money that we had a job struggling home with it.

I remember one year the butcher got so annoyed with her that he took off his striped apron and threw it at her shouting, "You might as well have the bloomin' shop as well!"

Mum countered with, "Throw in your straw hat, and it's a deal!"

Then we were off to the stall that sold Christmas trees. By now, they were really cheap; quite often we got one for nothing. Then the struggle home with our load. The first thing we did was to set up the tree in a bucket of soil wrapped in colored paper. Out came last year's tree decorations, and on they went. In those days we had no Christmas tree lights—we used to clip on little candles and light them—imagine the danger of fire!

By the time we kids got to bed that night, it was pretty late. We were too excited to sleep, wondering what presents we would get. Finally my brother and I, who shared the same bedroom, fell asleep. But not for long. Our presents arrived at the bottom of the bed in separate cardboard boxes. The first one of us to wake up would let out a shout and wake up the other.

It was absolute magic—wind up toys, flash lights, mouth organs, snakes and ladders, Ludo, and jigsaw puzzles. My special present this particular year was a set of Western Six Guns in a leather belt—replicas of those used by Wild Bill Hickock. For my brother, it was an aluminum fighter plane powered by a thick black elastic band. It flew very well—so well, in fact, that it finally crashed into a chimney stack and left a wing in the roof.

How my mother provided all this, I will never know. It must have required 12 months planning on the money she was earning. Poor Mum, she didn't get to bed until the early hours of Christmas morning, only to have a mouth organ blasting in her ear at four a.m.

Christmas Day was a real family day. In the morning, we went out and flew my brother's plane—then back to a huge Christmas dinner. In the afternoon, we played cards and board games with our parents.

Sadly enough, there wouldn't be many more Christmases like this. War was approaching fast. Before it was over, my brother would have changed his model aircraft for the real thing—a Pathfinder Mosquito Fighter Bomber—and I my Hitchcock Specials for a 17-pounder, a gun mounted on the turret of a Sherman Tank.

Cat Memories

By Rose Moss
Northwich, Cheshire, England

[Dedicated to the memory of Marian (Marie) Josephine Moss, my dearly loved and much missed mother. 1913-1997]

It was the spring of 1997, and I was sitting with my mother on the front porch. It was painfully obvious that her health was failing. She was having increased difficulty in walking and needed her angina medication more frequently. But despite this, I found the facts hard to face, as my mother and I were inseparable companions. She had nursed me through numerous illnesses in my childhood, and since my poor health had meant I couldn't play with other children, she was more than a mother to me—she was also my best friend.

As Mum's health worsened, more and more our conversations turned to the past and all the memories we'd shared. Among other things, my mother and I have always shared a love for cats, and now, we especially liked to reminisce and talk about the cats we'd loved and lost throughout the years.

Two of our favorites were the topic of many front porch conversations in her last months. We remembered Mrs. White Puss, a beloved cat who had been my mum's constant companion. Mum had been very upset when Mrs. White Puss died, but she was consoled by the fact that Mrs. White Puss had attained a ripe old age before dying, and the pain of the loss had faded over the years.

We also talked at length about Tom, another of Mum's favorites. His death, however, was very recent and still distressed mother a great deal. Within a few months of his premature death at the age of seven, her health had declined rapidly until she became housebound, venturing no further than the front porch.

After Tom's death, Mum sent a donation to Britain's largest cat charity, *The Cat's Protection League,* in his memory, and became a member when the charity arranged for the new cats we had to be spayed or neutered. They sent her a bi-monthly magazine that was full of stories written by owners telling of their beloved cats both past and present.

One afternoon when we were sitting side by side in our chairs on the front porch, mother was reading the magazine when she suddenly said, "When I get better, I'm going to write about Tom and send them his story." I was surprised to hear her say that, as Mum disliked writing intensely and even put off writing letters for as long as she could. She always wanted me to write, though, and encouraged my clumsy attempts to write a novel. I remember that she was thrilled the time I won a runner's up prize in a poetry contest.

So the fact that she wanted to write about Tom, rather than suggesting I do it, was quite a shock to me. It made me realize just how much she missed him.

Within three months of that conversation, my mother suffered first a stroke and then a heart attack, and she died a month later. At the time, I was far too grief stricken to think about writing Tom's story and put her last wish to the back of my mind.

Two and a half years passed, and I finally had Internet access—something Mum had long encouraged me to consider. One day I came across a lady's tribute to her cat and it struck me—I realized it was time to carry out Mum's last wish and tell Tom's story.

By this time, *The Cat's Protection League* magazine had become a glossy publication filled with articles by professional authors. I wrote to them set on fulfilling Mum's final wish, only to be told the magazine had a huge backlog of articles and to try elsewhere. Undeterred, I started to write the story, determined that somehow my mother's last wish would be fulfilled. This is what I wrote:

I can't recall the exact day when Tom came to live with us. His moving in was so gradual that in the typical fashion of cats, we found we had one without being quite sure how! Maybe Tom sensed that we missed Mrs. White Puss and felt needed.

Mum said Tom used to follow her when she walked 'round the garden, so I imagine that was when they decided they were just right for each other. Often when we went out to the front porch, Tom would be sitting there waiting patiently for Mum to appear and then would follow her while she pegged out the washing or cleaned out the outhouse.

Our next-door neighbors, who've since moved elsewhere, had a tendency to acquire cats and quickly grow tired of them. They had two at that time—Suzy, a black and white female, and Tom, Suzy's grown kitten, who looked almost as if his mother had produced him from a negative. While she was predominantly black, he was very much white.

The two cats had as little time for each other as their owners did for them. Suzy eventually moved in with another neighbor, and Tom took to us.

Suzy would sit on the neighbor's porch and glare balefully at other cats that passed by, and when she and Tom occasionally met in our garden, they made a great comical show of pretending not to see each other.

Tom liked everyone but was very much my mother's special cat. He was gentle, affectionate, intelligent, and playful. His meow was so expressive that on several occasions, we swore he actually said, “Hello!”

Every morning Tom waited outside for my mother, who was always the first downstairs, to let him in. He sat by her chair as she ate her breakfast, but before she had finished would demand to get on her lap and be cuddled. He was happy to let other people stroke him, but he only sought out my mother’s lap to sit on.

I still laugh at the memory of the day Tom decided he wanted to sit on a chair in front of the fire—a chair that was occupied by my mother. Tom knew he was forbidden to jump on our antique sideboard, but that evening he kept doing so repeatedly until finally my exasperated mother got up to lift him off. Quick as a flash, he was on the chair he wanted. We were so amused at him that we hadn’t the heart to deprive him of his prize.

Tom loved Christmas because we always had turkey—his favorite food. His love of turkey created a dilemma for us, however. We had a hard time deciding where to put the turkey to cool after it was taken out of the oven. We decided the safest place was on top of our high fridge freezer. Of course, Tom could smell it and took to sitting by the freezer staring up at it with an expression of devout adoration on his face, like a worshipper venerating an icon. Occasionally, he’d let out a plaintive meow until Mum couldn’t take it anymore and finally cut him a slice.

During the summer of 1996, Tom lost his appetite and began to drink huge amounts of water. We suspected kidney failure, but the vet diagnosed an infection and dismissed our concerns, despite repeated visits. On several occasions Mum steeled herself to say “Goodbye,” only for the vet to say the infection just needed another expensive injection to cure it.

One day in September, Tom died peacefully in his sleep. He was only about seven or eight years old, and Mum was distraught. She gave Tom's food to the new cats, but wept as she did so. I tried to comfort her to no avail. Though I missed Tom, too, I lacked the bond with him that she had shared and was unable to fully comprehend her grief.

Tom had given her a reason to start each day—with his affectionate meows and his obvious pleasure in seeing her.

Mum never recovered from the blow of losing her companion. The following January, she had a minor heart attack. It was a cold winter, and we longed for the spring when I hoped she'd be able to go down to the garden with the new cats. Mum was never able to do that. Instead, we sat watching the new cats from the front porch as we talked of happier times and remembered all the things we'd shared together, making the most of the last precious weeks we had left with each other.

I can't sit on the front porch now without thinking of my mother and how much love she had to share. She was a sweet natured and gentle lady who never spoke ill of anyone. She dedicated her whole life to the welfare of others—whether that was me, her cats, or the Brownie Pack she ran for almost 50 years.

Mum's last wish was to have Tom's memory kept alive—he meant so much to her. Now when I sit on the front porch, a warm feeling comes over me when I think of Mum. She did so much for me. I'm happy that through this story, I could do one small thing for her.

Three Perfect Roses

By Nellie Virginia Caudill Compton
as told to Bonnie Compton Hanson
Santa Ana, California, United States

"Mommy!" I cried. "Your roses are blooming!" I ran up to the front porch steps impatiently. "Come out and see!"

Although it was still May, summer was already here. The rolling mountains all around were covered with new-green forests, and the creek that ran through the thriving cornfields was almost warm enough to wade in—that is, for people who weren't afraid of water snakes and lizards, as I was. Of course, at 12 years of age, I was almost too old for that kind of play anyway.

Mommy's vegetable garden was full of sweet peas and green tomatoes. Lilacs and forsythia colored the back yard, and tiger lilies and daffodils brightened the flower garden. I had been weeding the flowerbeds when I discovered the blooming roses.

Those roses were Becky Caudill's pride and joy, next to her eight children, of course, and I knew she'd be thrilled with my news. But instead of my mother, old Mrs. Easton appeared at the door.

"Nellie, dear," she said, "you can't come in right now. Go stay in the store with your Poppy. That's a good girl." Then she shut the door.

Puzzled, I walked from the house side of our big wooden building to the store side, where a huge sign announced: Tilden Caudill's General Store, Waltz, KY. I rushed in, letting the screen door bang behind me.

"Poppy, what—"

He was busy talking on the wall crank phone. As soon as I saw his face, I knew something was wrong. No, not another one of my mischievous brothers needing a lecture behind the wood shed. Nor a problem with his store or sawmill. Not even with the crops. If so, Papa would have been studying the store ledgers or out talking to the hired hands.

"Yes, Ma'am, I'd sure appreciate it if you could come and help my wife soon as you can," he said. "The Doc's already on his way."

Our tiny farming hamlet of Waltz nestled in a picturesque valley far back in the Appalachians. The nearest town was hours away by mule-drawn wagon. The only road from town crossed a wide creek several times—with no bridges. After every rain, everything was a sea of water and mud. Because of that, people didn't ask doctors to come out unless lives were in danger. So Mommy's life must be in danger—or else the baby was coming.

I'd loved being part of our big, sprawling family of five brothers and two sisters. My older sisters, Maude and Carrie, were teen-agers now. They were the only girls—besides me. Bessie had died as a baby. Sometimes Mommy still cried, thinking about little Bessie.

Now Mommy was going to have another baby. What fun it would be to babysit. *Oh, please, God*, I prayed to myself, *let Mommy and the baby be all right.*

When Poppy hung up, he put his arm around my shoulder. "Nellie, girl, you've got to take over the store for a while. Maybe you can straighten up the yard goods for me. I need to take care of things at the house." Then he left.

I always enjoyed working with all the colorful bolts of fabric stacked neatly on the wide store shelves. Muslin, batiste, flannel, broadcloth, and linen—they all felt and smelled so wonderful and new. I'd try to imagine all the new clothes that could be made from each one—especially ones I could make myself, now that I was old enough to sew.

As I stood on a pickle barrel to reach the highest bolts, I saw a stream of people outside hurrying to our home. Mrs. Ball and Mrs. Thompson, mother of my good friend, Mamie. Then Mrs. Kirk, and finally plump, good-natured Aunt Betty Hamm. Aunt Betty wasn't a trained nurse, but she knew how to help doctors, especially when babies were ready to be born. That meant Mommy's new baby must be coming very soon.

I was so excited I almost fell off the pickle barrel! Last of all came Dr. Davis' buggy. Poppy ran to help with his horse. Then both of them disappeared into the house.

Just then my big sister, Carrie, came into the store. "Nellie," she said, "I'll take over the store now. Mommy wants you to go to Mamie Thompson's house for the night."

"No fair! I want to stay here and see the new baby when it comes!"

Carrie's black eyes usually sparkled. But now they were troubled. "Nellie, Mommy's very sick. She can't cook or take care of anyone today. Maude and I will watch out for the boys, but you need to go stay with neighbors. You can come back tomorrow. Hurry now, while it's still light."

The dusty country road to Mamie's cabin was bordered with daisies and violets. Birds and butterflies fluttered everywhere. Pine trees shaded some spots, while others were bordered with golden honeysuckle. The sun was warm and glowing, even though a few gray clouds were building up here and there. When I reached the creek, I took off my shoes and stepped carefully across on big stones so I wouldn't fall into the water—and maybe on a water snake. But at least that was better than having to cross that scary-looking footbridge high above. All during my trip, I kept praying, *Dear God, please help Mommy and the baby be all right.*

When I arrived, Mamie stood at her cabin door, waving. What fun seeing my friend again, now that school was out for the year. Since Mamie's mother was back helping at my house, Mamie's older sisters cooked dinner that night. They even baked a huckleberry pie. Afterward, I helped draw water from the well to do the dishes.

"Look, Nellie," Mamie remarked, pointing up to the sky. "It's really cloudy. Betcha it's going to rain."

"That's okay," I answered. "Poppy says we need some for the corn right now."

When the dishes were clean and put away, we chattered until bedtime. Mamie helped me pull out a small feather mattress to sleep on. "So which do you want," she whispered, "a little brother or a little sister?"

I thought a minute. "Either, I guess. But wouldn't a little sister be great? We could dress her up in ruffles and brush her curls—like a great big doll."

"Then baby sister it is. Let's pray for one right now!"

Just as we finished praying, the rain began pouring down, lulling us to sleep. The next morning, all was bright again. Just as we sat down to breakfast, Mamie's mom rushed in—wet and mud-splattered, but beaming. She walked straight up to me and threw her arms around me.

"Nellie, love, how many sisters do you have?"

My eyes sparkled. "Two." She knew how many sisters I had—that must mean our prayers had come true!

Mrs. Thompson laughed. "Not any more."

Mamie clapped her hands. "I told you so! You got a baby sister!"

But Mamie's mother shook her head. "No, not one—three! Nellie now has three baby sisters! Triplets!"

Triplets? I was so shocked, I didn't even finish my sausage and hotcakes. Instead, I jumped right up out of my chair and ran straight for home.

Because of last night's rain, the road was full of puddles, slippery rocks, and mud. It would take me forever to get home. And I just had to see this awesome answer to my prayers with my own eyes—as quickly as possible. Daringly, I decided to take a shortcut through our bottomland pasture. At first I ran. But most of the pasture had turned into a swamp from the rain, so I soon began sinking in mud. My feet and skirts were soaked, and blackberry briars tore at my legs. The grass and bushes were so thick, I couldn't even tell if there were snakes or lizards hiding there. I could hardly wait to cross the creek and be home again, safe and sound.

But what was that roar?

Overnight, our mild little stream had turned into a raging torrent, so deep I couldn't see the big crossing stones. The only way to the other side now was that scary swinging bridge high above—the one I always avoided unless someone was with me to hold it steady.

The ladder up to the bridge consisted of pieces of wood nailed to the trunk of a huge tree. The bridge itself consisted of small slats of wood fastened together with two long ropes.

With my first step, the bridge began swaying wildly. "I can't do this, God!" I cried. "It's impossible!" Then I remembered: I had asked for one baby sister and God had given me three. That was above and beyond anything I had asked for, hoped, or even dreamed about. He could do the impossible, including help me cross this bridge.

Step by step, I inched forward, swaying back and forth, praying all the time. Sometimes the wood slats tipped so much my feet flew right out from under me. I had to hold onto the side ropes to keep from falling. But, step by step, I made it.

Quickly scampering down the ladder on the other side, I ran straight for home. When I arrived, Poppy was standing out on the front porch talking with some men. Even though I was covered with mud, he caught me up in his arms.

"Nellie!" he cried. "We were so worried. Mrs. Thompson's family looked everywhere for you. These men were just heading off on a search party. Here, take off those muddy shoes and come see your new baby sisters. But don't touch anything."

Mommy was in a big bed in the front parlor. Beside her in the old wooden cradle were indeed three tiny babies. Three identical baby girls—all well and healthy—as beautiful and perfect as rosebuds, and right beside them lay three just-as-perfect roses Poppy had picked from Mommy's garden. Though too tired to talk, Mommy reached out for my hand and blew me a kiss.

"I love you, Mommy!" I whispered. "Oh, I wish I could pick the babies all up right now and hug them!"

Poppy laughed. "Filthy as you are, girl? There'll be plenty of time for that later. For now, go wash up and change your clothes. Then see if you can help your big sisters in the kitchen."

"Yes, Poppy."

Dutifully, I headed out to the well to pump water for the wash pan. But this time I didn't step in any mud. My feet were flying too far off the ground.

The triplets were named Nina, Tina, and Ina. My grandfather had a formal picture made of his three infant daughters with long, long skirts and the three roses, which is still in the family. Of the triplets, Nina (Gearhart of Ashland, KY) is still alive and well and a delight to be around.

Don't Forget Me

By Helen Kay Polaski
Milan, Michigan, United States

As I turned into the driveway of my childhood home, a million memories tugged at my mind.

How many times had I raced in and out of this driveway with a dog hot on my heels or skipped to and fro, caught up in the excitement of bicycles or kites or childhood games? How many times had I jerked up and down the driveway as I learned to drive in my mother's 1967 blue, four-on-the-floor Chevrolet?

My eyes traveled across the pointed roof and gently caressed the northeast edge where the lilac bush grew. How many secrets could one house hold before the secrets began to slip away, one by one? Surely this house held more than its share.

My gaze settled on the porch. I suddenly realized our front porch was not much to look at, nor was it very big. How had that tiny area maintained a cool spot throughout such hot summers or sheltered so many through the million and a half thunderstorms we'd witnessed? A sigh escaped. The front porch on this simple cinderblock house was the keeper of more memories than any place else in the small hamlet I still called home, though I lived hundreds of miles away.

Our house, so small to have housed a family with 16 children, stared back at me from the middle of the yard as if to say, "Am I good, or what?"

As a child, I had always imagined the house was alive. The front, facing the rising sun, was of course the face, though how I figured it could be is quite humorous. The door, which had opened and closed on a regular basis as children ran in and out, was the mouth. You needed more imagination when it came to windows being eyes, but I guess I wasn't concerned about having a three-eyed house.

Its tongue lolled out and made up the front porch steps that slid down into the dirt at the end of the gravel driveway. No one knew exactly how long that tongue was, for the house never rolled it up and tucked it back inside as children were always told to do.

As my mind wandered across my childhood stomping ground, the house opened its mouth, and my father stepped onto the porch. With one hand on the screen door, he stood watching, waiting for the company he always welcomed. I couldn't help but notice the bright splashes of color at his feet, and a smile tugged at the corners of my mouth. They were there to greet me again this spring. No doubt they had made Dad's days brighter. Who could resist those tiny little purple and yellow faces?

"Here, take one," Dad said, thrusting a pot of pansies toward me as soon as I opened the van door.

"Oh, I will, Dad," I answered, giving the door a back-handed shove. I peered at the pansies closely and smiled. "I'll take as many as you're giving away!"

Just like Dad, pansies have always been one of my favorite flowers. Mom had loved them, too, though they weren't her favorites. To help cheer Dad up the year after Mom's death, I'd bought a whole flat of tiny purple, yellow, and blue pansies, and with the help of my sister, Karen, who donated another flat of flowers, planted them in the yard near the cherub statue a bunch of us had purchased in honor of Mom and Dad's 50th wedding anniversary the year before.

Though Dad loved flowers, he lost sight of the big picture for a while after Mom died. That was when I realized Mom had been his special flower. Without her, Dad's day had no color, no beauty. He hadn't cared much for anything those first few years.

But the pansies hadn't taken offense to his neglect. They had grown well and seeded all over the yard. This year—four now since Mom passed on—appeared to be a turning point for him. I'd heard from other sisters that he was spending more time in the gardens and yard this summer. He'd even talked about putting in some tomato plants. It was refreshing, yet humorous, to imagine my big strong father digging up delicate pansies and lovingly potting them in whatever available container he could find.

As if reading my mind, he sputtered. "They're all over the yard!" He waved his arms around to indicate he really did mean everywhere. "I gotta stop the mower every couple feet." He drew his eyebrows together and squinted at me to make sure I understood the enormity of his statement.

I chuckled, pleased my sister and I had caused such a phenomenon by merely planting flowers. "That many, huh?" I reached for the pot he was holding. "Oh, but they're so pretty. Don't you just love these little flowers?"

Unexpectedly, when my hand touched the margarine tub that held his precious gift, my mind flashed backward in time. In an instant, Dad's tall lean form seemed to shrink. His angular shoulders rounded out softly, and his smile widened. His blue eyes turned hazel, and Mom's country twang answered me, just as she had done six years ago on this very spot. Though time seemed to stand still, the sun still beat down warmly on our backs, the birds still chirped from the tree tops, and the scent of lilacs was still heavy in the air. The only difference was that the margarine tub Mom held before me had one single pink English daisy in it.

"Go on, take it," she said. "They're coming up all over the yard."

My hand trembled as I took the flower. I turned quickly and walked toward the driveway. Blinking away my tears, I set the pansy near the van and then turned back to Dad. His eagerness was evident, and I couldn't spoil the mood by saying my thoughts had strayed to mom and tears now threatened. We all missed her, but perhaps no one as much as he did.

"Come on, I'll show you," he said. With one hand, Dad swooped up the shovel from where it rested against the front porch and picked up a couple margarine tubs. "You want some more?"

I nodded and cleared my throat, swallowing the lump that had formed. "How many have you given away already?"

He leaned on the shovel handle and ran his free hand across his head gently, ruffling the graying hair against his sun-darkened neck. "Oh, jeez… Too many to count. And there's plenty more where these came from."

I glanced at the front porch. There must have been half a dozen pots filled with cheerful little faces moving gently in the breeze. "Well, you don't have to dig 'em up right now. I'll take a couple pots from the porch."

"No, I'll dig up a few more—they're already smiling at me, waiting." He tried to frown, but I saw right through it. "I can't get nothing done—always stopping the mower." With a loud sigh, he looked me in the eye.

"I can't keep mowing around 'em."

My heart skipped a beat. My 77-year-old Dad was saving pansies from the mower! Life doesn't get better than that. I laughed out loud, the tears threatening to spill again. The big softy! "No, Dad, I guess you can't keep doing that."

He managed to wrinkle his brow, but his gray-blue eyes sparkled with mischief. Suddenly he leaned the shovel handle against his chest, dropped the margarine tubs, and framed his face with his hands. He wiggled his hands and moved his head slightly as if it were being pushed by a soft breeze. "How you gonna mow 'em down when their little faces are smiling up at you like this?"

I laughed again and picked up the tubs. "You can't! I know. Anytime I see them I have to dig 'em up too!"

He nodded in agreement and resumed walking. After a couple more strides, he stopped and pointed the shovel toward the ground. "See, there's one right now. Looking up at you. Smiling." In one easy movement, he had stuck the tip of the shovel blade into the grass and tapped it with a worn brown work boot. When he placed the pansy into the empty container, I froze again as his leathery calloused hand changed. The hand before me had no trace of Dad's bulging rheumatic knuckles, but plain as day were the brown sun spots Mom seemed to have had for a lifetime.

"These daisies are all over the place," she said as she stuck the shovel tip into the grass again and applied pressure with one dirty white gardening sneaker. "They don't need much watering or care. And they bloom before there's even any leaves."

Dad plunked the second pansy into the tub and straightened. He put his forefinger and thumb together. "An inch tall and there's a flower on it already." His brows rose nearly to his receding hairline, and he smiled big and full. "There's a couple over here," he said and continued toward the back yard.

For the next few minutes, I toured the yard with Mom and Dad. Everything Dad did was so similar to what Mom would have done had she been there—it was as if she was with us. We left a trail of divot holes—divots no one worried about so long as the flowers were okay. And as we walked, I watched for English daisies. But it was as if Mom's flowers had vanished and given Dad's flowers free rein. I was surprised that I'd forgotten all about the English daisies until that moment. Now that they had come to mind, I wondered what might have happened to them. The last ones I'd seen were the ones Mom had given to me that day so long ago.

I stopped in my tracks as understanding dawned. Maybe it had been an omen of things to come, but as happens frequently, we don't always take God's messages to heart.

For some reason, the two English daisies Mom gave me that day didn't come up the second year in my garden. Instead, a bunch of forget-me-nots sprouted in their place.

I had been shocked, to say the least, and remember calling Mom to tell her the news.

"Yeah? Isn't that something," she said. "There must have been forget-me-nots seeds in the ground where we dug."

"Well, isn't that strange, Mom? I mean, where did the seeds come from?"

"I don't know," she replied. "But for some reason the whole yard is full of forget-me-nots this year."

"You didn't plant them?"

"No," she said with a chuckle. "I have no idea where they came from."

Her laugh, always ready and full, warmed my heart, and I smiled. Mom's laugh was contagious. Many times I'd seen her laugh so hard tears rolled down her cheeks.

Simultaneously, we'd joked, "Maybe the forget-me-nots are so you don't forget me." We agreed that must have been the reason. Since then, every time I come across a forget-me-not, my mother's laughter comes to mind and her voice fills my mind, "...don't forget me."

As Dad bent over to dig up another pansy, I realized his smiling face—with his leathery, calloused, rheumatoid hands waving comically on either side—would come to mind every time I saw a pansy, and I couldn't think of a better way to think of him. And Mom—well, who could ever forget her?

Several days later, I stepped into my backyard garden and marveled at how much my morning glories had grown in two days. I stopped to drink in nectar from the pink, yellow, and white roses that graced the fence and frowned when I noticed that some of my stately hollyhocks needed staking. I hugged a pot of pansies to my chest and scanned the garden for the best location. As my trained eyes wandered across the familiar territory of my herb gardens, I noticed the chives had been cut. Good. My family took advantage of their pungent and savory flavor in my absence.

I caught movement in the shadows and watched as a bunch of blue forget-me-nots danced alone in the wind's rhythm. I grinned. Pansies, of course, should be planted near forget-me-nots. I planted them close. So close they touched.

When I finished, I stood up and viewed my handiwork. Now, as it should be, the pansies could dance with the forget-me-nots, and I could pretend all Dad had to do is reach out and hold Mom in his arms again.

About the Author who compiled this book

Helen Kay Polaski

My claim to fame? I am number seven in a family of 16—12 girls and four boys—and have somewhere in the neighborhood of 70 nieces and nephews. More important than size, however, is that we are very close. We grew up believing in the Lord and we thank Him for all of the generous blessings He's bestowed on our family. For us, it's not just a phrase, family really does come first.

My siblings and I grew up in Michigan's lower peninsula along the shores of Lake Huron, just 60 miles southeast of the Mackinac Bridge. Like wildflowers dancing to the beat of our own drummer, we bobbed to and fro in the cool lake breezes and became one with our environment. Dad kept our home safe and secure and in the way of mothers, Mom kept the real world at bay. Though we lost shoes and mittens and school books and lunch pails, she made sure we kept track of our rose-colored glasses. I thank God the world was an easier place to live in when I was a child for Mom had her hands full trying to keep us on the straight and narrow. For the most part she succeeded—though how is a mystery that surely will never be unraveled!

One thing is certain, growing up in a small hamlet that I believed was covered in fairy dust was for a child like waking up every morning to a brown sugar sandwich. Life was sweet and delicious from the moment the smell of bacon floated up through the floor register until darkness descended and Mom and Dad's voices called good night through the register.

I married my high-school sweetheart, Tom, and together we have three wonderful children, April, Alissa, and Nathan. This year we celebrated our 26th anniversary. While Tom kept our home safe and secure, I attempted to make our children's life as full of sugar and magic as mine had been. That's when I realized how blessed my own childhood had been and decided to commit some of my experiences to paper. My fondest wish is that my writing will one day touch the hearts of others in a positive way.

Another dream has been to include illustrations by my sisters, Sandy and Melissa, and my eldest daughter, April, who all are artists. Though I have had numerous stories published in various anthologies, *Forget Me Knots...from the Front Porch* is special for it has helped me attain a big portion of my goal. Several of the stories within the book are from my own childhood and stomping grounds, and the child on the cover is standing on our family's front porch. The little girl is my sister, Karen's, youngest daughter, Jillian Liedtke. The dog, Sassy, is a fixture in their home. And the illustration was drawn by my baby sister, Melissa.

I've had so much fun doing this book that I don't plan to stop. I have five additional anthologies in progress. They will all be *Forget Me Knots* books, but with different themes. The themes so far include: beneath the garden gate, along the shore, from the back pew, across the kitchen table, and within the school yard. If anyone is interested in submitting something for consideration in these anthologies, please email me at forgetmeknotsanthology@yahoo.com or check out my website at www.geocities.com/forgetmeknotsanthology.

About the Cover Artist

Melissa Jane Szymanski

Melissa Jane Szymanski received a Bachelor of Fine Arts Degree from Siena Heights College in Adrian, Michigan. Her major was drawing. Melissa's work has been exhibited in several art shows in Michigan, including Cranbrook Institute of Science in Bloomfield, Ella Sharp Museum in Jackson, Buckham Gallery in Flint, The Orion Center in Lake Orion, and Paint Creek Center for the Arts in Rochester.

With a great eye for detail, portraits and figures have always been her strong point. Diana, her framer, says, "When Melissa does a portrait, it almost breathes."

Melissa's recent works include children and pets portrayed as angels done in colored pencil. She currently resides in Metro Detroit with her husband, Sam Mau, and their two Australian Cattle dogs, Wally and Rodeo.

You can email Melissa at: forgetmeknotsanthology@yahoo.com.

Contributor's Bios

Jozette Aaron has been a published writer since 2000. Her work is available on many sites across the Internet. Her ebook, *Next Stop*, written under her pseudonym, Georgie DeSilva, is now available in print and on CD. Her first full-length novel, *If I Would Love Again,* will be released in November 2002. Jozette lives in Ontario, Canada, where she works as an R.N.

Maureen Allen has been writing for Bellaonline.org since 1999 where she writes three weekly columns: Classical Music, English Culture, and Scottish Culture. She lives in Newcastle, England, with her husband, Dennis, with whom she co-authored the romance novel, *No Hiding Place,* under the pseudonym Maureen Dennis. Currently Maureen is at work on a novel about Scotland's role in World War II.

Violet Apted tutors creative writing and has won many writing competitions. She has had her writing published in magazines in four countries. Her first novel is ready to send to a publisher, and she's working on her second novel. She also is a member of an online writers' group.

Nancy Baker retired from Texas A&M University, and has since pursued her lifelong love of writing. She is published in several magazines—*Eucharistic Minister* and *Deacon's Digest*—and anthologies including *Cup of Comfort for Friends, Cup of Comfort for Women*, and *911: The Day America Cried*. Nancy currently is writing her grandmother's life story called *Laura's Legacy.*

Georgiann Baldino is a novelist and graphic artist who lives with her husband near Chicago, Illinois. Her first novel, *The Prodigy*, was published in multimedia format with classical music files imbedded in the text. Her short fiction, nonfiction, and cartoons have appeared in several publications.

Maureen Beaman is a freelance writer, a wife, and the mother of two young children. With a 15-year background as a Veterinary Technician, her specialty is writing anything and everything about companion animals. Her work will be published soon in *I Love Cats* magazine, as well as others. You may e-mail her at Bralen@prodigy.net

Carole Bellacera is the author of three mainstream fiction novels published by Forge/Tor Books. *Border Crossings*, her first novel, was a 2000 RITA finalist, a 2000 Romantic Times Reviewer's Choice finalist and the winner of the 2000 Laurel Wreath Award. *Spotlight* was a 2000 RIO Nominee in the Dorothy Parker Award for Excellence in Fiction (Best Romantic Suspense), a 2001 Holt Medallion Finalist for Best Mainstream Novel, and a 2001 Booksellers' Best Awards Finalist. Her latest release, *East of the Sun, West of the Moon* is a 2001 RIO Honorable Mention award winner in the Dorothy Parker Award for Excellence in Fiction.

Dale Davies is 17 and lives in the United Kingdom. Though Dale currently is employed at the local McDonalds, his goal is to write, write, write. He noticed the advertisement for the Forget Me Knot Anthology at a children's writers' group he belongs to and decided to submit a story about his own childhood. He hopes his writing will help readers think about their lives in a different way or maybe just feel happier. His website is at http://www.dale-davies.cjb.net and you can email him at: daley_davies@hotmail.com.

Barbara Deming started writing at age 10 when she climbed to the top of a mulberry tree with a Big Chief tablet to create her first story. She no longer writes in trees but has been published in *Grit, Cappers, Mystery Time, A&U Magazine, AIM,* and *The Rockford Review* among others. She is currently working on a novel set in East Texas.

Martha Dillon is a widow and a single parent of two grown children. She stayed at home with the children for the first 10 years, then went back to work and college. During her three years at school, she completed four years of education (magna cum laude), tutored during open periods, worked part-time, and was at home every night with her children to help them with their homework. One of her greatest pleasures is writing about her life experiences.

Fran Finney began a second career of writing following a 35-year career teaching American history and English to ever-so-grateful adolescents in Kansas and Pennsylvania. She is a member of Romance Writers of America and Wichita Area Romance Authors.

Rusty Fischer is a freelance writer whose work has appeared everywhere from *Seventeen* magazine to *Chicken Soup for the Volunteer's Soul.* Currently, his two books for writers—*Beyond the Bookstore and Book Marketing Made Easy*—can be seen at www.bookbooters.com.

Trish Gallagher is a writer living in country Australia. After a career as a journalist for some 20 years, she has turned to writing short stories, poetry, and children's stories. She was born and raised in New Zealand and left home at 16 to study English at university. She completed her BA several years later in Western Australia. Now 48, she has fond memories of her childhood in a quiet farming area of New Zealand.

C. C. Hammond has had a lifelong interest in theology and writing, has a MA in psychology, and has made an extensive study of world religions and the paranormal. Her books cover all her interests and emphasis her understanding that most of what we are taught is unreal is actually real. Web site : www.cchammond.com Currently available books : *The Other Side of the Door, Compassion's War* (www.echelonpress.com) and *The Six Lessons of Alpha Centauri* (www.Amazon.com).

Bonnie Compton Hanson is an artist/speaker and the author of several books, including the new *Ponytail Girls* series, plus hundreds of articles, stories, and poems. Her mother, the "Nellie" of this story, eventually had 15 brothers and sisters. You can reach Bonnie at: (714)751-7824; bonnieh1@worldnet.att.net; 3330 S. Lowell St., Santa Ana, CA 92707.

Veronica Hosking lives in Arizona with her husband of six years and two wonderful daughters. She received a Bachelor's degree in English Education at Buffalo State College. Now she's a stay-at-home mom and enjoys reading and writing in her spare time.

Dave Huggins has been writing all of his life. He recently had work published in an anthology of memories published by Queenspark Books. He also has a "memories" article in a history book for teenagers to be published in late 2002 by Hodder and Stoughton and another in an educational book for Letts. Dave is 75 years old.

Lynn Huggins-Cooper lives on a farm in County Durham, England, with her husband and three children—and too many animals to count! She has written many books for children including six "science through story" books for Franklin Watts featuring her family and her animals. She writes a weekly column for the Times Educational Supplement and articles for parenting, women's magazines, and those with a Christian perspective. Look for her Dad's (Dave Huggins) piece also in this book—it's a family affair!

Bette Milleson James, a Kansas writer and poet, is a former English/ Composition teacher and grant writer. She and her husband raised their three children on a family farm in northwest Kansas where they still live. Recent publications include poetry in N. A. Noel's book of angel paintings, *I Am Wherever You Are*, and stories and poetry in the veterans' anthologies *Let Us Not Forget* Vol. I and II.

Karla Jensen has enjoyed 14 years in the radio, television, and magazine publishing industries, amusing and enthralling a variety of audiences through commercials, print ads, profiles, and numerous articles in national magazines. Augsburg Fortress Publishing has published several of her church dramas and reader's theatres. She particularly enjoys writing for children.

Kathryn Jones has been a published writer since 1987. She has published various newspaper and magazine articles for teens and adults and is also the author of *A River of Stones* found at www.pdbookstore.com/InspirationalN.htm. To contact the author, please send e-mail to kathy.jones3@attbi.com or visit her website, www.ariverofstones.com.

Kristin Dreyer Kramer, a native of small-town Western Michigan, now lives with her husband, Paul, in Massachusetts. She is a freelance writer and Editor in Chief of NightsAndWeekends.com. Kristin can be contacted at krdrkr@hotmail.com.

Heather V. Long is a freelance writer who resides in Virginia with her husband, Scott, and her daughter, Cassidy. She makes quilts, raises horses, and recently completed her first novel. She is diligently working on a second novel while completing her Bachelor's Degree in English. Heather hopes to add the accomplishment of teacher to her resume some day, as well as author. Her website is: http://www.heatherlong.com.

Gloria MacKay now lives on Camano Island, a spot in Puget Sound not far from Seattle. She digs clams, drops crab pots, gardens, weaves, and almost every day—rain or shine—writes. The focus of her writing is a weekly radio program on KSER where she is free to express whatever she feels. Gloria's work has appeared in *The Seattle Times*, *The Philadelphia Inquirer,* and various print and on-line magazines and she has written a book, *The Bubbles Go Up*. She answers to: glomac@whidbey.net.

Steven Manchester is the published author of *The Unexpected Storm: The Gulf War Legacy* (P.S.I. Research, Hellgate), among other works. When not spending time with his sons, Evan and Jacob, this Massachusetts author is either writing, promoting his published books/films, or speaking publicly to troubled children through the "Straight Ahead" Program.

Margaret Marr lives in the mountains of western North Carolina where she divides her time between her two sons, the great outdoors, and romance novel writing. She's had numerous short stories, poems, and two books published, and has been involved with several anthologies. Her latest romance release, *Moon of Little Winter,* is due out in August of 2002. *Between Earth and Eternity* is coming soon from Treble Heart Books. Visit her online at: http://www.margaretmarr.com or drop her a note to say howdy at: mizz_scarlett@hotmail.com

Gwen Morrison is a freelance writer and mom of four children, ages six through 17. She has definitely "been there, done that." She claims that her family life alone could keep her in writing material for decades…she is never bored.

Rose Moss is 44 years old and English. A student of English and Sociology, Rose has had her work published on a variety of websites and an article published in the 2002 April edition of *Whispers From Heaven*. Learn more about Rose at: http://pages.ivillage.com/louisamaydew/rosesphotosandarticles/.

Vanessa Mullins is an eclectic writer. Having been featured in several anthologies, she recently ventured out and compiled her own anthology with writers from around the globe titled *Nudges From God – An Anthology of Inspiration*, published by Obadiah Press. Email her at: vkmullins@comcast.net.

Glenys O'Connell has worked as a journalist in the UK, Canada, and in Ireland where she now lives with her family. She writes for both children and adults and has recently completed a series of interactive children's stories for MyCDStory.com (www.mycdstory.com) Her first romantic suspense novel, *Judgement By Fire*, is set in rural Ontario, Canada, and published by Puff Adder Books, United Kingdom, as an ebook (www.puff-adder.com). Currently she is working on her third novel and another series of children's stories. Contact her at: oreo@eircom.net or www.geocities.com/writerinireland2002/.

Helen Kay Polaski, number seven in a family of 16, hails from northern Michigan. She and Tom, her husband of 26 years, have three wonderful children. Helen has been a newspaper reporter for 16 years and has had numerous articles published online and in anthology books. She will be putting together more *Forget Me Knots* books in the near future. If interested in submitting a story for consideration, contact her at forgetmeknotsanthology@yahoo.com.

David Ritchie is the Northwest Regional Vice President of the Washington Poets Association. His poetry and fiction have been widely published in the U.S. and abroad, including in *Mountaineer's Magazine, The Animist, The Paumanok Review, Red River Review, Drexel University's On-line Journal, Albany University's Offshore Journal, BuzzWords UK, Parnassus Literary Review, BigCityLit-New York Edition, Rue Bella,* and *Short Stories Magazine*. He lives in the San Juan Islands.

Kimberly Ripley is a freelance writer and published author from Portsmouth, New Hampshire. Her work has appeared in collections including *Chicken Soup for the Soul, A Cup of Comfort,* and the *Virtue Victorious* series from Red Rock Press. Her award winning book for freelance writers, *Freelancing Later in Life,* has become a national writing workshop. Visit her site and sign up for her free newsletter at: http://www.freelancing1.homestead.com.

Linda L. Rucker lives in Northeastern Tennessee with her husband and pet wolf, Zo. She has been writing since the age of 13 and is the recipient of a national writing contest award. It was the beginning of a lifelong love affair with writing. She recently completed her first full-length novel and is working on a second. She has also had a short story and a poem posted on a website for fantasy writers.

Eileen Sateriale lives in Bowie, Maryland, with her husband and two girls. She is the public relations liaison for her younger daughter's school. For the past several years, she has been drafting a novel. She has had some poetry accepted in *Sol Magazine* and had a short piece published in the *Let Us Not Forget* anthology.

Janet Elaine Smith is the author of best-selling *Dunnottar,* as well as eight other published novels, and has been widely published in many magazines over the last 20 years. She is married, has three adult children, was a missionary in Venezuela for nine years, and for 31 years has run a charitable "Helps" organization with her husband.

Dorothy Thompson is a freelance writer, children's book author, and anthologist from the Eastern Shore of Virginia. She writes nonfiction articles on the craft of writing for both online and print publications, as well as for her own site, The Writer's Life (http://www.thewriterslife.net), one of Writer's Digest Magazine's Top 101 Websites. Her children's book, *No More Gooseberry Pie,* is published by Writers-Exchange E-Publishing (http://www.writers-exchange.com/epublishing/dorothy-book1.htm). She has been included in many anthologies as well her own, *Romancing the Soul—True Stories and Verse of the Existence of Soul Mates Around the World and Beyond*, which is pending publication.

Nanette Thorsen-Snipes has published articles and stories in publications such as *LifeWise, The Lookout, Mature Living*, and in 15 compilation books including *Stories for a Teen's Heart, Book 3, Chicken Soup for the Christian Family Soul, God's Abundance, Nudges From God*, and others. She lives in Buford, Georgia, and has been married to Jim for 25 years. She has four grown children and two grandchildren. E-mail: nsnipes@mindspring.com. Check out her website at: www.nanettesnipes.com.

Avis Townsend has been writing since 1987, first as a newspaper editor and columnist, then as a writer of short fiction. She has finished her first novel, part of a three-quel, and is halfway through number two. She lives in Appleton, New York, where she enjoys her menagerie of dogs and cats, six horses, one husband, two children, and four grandchildren.

Rita Tubbs lives in Michigan and balances her time between homeschooling her five children and freelance writing. She has written for *Brio* and *Discoveries* and recently finished a children's book about Great Lakes shipwrecks.

Anne Culbreath Watkins has been a freelance writer for nearly 20 years. Her work has appeared in 10 Guideposts Publications hardcover books; in their magazine, *Angels on Earth*; and is scheduled to appear in two upcoming *Chocolate for Women* sequels. Her credits include pieces in numerous print publications and articles for several online magazines. She is the author of the book, *A New Owner's Guide to Conures.*

Darlene Zagata is a freelance writer, poet, and editor. She is the mother of four children and grandmother of two young grandchildren. Born in Georgia, Darlene currently resides with her family in Pennsylvania.

Permissions:

That November printed by permission of L. L. Rucker. ©2002 L. L. Rucker

Wildflowers printed by permission of Nancy Baker. ©2002 Nancy Baker

The Village Boy printed by permission of David Ritchie. ©2002 David Ritchie

War Through the Eyes of a Child printed by permission of Violet Apted. ©2002 Violet Apted

The Cousin Danny Story printed by permission of Maureen Allen. ©2002 Maureen Allen

He Sat Alone printed by permission of Steven Manchester. ©2002 Steven Manchester

Popeye in the Outhouse printed by permission of Darlene Zagata. ©2002 Darlene Zagata

Burning Memories of Dad's Easy Chair printed by permission of Avis Townsend. ©2002 Avis Townsend

The Cave printed by permission of Anne Watkins. ©2002 Anne Watkins

Five Dollars Up printed by permission of Helen Kay Polaski. ©2002 Helen Kay Polaski

Carousel printed by permission of Veronica Hosking. ©2002 Veronica Hosking

A Place Called Home printed by permission of Vanessa K. Mullins. ©2002 Vanessa K. Mullins

Stop Wishing Your Life Away printed by permission of Margaret Marr. ©2002 Margaret Marr

The Dollhouse printed by permission of Martha Dillon. ©2002 Martha Dillon

My Summer Job printed by permission of David Ritchie. ©2002 David Ritchie

Just Lavendar Polish printed by permission of Glenys O'Connell. ©2002 Glenys O'Connell

Gifts on a Porch Swing printed by permission of Barbara Deming. ©2002 Barbara Deming

Lullaby printed by permission of Kimberly Ripley. ©2002 Kimberly Ripley

The Sanctuary printed by permission of Dorothy Thompson. ©2002 Dorothy Thompson

Broom-Swinging Grandma printed by permission of Janet Elaine Smith. ©2002 Janet Elaine Smith

The Road Trip printed by permission of Heather V. Long. ©2002 Heather V. Long

Porch Swing Cocktails printed by permission of Rusty Fischer. ©2002 Rusty Fischer

Bubble Gum in Disguise printed by permission of Georgiann Baldino. ©2002 Georgiann Baldino

What Grandpa Taught printed by permission of C. C. Hammond. ©2002 C. C. Hammond

Miss Fitchett's House printed by permission of Jozette Aaron. ©2002 Jozette Aaron

Walks Through the Woods printed by permission of Kristin Dreyer Kramer. ©2002 Kristin Dreyer Kramer

It's All About Yellow printed by permission of Rita Tubbs. ©2002 Rita Tubbs

I Feel So Free printed by permission of Bette Milleson James. ©2002 Bette Milleson James

A Pitch in Time printed by permission of Gloria MacKay. ©2002 Gloria MacKay

When Fairies Danced printed by permission of Carol Bellacera. ©2002 Carol Bellacera

Our World printed by permission of Helen Kay Polaski. ©2002 Helen Kay Polaski

A Faithful Friend printed by permission of Nanette Thorsen-Snipes. ©2002 Nanette Thorsen-Snipes

The View From the Porch printed by permission of Maureen Beaman. ©2002 Maureen Beaman

Porch Swing Memories printed by permission of Fran Finney. ©2002 Fran Finney

Someday My Kiss Will Come printed by permission of Kathryn Jones. ©2002 Kathryn Jones

The 1967 World Series printed by permission of Eileen Sateriale. ©2002 Eileen Sateriale

Behind the Tractor printed by permission of Karla Jensen. ©2002 Karla Jensen

My Kingdom for a Book printed by permission of Helen Kay Polaski. ©2002 Helen Kay Polaski

My Own Personal Lifeguard printed by permission of Dale Davies. ©2002 Dale Davies

The Simple Things printed by permission of Gwen Morrison. ©2002 Gwen Morrison

Our Memories Make Us What We Are printed by permission of Lynn Huggins-Cooper. ©2002 Lynn Huggins-Cooper

The Shopping Expedition printed by permission of Trish Gallagher. ©2002 Trish Gallagher

The Barn printed by permission of L. L. Rucker. ©2002 L. L. Rucker

Christmas 1938 printed by permission of Dave Huggins. ©2002 Dave Huggins

Cat Memories printed by permission of Rose Moss. ©2002 Rose Moss

Three Perfect Roses printed by permission of Bonnie Compton Hanson. ©2002 Bonnie Compton Hanson

Don't Forget Me printed by permission of Helen Kay Polaski. ©2002 Helen Kay Polaski